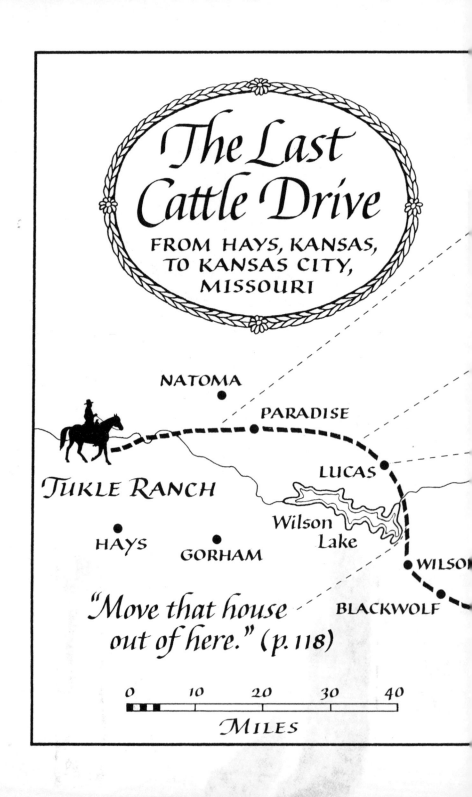

# The Last Cattle Drive

## FROM HAYS, KANSAS, TO KANSAS CITY, MISSOURI

NATOMA

PARADISE

LUCAS

Tukle Ranch

Wilson Lake

HAYS

GORHAM

WILSON

"Move that house out of here." (p. 118)

BLACKWOLF

0   10   20   30   40

MILES

*"We need some film of
these babies running."*
(p. 99)

*"...all of you standing in
this road are guilty of
a FEDERAL CRIME."*
(p. 107)

*"...I have a cement angel
outside...to take me up."*
(p. 113)

SALINE RIVER

SALINA

WOODBINE

BROOKVILLE

HOLLAND

*"You cook the dinner and
I'll do the dishes."* (p. 146)

N
W E
S

*continued on back*

# The Last Cattle Drive

# The Last Cattle Drive

A NOVEL  Robert Day

## 30th Anniversary Edition

FOREWORD BY HOWARD R. LAMAR

 UNIVERSITY PRESS OF KANSAS

© 1977, 2007 by Robert Day
© 2007 by University Press of Kansas
First hardcover edition, 1977
Reprinted, 1983, by arrangement with the author's literary representative,
Russel & Volkenning, Inc.
30th Anniversary Edition, 2007


Published by the University Press of Kansas (Lawrence, Kansas 66045), which
was organized by the Kansas Board of Regents and is operated and funded by
Emporia State University, Fort Hays State University, Kansas State University,
Pittsburg State University, the University of Kansas, and Wichita State University


Library of Congress Cataloging in Publication Data
Day, Robert, 1941–
  The last cattle drive : a novel / by Robert Day ;
foreword by Howard R. Lamar. — 30th anniversary ed.
    p.   cm.
  ISBN-13: 978-0-7006-1463-9 (alk. paper)
  ISBN-10: 0-7006-1463-X (alk. paper)
  1. Cattle drives—Fiction. I. Title.
  PS3554.A966L3 2007
  813'.54—dc22                                    2006025733


Printed in the United States of America


10 9 8 7 6 5 4 3 2 1


Portions of the *Pictorial History of the Cabin Home in the Garden of Eden* by S. P.
Dinsmore are reprinted with the kind permission of W. S. Naegle, proprietor of the
Garden of Eden, in Lucas, Kansas.

*This book is for Virginia,*
*and also for Edgar Wolfe, Edward Ruhe,*
*and Treva and Ward Sullivan*

# Contents

# The Last Cattle Drive

The typical cowboy wears a white hat, with a gilt cord and tassel, high-top boots, leather pants, a woolen shirt, a coat, and no vest. On his heels he wears a pair of jingling Mexican spurs, as large around as a tea-cup. When he feels well (and he always does when full of what he calls "Kansas sheep-dip"), the average cowboy is a bad man to handle.

—D. W. WILDER, *Annals of Kansas*

# Foreword

As a devoted teacher of the history of the American West for the past fifty years, I have long been fascinated by the saga of the action-packed, heroic cattle drives on the Chisholm Trail from Texas to the Kansas railhead towns of Abilene, Wichita, Dodge City, and Caldwell, as well as the story of other trails leading from Texas and Colorado to Montana. To me two of the most delightful yet accurate accounts are to be found in Charles Siringo's rollicking 1885 autobiography, *A Texas Cowboy*, and Andy Adams's 1904 wonderful *The Log of a Cowboy*, which, although written as a novel, was so autobiographical that Adams is still acknowledged as "the most articulate spokesman for the authentic 'Old West' of the cattle kingdom."

Then in 1978 I read Robert Day's delightfully readable, humorous, and plain-spoken novel, *The Last Cattle Drive*, which I quickly realized was yet another truly classic trails narrative, but this time about a mid-twentieth-century drive in the state of Kansas. In rereading his novel over and over for nearly three decades I came to appreciate not just the lively account and its impressive understanding of a surviving cowboy-ranching life style, but also the varied personalities of men and women in Kansas, both rural and urban, and how the physical environment—and the seasons and weather—shaped life in the state. Thus when Bob Day asked me to write a foreword for a deluxe new edition of *The Last Cattle Drive*, I felt honored and privileged to have the opportunity to express my enduring admiration for the author and the book.

Day's book manages to include references to most familiar trail experiences and challenges facing the earlier cattle drives, but in a new context. The physical obstacles are no longer just rain, hail storms, tornadoes, and swollen streams or Indians and rustlers, but modern highways, automobiles, bridges, state and local police, and the problem of how to find a place in the many towns along the route to bed down the herd of Spangler Tukle's cattle. As Leo Murdock, the novel's narrator, comments, our fears of failure were different from those who were guiding the nineteenth-century trail herds.

The novel's five chief characters, three men and two women, are all very believable persons, but each has a very different and surprising story to tell. Leo Murdock, the Kansas City boy who opted to be a cowboy on this last trail drive, is not the usual naive eastern dude making a fool of himself in the West, because he already knows Kansas, has been an elementary school teacher in the state, and is now trying to learn about cattle ranching. In stark contrast Jed Adams had spent his whole life working on the Tukle ranch and had actually been on earlier cattle drives. He is the one genuine old-timer.

Spangler Tukle, the earthy, muscular, handsome, bright, and ambitious owner of the Tukle ranch, and the hero-protagonist of *The Last Cattle Drive*, is not another John Wayne or a dignified Texas cattleman like Charles Goodnight, but someone who has been to college, likes pretty women and jukebox popular music, and while a superb horseman and a believer in guns for both hunting and human disputes, lives in his truck, has all the modern conveniences, and runs the ranch as a modern business operation. He enjoys male company in Kansas restaurants and beer taverns, loves his Green Gables scotch whiskey, and has a flair for such outrageous vulgar language when angry that some stunned listeners have called it "inspired obscenity." Yet Spangler Tukle still has great admiration for the surviving cowboy–cattle ranching life-style; he secretly harbors a desire to undertake a last cattle drive.

Still another original feature of the novel is that it is not romantic or heroic, but factual—yet the facts are always insightful and full of new information that you realize is crucial to the narrative. Indeed the factual accounts often depict hilarious events such as Leo trying to learn to ride a horse or to rope cattle, or getting soaked in poisonous cattle dip. His experiences remind one of Mark Twain's stories in *Roughing It* about dudes in the West.

The novel's fourth character, Heather, is a rich Kansas City girl determined to get Leo to marry her. Although she is not the traditional "soiled dove" seen in the nineteenth-century cattle town saloons, she does use every sexual enticement to win him. And when he finally rejects her to stay on the cattle drive with his horse, Chief, he realizes that as in the western movie cowboy tradition he, too, has chosen the horse rather than the girl!

The novel's fifth central character is Spangler's wife, Opal Tukle, who is also a surprise, for she proves to be a better businesswoman and ranch manager than her husband and, indeed, emerges as the heroine who plays a key role in planning and making the cattle drive to Kansas City a success. But such is Bob Day's love of ironic and absurd situations that produce smiles and laughter in the reader, he cannot resist portraying the Tukles' only son, Harold, not in the character of a rebellious western James Dean, but an unattractive college nerd who has gone into drugs, chosen to major in drama and Japanese, and spite his meat-raising parents by becoming a vegetarian.

To me, however, the most powerful and successful original feature of *The Last Cattle Drive* is Bob Day's talent for effective writing. His portrait of his beloved home state of Kansas, often saddled by stereotypical images of being sternly Protestant, conservative, and teetotaling, instead becomes an example of a vibrant, varied society of free-wheeling individuals, rural and city men and women, who enjoy their tomato beer and whiskey and have strong opinions about what is wrong with the U.S. government and incorrect television and film versions of Kansas and the West.

Yet Day's effective mastery of a clear and precise writing style, often with rough, blunt dialogue, can be matched with eloquent and moving passages—especially when he has Leo come to admire the Kansas terrain, the seasons, sunrises and sunsets, and as always, what is going on in the sky.

Equally eloquent is his admiring depiction of the ranch's loyal horses: Jed's Duke, Spangler's Canyon Snip, and Leo's own Chief. The appreciation extends to cattle, his difficult heifer, the stray cat, and the doves, pheasants, blackbirds, and pigeons present everywhere. Somehow there is a totality of coverage that makes Kansas a distinctive region and society.

Spangler's denunciations of western movies and such Hollywood producers as Cue Ball, along with television and newspaper reporters, reveals that once again he still dreams of a real, honorable West, a dream that is epitomized by his undertaking a last cattle drive. Yet he is not alone in his dream. Time and time again during the drive he encounters other Kansans who have equally fond memories of an older, cowboy-ranching West and who come forward to assist in this historic last drive.

Ralph Waldo Emerson once remarked, half in jest, that the trouble with the West was that it was all "out of doors." Bob Day's signal accomplishment in *The Last Cattle Drive* has been to tell us not only about Kansas "out of doors" but to depict its "indoor history" as well by describing the life-style and values of its citizens, the unique qualities of the state, and a vigorous, ongoing cowboy-cattle ranching heritage.

Howard R. Lamar
Yale University
March 2006

# This Book Is for Jed

JED WAS SEVENTY THE SUMMER I MET HIM. *Like a lot of cowboys, he had prostatitis, even though he seldom drank. He had been raised by parents who were deaf mutes, and so he learned to speak as if it were a bodily function. He didn't talk much, but when he did, he said complete sentences. Like the ones you learn in school. Subject-verb-object. It made it easy to understand what he meant: "Leo needs a horse." "You do not drive the truck backward. We will crash." "The bulls are coming at you." "Give me the pistol. I am going to kill the steer." "The tornado has turned the corner. Drive the truck fast." He never used the passive voice. The gate did not "come open." "You left the gate open," he told me one day after I had left the gate open, and thirty steers had trampled his garden.*

*The doctors wanted to cut on Jed. They said he'd live longer if he'd get castrated. Jed never talked about it and neither would Spangler, but Jed wouldn't see the doctor again. Spangler thought the prostatitis was drifting into cancer and Jed was pretty much through working. He figured Jed would just sit out his days in the old ranch house where he had lived ever since the Tukles had moved to town. Spangler told me Jed would be dead by spring. It was odd, but Spangler had noticed that lots of old people die in the spring. He read the obituaries one year and developed a theory that old people made it* through the winter, but it took all their strength and they died when warm weather hit. He also said they'd die not long after a birthday or Christmas or an anniversary. Jed was born on New Year's Day. Spangler figured he'd find Jed dead in April, if not the second of January.

"You think you want to come along on this deal?" Spangler said to Jed one day when we were putting together the drive.

"Yes."

"I mean, we need somebody to stay with the ranch. You could help us out there. I'd hate to leave that to Harold."

"I will go with you," Jed said and fiddled with his hat.

"You can ride in the truck with Opal. She'll need some help driving."

"I will ride my horse," Jed said.

"Maybe you can get your old ass down the road one more time, but that leather bag of cat food you call a horse will be in a can by the time we get to Gorham." Spangler handled delicate moments by crushing them. Jed said he and Duke would make the trip.

"He'll be pushing up daisies before his time," Spangler said to me after Jed left.

Jed had been with the Tukle family fifty years. He had never married. He owned a half-section in Rooks County that he drove over to see once a year and made some deal to lease it out. It was the only trip he'd make. He didn't swear. He didn't go to church. He was considered by the ranchers in the county to be the best hired man in their memory. Spangler paid him ten dollars a day, plus a house and a truck, and dinner at the big house in town any time he wanted it.

When Jed died this spring, he left his money and his saddle to Spangler. All the rest of what he owned—his clothes (two cold weather outfits, two hot weather ones, two hats, and two pairs of Hyer boots), and some pans and dishes—he put in a box and put the box in the storeroom the day before Spangler and I were to take him to the hospital. He died naked in a clean house, leaving only the sheets to be changed and the bedding to be aired. He was the only one who knew what we were doing when we took the herd East last fall.

# Before the Beginning

The papers have it all wrong. The lawyers never did get the story straight. And every once in a while I hear a botched version at a bar, and I'm tempted to break in and set things right. But I don't. It's too complicated, for one reason. Besides, you'd have to know everybody. You'd have to know Spangler.

I first met him when he picked me up between Russell and Hays on a scorching day in August. I was on my way to Gorham, where I had a job teaching at the elementary school, when my yellow MGTC (right-hand drive, wire wheels, white top-up) stopped. I was in trouble.

Hitchhiking in Kansas is tough. You can spend days getting halfway across the state, and the only reason you get anywhere at all is because the local sheriffs will drive you to the edge of their county just to get you out of there. I didn't see much hope that I'd get a ride standing beside a yellow MGTC in a pink and white shirt, white slacks, and kangaroo leather loafers. Not that I'm a queer.

I got the car from Heather. On the promise of my teaching job, her father's bank loaned me the balance. Heather picked out the clothes. She got a kick out of doing things like that. Not that they chaffed. I grew up in the suburbs of Kansas City, and as long as what you wore was clean, it didn't make much difference. I was a little overdressed, though.

And I didn't know anything about cars. Gorham was ten miles up the road that merged with the power lines on the left and the train tracks on the right. Pickup trucks with shotguns hanging across the rear windows were zipping by me like bullets. Every once in a while, somebody would look back at me through the gun rack and grin. I sat on a fender.

A train went by on the right, its light making futile eights on the sunny prairie. After it passed, I could hear the sound of distant oil wells pumping. Back down the road I could see a red pickup coming at me. I was embarrassed. I still am, now that I think of it. If there is a cosmic scorekeeper of aesthetic effects, I'm sure driving a British artifact of a sports car into the cattle and oil country of western Kansas is a minus seven. I'd get two off for the clothes and another four down for the shoes. Kangaroo shoes. The problem with embarrassing moments is that when you relive them, you can't find anyone in your mind's eye to blame them on but yourself. I got off the fender just before the truck passed, not to thumb a ride but to get walking.

It rushed past me, bigger, I remember, than other pickups I'd seen, but with the same rack of guns in the rear window. The driver turned his head abruptly and then, without looking ahead again, brought the truck to a vicious stop. Rolls of new barbed wire sprang forward against the cab, tools shifted, a shovel stood up briefly, then fell against the side. The bed of the truck was a dust storm for a moment. The driver laid his arm out along the top of the seat and backed up straight and fast.

"Need a lift?" he said as he got out of the truck.

"Yes, or a tow," I replied.

"What's the matter with her?" he asked, pointing at the car.

"I don't know."

"Probably out of gas," he said, looking me over. He as bigger than I was, and I'm nearly six feet tall. "Is that it, pistol? She run out of gas, did she?" He took off his tan straw hat, wiped his brow with his forearm, and put his hat on again.

"I don't think so. I don't know much about cars, but I can read a gas gauge," I said, remembering that I had no idea how much gas I had. "It was full when I left Kansas City."

"They always are. They run out about here. Here or the other side of Hays. Keys in it?" he asked, approaching the car.

"I don't think you can fit in. It's tight for me. I'm pretty sure I got gas."

"I've never been in one of these," he said, as he opened the door and bent over and peered into the inside. "Drives from the wrong side, does she. Well, now, that's something."

He went around to the other side, put his hat on top of the car, and began to shoe-horn his way in. There was some unidentified popping and ripping. The top of his head bulged against the top, slightly to the right of his hat, then absurdly under it.

"I'm in it now. I'm all in. It's snug, that's for sure. My body's all over the dash. How the hell do I start the thing? Never mind." He cranked the engine. It started, then died. He cranked again. Nothing. "Sounds all right." More banging and ripping as he stirred around inside. His hat slid off his head and onto the hood.

"I'm out," he announced after he had unfolded from the car. "You could get sick cramped up like that." He paused. "Nice steering wheel though." He looked at the car with amused disgust. I'd see that look later when he'd have to deal with a crippled calf or a broken riding lawn mower. He'd frown by pushing his lips and nose together, and I could tell he didn't think whatever was in front of him was worth his time. But he'd fix it. Walking around the MG, he plucked his hat from the hood, then went over to the truck and brought back a shovel. I figured he would bash the car in the grill first, then bury it.

He took off the gas cap and pushed the shovel handle into the tank. It came out dry. Of course.

"Let's get you some gas," he said, and led me over to the truck.

I cleared a space on the truck seat, shoving tools and machine parts and gloves into a pile between us.

"Push that crap on the floor, if you want to. Clean yourself a spot there." I leaned back and banged my head against the barrel of a shotgun. I tried to roll the window down.

"That don't work right," he said. "You got to roll the handle all the way down and then push the window down with your hands." I said never mind.

"I'll take you up the road and back," he said as we started up. "I don't guess you'd get far coming back." He looked me over again in a glance and grinned. When we got to Gorham, he did the talking and got the gas can; he told me to stay in the truck. On the way back to the car, he whistled the theme from *Giant*.

After he got me going (he had to pour some gas into the carburetor) he followed me into Gorham and then took off down the road toward Hays. I returned the gas can. It turned out I didn't speak to him again for nearly a year.

In Gorham I rented a small apartment behind the post office for forty dollars a month, and took up teaching the seventh and eighth grades in a three-room schoolhouse. Tradition had it that the seventh- and eighth-grade teacher was the principal. In the Gorham school that meant that once a month I took a large brass hand bell out of the storage closet and rang it for a fire drill. I timed our exit from the building and sent the time to a state office in Topeka.

The other two teachers in the building were pleasant, plump women who had taken to teaching thirty years ago because they had been the brightest students to graduate from the then brand-new high school. They had never gone to college and while I was there, the state, in a spasm of efficiency, found them out and declared they were TEMPORARY and issued them only "provisional certificates." This message from Topeka was filed in the trash can the same day it was received.

I liked these women. They knew that the students who moved from their grades to mine could spell, name the parts of speech, recite the multiplication tables, and name the capitals of the states and the counties of Kansas. If the students forgot any of that, it would be my fault. Also, there was never any notion that the students these women taught would go on to more schooling; they might, for instance, drop out of school before the seventh grade and work on the ranch or go to Hays and work in a store. The students, therefore, had to get all they could from school before they left.

The state required that new teachers be observed and that a report be filed in Topeka. The school board members at Gorham were all ranchers, except for Tom Woods who ran the railway station and couldn't get away during the day. Most of September had gone by when one day the carrot-haired cook who baked the rolls and bread in the school kitchen came into my room, wiping her hands on her bib apron.

"I'm Ed Chaney's wife," she said, by way of explaining that she was more than Treva, the cook. She sat down on a folding chair underneath the flag and just behind Lucas Schmidt.

I'm bad at names, but I thought I remembered that Ed Chaney was one of the men I met the night of the opening-of-school-dinner. I guessed he was a member of the Gorham District School Board, and that this was my observation.

I was teaching poetry, some overwritten lyrics by Sandburg (and by coincidence the one about the red-haired waitress). Treva Chaney sat there, her white cooking apron discolored with old and fresh stains. She wiped her hands. I taught. She looked around the room, peered wistfully over Lucas's shoulder, frowned, then looked out the window at the stale September day. She sat there about ten minutes and then left.

Later in the day I helped her fill out the forms that were to go to Topeka. The formality was over. I had not been judged—that would take time and the people of Gorham wouldn't do it by observing me in the classroom. They just hoped that I wasn't a drunk, because the last man they had was a drunk and the one before that a queer. I put a scare into them when I drove up in the yellow MG.

When I rented my room, the lady at the phone company (who walked to another desk and became the lady at the electric company) told me that there wasn't much happening in Gorham. The Viet Nam war had taken all the men, and the girls had moved to Hays where there was a college. They didn't come home, even though it was less than twenty miles away. Gorham could still be proud of Betty's Tavern, though. Betty was her sister and in the evenings the phone lady/electric lady became the barmaid at Betty's Tavern, two doors down.

I enjoyed the year. It was lonely at times, but I got to enjoy that too. I took dinner at Betty's and drank my beer in Hays. I avoided going back East. I didn't write Heather and except for one time, didn't see her.

I read a lot. I read all of Conrad, because a professor at the college in Hays was apparently giving a course in Conrad and all the books were in the college bookstore. I made some friends and dated a girl from Hill City. Mostly, I taught my classes and watched the country change with the seasons and watched the people work in it.

I had never been in a place where the weather had so much to do with the lives of the people who worked. If it was a cool autumn day in October and the sky was a deep blue and there was no wind, they could think that whatever they did would go well. They could plant wheat this year and the green bugs would stay the hell out of it; they could run cattle and the winter would be mild enough to bring them through; they could put in milo and not have it buried by an early snow or beat to death by a hail storm. But in January when the wind was over fifty and snow had been on the ground for thirty days, they'd wonder how anything ever made it through the winter and if it did why it didn't go mad.

In the winter I'd stop by the Co-Op after school and stand around and listen to the farmers and ranchers and oilmen talk. There was nothing else to do but talk, or drink. And they didn't like to drink unless they were working, so they swapped lies about hunting and made up stories about how the government was doing this or that, and then cursed the government for doing this or that.

Spring is painful to the prairie. It hurts to thaw out. The frozen crust of snow and the ice and the frozen mud have been around too long to be forgotten right away. Besides, spring blizzards lurk in the Dakotas. The wind comes up again. I remember watching the weather channel on cable T.V. one night in April. The camera would rotate from one gauge to another: Humidity 50; Temperature 32; Time 8:36; Wind (the needle whipped back and forth between forty and seventy). The camera went on: Humidity 50.

By the first of May, I had sold the MG and bought a jeep. I had agreed to teach another year (a hundred-dollar raise to $6,100). I thought I'd look for summer work.

Spring had settled in, the wind backed off, the wheat began filling out the fields. I had never worked before, unless you count lifeguarding at a country club pool as work. I asked around, but without much luck. Money was getting tight and everybody was trying to stay lean. It was in May, two weeks after school had closed, that I ran into Spangler again.

I had seen him a few times around town in his truck. The reason it looked bigger than other pickups was that it had four-wheel drive and sat up higher off the ground. I'd see him alone or sometimes with a small woman whose eyes peered over the dash or out the balky cab side window. But more often than not he'd be with a very old man in a flat cowboy hat who'd beat his hat against his leg when he got out of the truck. Once or twice I saw Spangler in the Brass Rail Tavern getting a tomato beer and sitting by himself at the end of the bar. We'd nod at each other, but I never joined him and I wondered if he remembered me. Sometimes he'd take lunch at Betty's, I learned. But I was in school and so never saw him there. He was around Hays and Hays was small enough so that you'd notice him. You'd notice other people too. Like the Ukrainian who taught German at the college and rode a Mo-Ped everywhere. Or the Burger Shack man in his El Camino car-truck painted day-glow orange. Or the local sculptor in his army fatigues and open jeep.

One night I drank late at Betty's and got drunk. I slept in the next morning and when I got up, I figured the easiest thing to do was to return to Betty's and get lunch. Spangler's red pickup was parked in front, right beside my jeep, left there from the night before. I stopped by and pulled out the keys (a little late, of course) and checked to see if anything (flashlights, jack, tools) had been taken. Then I walked into Betty's and ordered a beer, two cheeseburgers, and french fries.

"You want to sell that jeep?" Spangler called to me from a table by the front window.

"No. I just bought it."

"You get it off Norman Dreiling?"

"No. It's new. I traded a sports car in on it. In fact . . ."

"I thought so, pistol. I knew I'd seen you from somewhere. Bring that beer over here and join me, why don't you?" I did.

"What'd you sell that car for?" he asked.

"Eight hundred dollars."

"I mean why? I mean it was a sporty kind of car. Not one like it anywhere around here. Now where the hell has it got to? Back in the city. Some Kansas City dentist bought it for his wife so she can drive downtown and have a thing in the Muehlebach Hotel. Right?"

The story seemed probable enough to me, so I said so. In fact, I didn't know what had happened to the car. It wasn't on the jeep dealer's lot in Hays.

" Now you got a jeep," he said, looking out the window at it. Betty brought him a dark-red beer and a plate with scrambled eggs at one end, a steak in the middle, and hash browns at the other end. "Everybody's got a jeep. Next you'll want a truck. Then it'll turn out you want to work on a ranch, be a cowboy." He drank his beer; it left a thin red line across his upper lip.

"I *am* looking for summer work," I said.

"You've been watching television too much," he said. I didn't say anything. He cut his steak and it bled into his eggs and potatoes.

"You've been watching the Marlboro ads. They film those down in Oklahoma where the weather is nice and they got enough oil so they can sit around and have their picture taken."

"They are going to take those off the air," I said. "If they haven't already."

"Good," he said. Betty brought my food. I decided I'd try again.

"Know anybody who might need help this summer?" I asked.

"What can you do? Can you rope? Can you string fence? Can you pull calves? Can you drive a grain truck?"

"I can drive a truck," I said. He finished off his beer and held his glass high in the air to signal Betty he wanted another one.

"O.K.," he said.

"What?"

"O.K. Ten dollars a day plus lunch. O.K.?"

"Sure."

"My name's Spangler Star Tukle. And that man there," he pointed to the very old man crossing in front of the window and coming into Betty's, "that man is Jed Wilson Adams." Jed Wilson Adams beat his flat cowboy hat against his leg and knocked considerable dust out of the pants and into the air around the table. He pulled up a chair and, putting his hat on the floor under it, sat down.

"I'm Leo Murdock," I said after Jed got settled. He grunted.

"Leo's going to give us a hand this summer, Jed." Jed didn't grunt. He looked at the table. Betty came up with Spangler's beer and asked Jed if he wanted the usual. He nodded.

"Jed doesn't say much," Spangler said. That was for sure.

It was a week before I heard him say anything. He'd talk to Spangler on the other side of the truck, or up a fence row before they'd come down. After a week, he'd talk to Spangler in front of me: "Tell him to string the bottom wire down low so the calves don't run out," he'd say to Spangler while I was standing there. It was about two weeks before he said anything to me directly. I was driving the truck and had backed it up to a trench silo to dump some corn. When I got back in, Jed got in on the other side. I forgot to put the truck in forward and was about to back it over the edge, when Jed said that if I wanted the truck to go forward I should use first gear, not reverse. I could do as I pleased, but he'd like to know what that was. Forward or backward. If backward he was getting out.

A week later he spoke to me twice, once to tell me that if I wanted to stand in the cattle chute (I was painting the fence) that was all right with him, but since he was putting the bulls through there, I'd get killed presently. He wanted me to know. Later in the day, after bean soup lunch at Betty's, he said that his truck wasn't an outhouse, in case I needed one. Speaking to me twice a day, that was about his limit. At least until we drove the cattle.

Jed's usual came: milk, liver, and two hardboiled eggs. Spangler wanted to know when I could get started. I said that afternoon. He said no, he had some banking to do. They'd meet me right here, in front of Betty's, tomorrow morning at eight. Spangler got up and went to play the juke box. Jed cut his liver into little squares and then stuck four or five of them through with his fork and drew them off into his mouth.

So. I had a job. It looked to me as I ate my cheeseburgers and drank my beer and listened to the juke box play "Wichita Lineman" that I'd have a lot to learn, but I thought I'd never been afraid of learning, even when it meant making a fool of myself. I thought I could work hard and that would make up for what I didn't know, and the harder I worked the quicker I'd learn. It seemed to me I could do the job, whatever it was. I ordered another beer.

"A red one," I said, when Betty took my empty glass.

# Heather

I drank the afternoon away. I sipped tomato beers and played the juke box and the pool table. Some of my students drifted in and beat me at eight ball. Around dinnertime, I asked Betty if she would sell me a couple of cheeseburgers and some french fries to go. A six-pack of Coors, too. I thought I'd go back to my place and eat and drink on the back porch. I could see the sun set from there. The early train was fun to watch come down the tracks from the west. I could see it coming for miles. A black dot against the setting sun. Getting bigger. I liked the way it scared me. I knew I was still alive when I'd hear it blow its whistle for the elevator crossing near where Spangler picked me up that first day.

I was pretty mellow when I left Betty's and walked past my jeep and down the block to my place. I thought it was a bit dubious that I hadn't moved my jeep from the night before because I'd been drinking at Betty's and here I was at it again. The west makes you buzz, I thought, as I rounded the corner to cross the street to my apartment. Parked on the other side, right in front of my door, was a yellow MGTC, wire wheels and right-hand drive. I figured I was in trouble, but after a dozen tomato beers I couldn't figure what kind of trouble I was in. Maybe the transmission fell out and the deal fell through.

I looked the car over. I peered inside to see if it still drove from the wrong side. It looked like my old car. How many yellow MGTCs could there be in Western Kansas? I put my bag of food and six-pack on the ground and got down and bellied underneath to see about the transmission. Nothing. It was cool and shady under the car, though. But a bit dirty. I thought about pulling my beers under with me, but then I figured there wasn't enough room to open one, let alone drink it. I heard a woman's voice. If that voice was as familiar as I thought it was, I knew what kind of trouble I was in.

I first met Heather at a funeral. A popular professor had died and many of his students had gone to the graveyard to see him buried. Heather and I had nodded to each other. She had sat behind me in Shakespeare, in front of me in Milton; and in Educational Psychology we both apparently cut so many classes neither of us knew the other was taking the course. I saw her the first day and then at the final. I thought she must be pretty bright to cut the whole year and then take the final. She told me she had thought the same thing about me. It was the first meaningful thing we shared—so she told me. Unless you count nodding at each other during the funeral. Heather said it was eye contact, not nodding. She had learned from her Psychology courses that eye contact is the first significant bonding between human subjects.

That funeral was the summer before my last year at the University. One thing with Heather led to another. It was like those high-school romances where you fall in love and just to make sure, you trade all kinds of objects back and forth. She wears your letter sweater; you have her forty-five collection and her goldfish bowl (your goldfish). She has the keys to your car, your Water Safety Instructor's patch, and your rubber-band bound copy of *Peyton Place*. If you fall out of love, all this has to be trucked back to each other. It is much easier to stay in love. Heather and I traded books to start with, then clothes (she liked oversized men's workshirts— she liked me in her brother's seersucker pants and Ban-Lon polo shirts with some creature on the left breast). There were other trades: she gave me a golden retriever that got run over by a school bus the weekend before hunting season opened. I gave her a cat (Ralph) who gave birth to eight kittens in her (divorced) mother's house over spring break and wound up in the Kansas City Pound, not to be traced, as if she and her kittens had vanished like a puff of smoke. There was a replacement cat (Ed) who pissed on my shoes. Heather bought me new ones. Kangaroo.

By the spring of our senior year, we were so much in love that it would have taken a U-Haul to break us up. Her father (banker) was talking marriage and wanted to know how I had done in my accounting courses.

"There are no short cuts in adding money," he said to me one day as he was turning the steaks over a Texas Weber Bar-B-Q. "Show me an A in accounting and I'll show you at least a Vice-President."

"Yes sir."

I took to hiding deep in the stacks of the Library during the day, and in the working-class bars at night. Heather wanted to know what the matter was.

"I think we need to talk," she said to me one day, as she caught me in a graduate cubicle near the oversized books.

"I don't want to talk," I said.

"You want to do something else," she said. She fiddled with her Kappa Kappa Gamma ring and shook her hair out of her eyes. I said I didn't know what the problem was, but that I needed a decade or so to think things over.

"Why are you drinking here?" she said to me when she found me sipping beer in the Eighth Street Tavern—a hangout for trappers and farmers along the river. I just looked in my beer.

"I think we need to talk," she said, looking around the place. She talked.

Being glib is easy when there is some distance between you and serious events. I haven't been fair about Heather, but then she was seldom fair about me. I guess I never thought being in love meant getting so intwined that our lives became gnarled in our early twenties. I felt like the old twisted ivy that grew up the limestone walls of Fraser Hall, and out of which birds sprang and flew away.

"There's a teaching job in Gorham, Kansas nobody wants," I said to her one day in late spring as we walked across the campus.

"Where is Gorham?" she asked.

"Near Hays."

"That's way in the west," she said. Western Kansas was the worst place you could go if you had lived in Kansas City and attended the university. That's where the hicks were, and the best people had long ago migrated to Kansas City and now lived (and banked) on the Plaza in Kansas City. I asked her what she thought. She said she didn't want to talk.

I didn't see her the rest of the spring. I had to go to summer school and take some education courses: *Audio/Visual Aids. Methods of Instruction.* It was in July and in the Rock Chalk Cafe when we met again.

"You didn't think you'd see me again," she said, as she sat down in my booth.

"I didn't know," I said. I had passed the months since we parted in a kind of gleeful solitude—it was like going to a movie by yourself when you had spent your entire life going to movies in pairs.

"I thought we should see each other before you left," she said. "I don't think the matter has ended. We are just taking a rest from each other." That was a fair enough way to put it, I agreed. She said there was also the matter of the car.

"What car?" I said.

"My father has this wonderful car the bank repossessed."

"No thanks," I said. I needed a car. I was desperate for a car. My 1951 Studebaker Commander had been impounded by both the campus cops and the city cops. The County Sheriff wanted a piece of the action, too. The campus cops got me for traffic tickets, the city police for pollution. The Studebaker used a gallon of oil with every tank of gas. It dripped other fluids as well. I used to pull into a filling station and tell the guy to fill it up with gas, oil, water, transmission fluid, and whatever they put in the differential. Toward the end, I was getting twenty miles to the gallon of everything.

"It's a sports car," she said.

"No," I said. I was giving in.

"My father can make you a loan. He told me to tell you that. A nice loan. I drove the car up. It's outside." It was outside. One thing led to another, as it always did with Heather. Our lives became entangled again and if it had not been for my job in Gorham, I might now be avoiding short cuts when counting money.

But we parted late that summer and I drove the MG west. Somewhere under the plate glass of her dresser drawer in her home off the Plaza there is a color Polaroid of me standing beside the MG, my left arm across its top, my pink and white striped shirt glowing. I remember shortly after that picture was taken she said it was time for me to leave, and that she'd come out west and see me. This was the second time she'd kept that promise.

"Leo. What are you doing under the car, Leo?" Heather said. For a moment she had me. I couldn't think what I was doing under the car. It was cool there and perhaps I had come out of the sun. But it was dirty in the dirt, and a tight squeeze. I put my nose to the ground.

"I'm back again," she said. "Why don't you come out and see me?" I remember thinking she would spoil the whole thing with the train. Maybe I should stay under the MG.

"No fair hiding," she said. "I've been here all afternoon. Where have you been? I thought we parted so badly in October, I had to come back." That was true. We had parted badly in October.

"Say something," she said.

"Where did you get this car?" I asked, looking at the rear axle. I wondered again if I might open a beer. I reached for the six-pack. Perhaps I could stay under the car, prop my head up into the engine compartment, drink my Coors, and talk to her through the grill. I could make the hood go up and down like a dummy's mouth. I popped a beer tab, but I had to do it sideways and the beer flowed out and onto the ground before I could get my mouth on it and suck away a mouthful.

"I heard that," Heather said. "Come out, Leo. We need to talk."

"No." It was easy to talk through the grill if you used short words.

"This is no way to start over," she said.

"Where did you get the car?" I repeated. A full sentence. The hood worked its hinges on that one. I poured more beer (sideways) into my mouth.

"Why did you sell it?" she said. "Father told me you sold it."

"I'm a cowboy."

"You can't sell a car without the bank knowing about it." Pure truth, I concluded, had a way of keeping my hood shut and my radiator cool. I looked toward my food. The grease that had soaked through the bottom of the sack had gathered a layer of dust. I wondered what Spangler would think of his new cowboy now. It was time to sober up and face the issue.

The best thing about Heather was the way she took off her clothes. She looked like one of Renoir's women—the woman in *The Swing*, wearing a blue dress with white buttons down the front and there are two men standing beside her, trying to get her attention. She is not looking at them. She is looking out of the painting at me. And if she is Heather, there's always a good chance that she'll move her left hand to the top button of her dress and undo it. That happened the evening of the funeral and at selected times throughout the following year. It happened in October, when we had last seen each other.

"There's a woman to see you, Mr. Murdock," said Lucas Schmidt, all grins.

"Who is it?" I asked. Not really thinking who it might be.

"She's wearing a red dress and a straw hat," Lucas said. A crowd of kids was beginning to gather around me.

"Back in your seats."

I had gotten used to living alone and was just now enjoying the first of what turned out to be two Indian summers. I had found myself the proud owner of a diffident and laconic state of mind. Nothing fazed me. The soft October days made me friendly and passionless in a way I never understood. I tended to forget who I was. I caught myself wondering who owned that yellow MGTC parked in front of the post office. Who owned those Kangaroo shoes on my feet?

I told my class to be quiet or I would put a hex on the Kansas City Chiefs for the entire season, and then I walked through the lunchroom and out into the schoolyard. Heather was sitting on the fender of her mother's black Buick (Electra 225). Heather was a car-fender sitter—she must have picked it up from a T.V. movie.

"I've come to see you. I think we should talk," she said.

"I'm working. I've got another hour to teach."

"I'll wait," she said. She shifted on the fender. Her dress had dusted part of it clean. I told her I'd meet her at my apartment. She knew where it was, she said.

"Who was the woman?" asked Lucas, as I was leaving school an hour later.

"A friend."

"You want to go fishing with us, Mr. Murdock?" he said, trying to keep a grin off his face. "We're going down to the Smoky Hill."

"No thanks," I said.

"Why not?"

"Get out of here or I'll put a special hex on Len Dawson." In my mind I could see myself plopping down on a river bank, a pole propped up by a forked stick, and my eighth-graders, the wholesome pride of Gorham, drinking Coors and smoking Camels. I had been there before.

"How can you live like this?" said Heather, as I came in the front door. "Not even a phone. I tried to call you and they said you didn't have a phone. I didn't believe them, but I've looked all over the place and you don't have a phone." She looked around again. Her red dress rustled slightly about her thighs and she twisted at the waist. "Why are you reading *Playboy Magazine*?" she said. "I think we need to talk. Who is Virginia?"

"A girl from Hill City," I said.

Heather would take off her clothes for two reasons. Well, one reason—it was just that there were two different moods that got her unbuttoning, unzipping, unsnapping, and shedding. When she was happy she'd become giddy and silly, and then she'd think of herself as a naughty girl. She liked the word "naughty" and she thought that a unilateral undressing was good and naughty. In this mood she liked to loosen all her clothes—unzip a dress down the side, unhook a bra underneath the dress, push her panties down so they gathered about her knees and then lift one foot out of them. Then the other.

She liked to be loose in her clothes, she said. It made her feel free. She would stand near the open window at the end of her room in the Kappa house and let the breeze blow through a gapping sleeve or an open blouse. She would shudder a bit and close her eyes, and then move her shoulders and waist and thighs, and clothes would shake loose and fall. A skirt would slide toward the floor, a dress might catch on a hip, her bra would jiggle from her breasts. She would take a deep breath and, eyes closed, take off what had not fallen off. Spangler would have said she was proof there was a God.

But she would also take off her clothes when she was angry. Not bitching-yelling-angry, but moody-pouting-angry. These moods were likely to come across her when she wasn't getting her way in long-term plans—like marriage and living on the Plaza, Marimekko on the walls, window boxes on a balcony patio, and multiple blenders grinding away at banana daiquiries. She would begin by saying we should talk, and end up by taking her clothes off. At these sessions, she didn't always realize what she was doing—or at least when she was starting the process. It usually began when she'd take off the Kappa Kappa Gamma Sorority ring and place it on the table. It wasn't until she'd slipped off her shoes that she knew what she was doing. She'd toe and heel them off and the sound of the second one hitting the floor would startle her a bit, and her eyes would open up wide, and her pouting lip would thin out a bit, and she'd stare out of the Renoir painting at me and know what she was doing, and what she wanted.

"Little things mean a lot," she said, as I offered her a can of beer that October, forgetting that she liked hers in one of the Pilsner glasses she had bought for me.

"It's October," I said. "I can't remember little things in October."

"What's so special about October?" she asked.

"Nevermind."

"Is it Miss October? In *Playboy*?" she said.

"I don't think so."

"We used to talk about things like that—like why we liked something. You don't want to share things with me anymore." She was getting to thick stuff quicker than usual, I thought. She sipped her beer. "It's been two months since we've seen each other. I thought we could talk things over."

"Six weeks."

"What?"

"It's been six weeks since we saw each other."

"I think it's nice that you've kept track. That's a good sign." Heather could create whole worlds of good will out of a phrase. "That's nice," she said again, and sipped her beer.

"It wasn't long enough," I said, pulling on my beer can.

"What?" Her eyes widened and her lower lip grew thick.

"You should have waited until I came back for Christmas. We could have seen each other over Christmas. I told you I needed to be away from . . . from you, I guess."

"You've *been* away. I agreed. That was part of the plan. But there are other parts to the plan. We need to talk over lots of things. Living at home is not an easy thing to do. Mother is wonderful. I spend some days with Father, and he is nice to me. But I am not going to spend my life like that."

"I don't know how I can help," I said. She had put her beer down and now twisted her sorority ring on her finger. It came off in her right hand, and she put it on the table next to her beer glass.

• • •

I scooted out from underneath the car. My hood was getting tired of talking anyway, and if I didn't pull myself together, I'd miss my train.

"It's good to see you at last," Heather said. She was standing in the doorway, behind the screen door. I must have wobbled a bit as I got to my feet. "Are you drunk?" she asked.

"Yes," I said, and leaned against the fender of the car.

"Is that nice?" she said. She was wearing one of those sleeveless summer dresses—halter dresses—yellow with big blue buttons down the front and straps that tied behind her neck. I didn't know what to say.

"Are you glad to see me?" she began. She propped the screen door open with her foot, then let it back.

"Give me until the fall," I answered, accidentally skipping over about twenty minutes of upcoming conversation. "I have a job."

"Your job is over," she said.

"I have a real job." I leaned back against the car, but the MG's fenders were much lower than the jeep's, and so my notion to lean back firmly and brace myself, tuck my thumbs in my jeans, square my shoulders—be a man—all that—it failed, because I wound up at a slightly oblique angle, tilted backward toward the tavern. I was too tight to admit a mistake—at least that mistake. "I have a job," I said again. "That's why I bought this car."

"*I* bought that car," Heather said with maternal patience. "You bought that nasty red jeep over there."

"Well. Yes. That's true. I have a job, though." I reached down and got my beer.

"What kind of job?" She had taken to leaning against the door jamb, and had finally—firmly—propped the screen door ajar with her right foot, which raised her summer dress along her thigh and made gaps and tight spots along the row of buttons. "What kind of job?" she said again.

"I am going to be a cowboy." I opened a beer and took a drink.

"What kind of job is that?" she said.

"I don't know, but I'm going to find out." My back was getting tired because I was at a bad angle.

"Stand up straight," she said. She paused while I readjusted myself and finally gave up the leaning-against-the-car pose and just plopped down on a fender. "Why don't you come in here and see me?" she said. "I've fixed a nice dinner." Using her foot, she bounced the screen door open wider a few times, then held it there. I could see the tan line on her right thigh where her Bermuda shorts had been. And then the leg went behind the screen, and into the dress.

"I brought my dinner," I said, and looked at my sack of cheeseburgers I had left on the ground. She bounced the screen door against her foot a couple of times.

"I've fixed a good dinner," she said. "I've cleaned your place up, too. Why don't you come in and see? I brought a bottle of wine. We could have dinner and talk."

I looked at her but didn't move. The shadow from the post office was edging toward me, but still I was in the sun. It must have looked like there was a spotlight on me. I'd finished one beer and started another. She fiddled with her ring, turning it around her finger, and then flipped the screen doorway open with her foot, but didn't catch it when it came back. Her sandal came off as she pulled her foot back. It plopped down a step to the ground. I could see her behind the screen—more clearly now—she shifted slightly then leveled off. Her smile became deeper and more thin-lipped. She shook her shoulders.

In October, her red dress, tailored, long sleeves, had a large brass ring fastened to the zipper that ran frankly down the front to the bottom. She smiled as she leaned back against the dark-brown chair in which she was sitting. She slipped off a loafer and rolled it over with her other foot. Her head rested over the chair's top and she tossed her hair so it fell down behind it. For a moment, she looked like a singer reaching for that meaningful phrase at the end of a meaningful note. Her mouth was slightly open and she closed her eyes slowly, then opened them to look at me. I opened another beer. I could tell she put me out of focus. She ran her left hand along her left thigh and up the trail of the zipper until it reached the ring. She closed her mouth into a thin smile.

The screen door was dusty. Someone long ago had put bandaids over holes near the top. The wood frame needed painting. Through the screen, Heather looked brown and impressionistic. She shook her hair out.

"I have a job," I said. "I am going to be a cowboy."

She leaned forward, placing her hands on either side of the doorway, bending forward frankly. The top button of her yellow dress had come undone and I could see the suntanned edges of her breasts.

"A train will be by soon," I said.

"One of my students might stop over," I said. She paused, then put her right hand behind her neck and massaged it, making her head bob slightly. She caught the brass ring with her index finger of her left hand and gave it a slight tug. She arched a bit, stretched out so the zipper line flattened. Her eyes were still open and I could tell she was taking me in and out of focus.

I couldn't see her eyes through the screen door. She held herself with her left hand against the door jamb and began undoing the blue buttons with her right. There was a white ribbon butterfly where her bra joined in front. When she reached the button at her waist, she stopped and again put both hands on either side of the screen. Sometimes looking through the screen, I couldn't tell if she was magnified or far away. She'd loom toward me and then fade into an image. A breeze stirred. The building's shadow formed a crisp line with the sunlight on the ground. She shifted against the doorway. She hunched her shoulders so the neck strap grew slack, and then twisted back and forth by pushing with one hand then the other, like a cat. I like white bras. I reached for a new beer.

· · ·

As the red dress parted along the zipper, I could see the light brown of a fading summer tan on her neck and shoulders, and below her white bra, on her stomach, and then along the tops of her thighs as they eased into pale-yellow bikini panties. Her head was back now and her eyes were closed. The dress was unzipped to the bottom, where its lock held it until she flexed her thighs a bit, shifted, and the dress opened across her legs and fell against the chair. She stretched her arms as if in a yawn, and the top opened wide.

The screen rattled slightly with a capricious breeze. It must have come through the windows in the apartment, because it stirred the yellow dress at the bottom. She stood up straight and gathered the bottom of the dress in one hand and undid the buttons with the other, looking at them intently. Now she was back from the screen just a bit, but standing full in it, her yellow dress hanging from her neck by its straps, now open, now closed, as the evening breezes edged back and forth through my apartment. It was a muted picture—the screen toning down the yellow dress and freshly bronzed legs and arms and stomach, the pale-green panties. Only the bra would not be faded by the screen or the shadows. It glowed. I could not see her eyes. She unhooked the butterfly and her bra fell open, her breasts fell free, white as her bra.

She had to arch her back off the chair in order to reach behind her and unhook her bra. It went slack and then jiggled a bit, as her breasts shook when she settled back into the chair. I finished my beer. She had me in focus with a steady stare, while I caught the slight twisting of her shoulders, the flexing of her thighs and hips.

I had seen it all before, I said to myself in both October and June, too. But from here on she could be capricious. She might leave for a back bedroom where you'd hear the easy creak of the bed she'd settled onto—saying nothing, waiting. More clothes—but never all of them—might slip, drop, slide off. Poses could be struck: wearing only a bra, she stands in a doorway, leaning against the jamb, legs crossed at the ankles. Bare-breasted but wearing a summer skirt that you can see through, she stands in front of a window, the streetlight shines through, her panties are in her hand. I had seen it all before, even the variety. Standing in the sun, looking through the screen, drinking beer—I began to see it all together.

A train whistle blew. She stirred in her chair and then hooked her thumb into the left side of her panties and raised her left leg out of them. They gathered like a bandanna around her right thigh. She reached behind her neck and untied the strap of her yellow summer dress. She smiled from the chair and arched her hip slightly. The dress fell away in a rustle to the ground. The train whistle blew. Her bra gaped open. I could no longer see the butterfly. She leaned back in the chair and closed her eyes and pushed her bra up high on her chest. She moved toward the screen and pressed her hips against it, the pale-green panties turned more to lime. She propped the door open with one foot. She arched, stretched her arms and hands behind her in the chair. Her breasts rose like muscles toward her shoulders. She lifted her hips off the chair. I could hear the train itself now. I put down my beer and went toward her. She smiled.

## II

I woke when the return train from Kansas City came through. That was usually around two in the morning. Heather was sleeping on her stomach, and the lone Gorham streetlight reached through my window and across the bed and glowed on her back. She stirred when I got up and put on my jeans and went outside. Something seemed wrong.

The empty beer cans reminded me that I was thirsty. I sat down on the step and leaned back against the screen door. The air was cool but heavy. I caught myself staring at the MG, thinking it was mine, and wondering if I needed to change the oil—I had forgotten to check the mileage lately. I shook my head and thought about Spangler and my job. I walked up to the corner and looked down toward Betty's. My jeep was still there, its snub nose against the curb, its windshield folded down on the hood. My students had done that—in the spring they'd wanted rides and they'd wanted the windshield down, and so their single act of vandalism was to put the windshield on the hood most every night. Bugs zipped around the streetlight. Far off down Highway Forty I could see headlights. When it gets late at night, you always think the only car on the road will be a cop. I started thinking about my job again and why Heather sleeping in my apartment seemed wrong. Before the car along the highway got to Gorham, I went back to my apartment.

I thought I should wake her up and tell her to get dressed and go home. At least go to Russell and stay in a motel. But I'm no good at things like that. I can't drive people away from me. Not because I need them—it's some feeling the other way.

I got a pillow and a blanket from the bedroom and went outside. I walked over to my jeep and took out the passenger's seat so I could stretch out and go to sleep. I still couldn't pin down what was wrong, but I remember thinking as I went to sleep that I hoped I'd wake up before Spangler came to get me so I could be out of the jeep. I didn't want to explain things. It seemed like mixing two lives together when one hadn't even begun. It turned out I woke with the morning light.

I took it as a sign of good luck that Jed picked me up, and not Spangler, or else Spangler would have noticed the MG. It also seemed to me lucky that Heather slept through the night. I left her a note on the MG, saying that I was going to Idaho and would not be back for a week. I'd write her. Even though I was tired and hung over, my luck made me feel strong again and I remembered how I felt early in the afternoon before, when I'd just gotten my job. Jed drove me to Hays in silence, his flat hat on the seat between us.

# Going to Work

**I**

**M**y first days of work, I rode with Spangler in the pickup. Jed was redrilling some milo in Graham County. I was costing Spangler time, because everything he did I'd ask about, and he'd be good enough to explain.

"How come you keep the horses and the cattle in separate pastures?" I asked, as we were cutting the horses out of a cattle pasture.

"Horses eat the best of the grass. Cattle just mow it down. If you let a horse stay in a cattle pasture, he'll pick out the best stuff. The little blues and clover."

"What are all those lumps up and down the lane there?"
"Cow shit."
"I see."

"Why does the wheat grow higher in little patches than elsewhere in the field?"

"That's where a cow pissed. That wheatfield was used as winter pasture."

. . .

"How come Jed doesn't talk to me?"

"He doesn't like you."

"I see."

"Am I going to need a horse?"

"Can you ride?"

"No."

"I don't think you'll need a horse."

"You want me to get out and unlock the gate?" I said, as we pulled up to the lane into the ranch.

"Either that, or fix the fence after I drive through it."

Work was tougher than I thought it would be. I mean it was harder work, harder on your body—stretching wire, cleaning out barns, hauling feed, painting barns in the hot afternoon sun, digging post holes. But working cattle was the hardest job.

One day Spangler lost two steers to modern-day rustlers. They cut his fence, drove in with a pickup (probably with a stock rack on it), and loaded two head out of a small pasture on the east side. We found the rest roaming up and down the road.

"The price of beef is getting too high," Spangler said. "I see the barber in town has got a steer tied to a rope in his backyard. It's time to sell when rustlers start cutting your fences and barbers start feeding cattle." He paused and looked at the open fence. "I'll cut their nuts out if I catch them."

Spangler decided we had to brand the cattle. Jed and Spangler rounded up the herd: nearly three hundred steers, about a hundred first-year heifers, and two hundred cows with their calves. The calves were too little to brand. The others we ran into a squeeze chute and put a large four-pointed star on their right hips with an electric branding iron. We gave the steers shots for shipping fever while we had them in the chute.

My job was to let one steer down the run (a narrow, fenced lane) to the chute at a time. That meant holding the rest of them in the pen where they felt crowded. It also meant getting the steer who realized he had made a rash move in dashing through the gate I'd opened and now wanted back with the herd—it meant getting him the twenty or so feet down the run to the chute. I'd beat him on the butt with a buggy whip, twist his tail, stick an electric prod in his ass (which would usually work), or finally I'd have to get behind him and, poking with the prod, push with my shoulder. Working behind the cattle that way I got kicked hard four times the first morning. And once, a small steer got turned around in the run and came back at me and pinned me to the gate at the other end. Jed beat his hat in the steer's face, but that didn't help much. I'd dropped the prod, but I finally drove the steer back by kicking him in the face a couple of times with my boots. By noon, I was a bruise from my toes to my waist and selected bruises the rest of the way up. I was covered with steer shit.

I skipped lunch and drove back to Gorham and went over to the school and borrowed some baseball equipment: shin guards (which I strapped under my jeans), a crotch cup (it was a matter of time, I figured), and a chest protector (which I covered with an extra-large sweatshirt). It would be a hot but less painful afternoon.

I must have looked a little bulky when I returned. Spangler kept glancing at me. Jed gave me a long, hard look when I first got out of the jeep. But they didn't say anything. It took me a while to get used to my gear, but once I did I worked well. Only my hands and face were vulnerable. They took a beating, but by the end of the day I learned how to duck flying hoofs and how to know when the steer was about to dump on you as you pushed him that last foot or so into the chute (the air thickens a bit just before). It would take us a couple more days to finish up the job, Spangler said, as we quit for the day.

By the third day, we were down to the heifers. Some of them were too small for the squeeze chute and they'd scoot down and Jed couldn't squeeze them tight enough. There they'd be, flat on their bellies in the bottom of the chute, and Spangler would have had to brand them too high on the shoulder.

I was feeling pretty good about all this. Heifers are smaller than steers, and my job had suddenly gotten easier. I thought it was about time the guys up at the other end had some trouble. There was a pause in the action as Spangler and Jed conferred. I was considering going behind the barn and getting out of the baseball gear; it was going to get hot and it didn't look like I'd need all that protection with the heifers.

"You ever play football?" Spangler yelled at me.

"Yes," I said with some pride. "Quarterback and middle linebacker. In high school."

"That's good," Spangler said, then talked with Jed some more. "I never played football," he said, walking up to me on the outside of the run. "Middle linebacker. You have to be a pretty good tackler to play middle linebacker."

"You're supposed to be the best," I said.

"Come on up here a minute," Spangler said, and motioned for me to follow him. I climbed the fence out of the run and walked up to the chute.

"You feeling all right?" he asked, looking at the way I walked.

"A little stiff."

"You putting on weight?"

"It's eating at Betty's," I said. He nodded. Jed stared.

"See that heifer in the bottom of the squeeze chute?" Spangler asked. I said I did. "Well, it turns out, as I'm sure you've observed from back there, that we can't get that pissing bitch off her belly so we can brand her on the side. And unless we start branding them on the back so only the ding-a-lings that fly around in helicopters can see the star, we gotta do something else."

"I see."

"Now what we're going to do is this: We're going to open up the front of the chute and when she comes out, bang, you're going to tackle her. Just like when you were middle linebacker. Knock her down, and then we'll brand her."

I looked at the heifer. I went up to the chute and took a close look at the heifer. "How much does that heifer weigh? I mean . . . I mean about how much does she weigh out at?"

"Two hundred," said Spangler. Jed slapped his hat against his leg. A slight breeze blew the dust away.

"What do I do again?"

"Stand right in front of the chute. I'd get in a little closer. You don't want her to get much of a run. Now tell us when you're ready." Jed moved over beside the chute. "Remember to give her a good belt."

"Wait a minute," I said.

"No. Let's just try this one. A practice run. Knock the green-shit out of her. O.K., Jed."

Jed pulled the chute gate open. The heifer got up off her belly and stuck her head out and peered around. I was poised. She bawled but didn't move. This was going to be easy. No problem. A piece of cake. I started toward her, figuring that I'd wrap a head lock on her and toss her down. Jed struck her in the ass with the electric cattle prod.

On her way over me, I caught hold of the left back foot and didn't let go. She pulled me about a hundred feet over to the water tank where it was muddy and where all the cattle go after we brand them. There they take a drink, piss themselves dry, and take a shit. I didn't let go. The mud slowed her down a little, and I got up on her leg a bit more, but then she began kicking me with the other hindfoot. Somebody hit her from the front (Spangler) and down she went. I looked up and saw Jed coming at us with the branding iron, the extension cord snaking out behind him. Spangler was laughing in the mud, body pressing the front half of the heifer. Jed said he'd run out of cord and we'd have to drag her over out of the mud, at least. We did. I held the hindquarters down and Spangler the front, and we branded her in the dust. We turned her loose and she bolted toward the herd.

"What happened?" Spangler asked, as we walked back to the chute.

"I'll get the next one," I said, glaring over at Jed, who was rolling up the extension cord over his hand and elbow. "I just hit a little low."

"I mean your leg," Spangler said. "That isn't your shin bone shining through, black and all polished." My jeans had ripped and the shin guards were showing. Jed said maybe I ought to hit them with a ball bat next time.

"You a catcher or a middle linebacker?" Spangler said.

"I'm a smart cowboy," I said. Spangler laughed and said he'd see about that.

The next couple of heifers were big enough to brand in the chute. Then there was another small one (that is, one around two hundred pounds).

"I'm ready," I said. I had taken my sweatshirt off and was down to the chest protector and T-shirt. I gained mobility, but ridicule as well. All Spangler said was, "Tell us when."

"Go!" I yelled. This one came right out and turned a little to the left. I hit her high, around the neck, and twisted her head into the dirt. Her body followed with a thud. I held her front quarters down while Spangler tied her feet. Jed branded her while she bawled and her eyes rolled back into her head and she drooled all over my arms. Even in the chute, they'd do that every once in a while, and we'd have to get some water and bring them around by throwing it in the face.

I felt better about that second one. I had done the job clean. About every other one from then on out was too small for the chute and I'd get the call. Sometimes no matter how hard I'd hit them, they'd dump me and all I'd get was a leg and Spangler would have to dive in. Twice more I got dragged through the mud and piss and shit. The cattle standing around the tank would scatter a little and watch me getting dragged through the dirt and mud, and see one big man in his forties running after me with his head down, and an old man after him, with a branding iron held high, checking back to see how much cord there was left. We were done by early afternoon. Spangler said to forget the last heifer in the holding pen.

"Why?" I asked.

"She's bingy." I looked over the gate and there was a small heifer with short black ears that seemed oddly deformed. She was leaning against the fence. I opened the run-gate and she immediately crouched down, lying flat on the ground, her head between her outstretched hoofs.

"She thinks she's hiding. When we round them up or even move them from pasture to pasture, she falls out and tries to hide behind a clump of grass or one of those scrub oaks out there," Spangler said.

"What's the matter with her ears?" I asked.

"Frostbite. She was born in a blizzard. I think the cold messed up her brain. I guess I should have shot her then, but I don't seem to ever get around to it." He looked at her the same way he had looked at my car, his nose and his lip coming together. "You want her?"

"I guess so. What could I do with her?"

"Keep her out there. I won't charge you pasture fee on a bingy heifer. She might come around. You did a good day's work. You can have her, if you want her."

"O.K."

"Do you want to brand her?" Jed asked. I looked at him.

"I don't have a brand," I said to Spangler.

"I think we've got a bar brand around here. We can make about any brand you want. Save a circle. Not that we can't spot her. Or anybody'd steal her."

I looked at her. She had moved some and was now hiding her two hundred pounds behind an old dried cow turd.

"Let's brand her," I said.

"If this were for real, you'd have to have the brand okayed by the state. But I don't think we need to do that. What you got in mind?" Jed had gone off to get the bar brand.

"How about a plus sign."

"That's Norman Teems' brand. How about a double plus? Like a tic-tac-toe square. Those kids you teach still play tic-tac-toe, don't they?"

"Sure." We carried her to where the extension cord would reach. I branded her myself. Jed sat on her hindquarters, but she didn't put up much of a fight. He had to beat her with his hat to get her up. She looked at us over her shoulder as she walked, her rear hips out of line with the front of her, toward the water tank and the rest of the heifers we had branded that day.

"Tomorrow we move them back to the north pasture," Spangler said. The three of us got in the truck and we drove over to Gorham and took a late lunch at Betty's.

# II

"Leo needs a horse," Jed said to Spangler, putting a stack of cut-up liver bits into his mouth.

"Think so?" said Spangler. Jed didn't respond. "Jed thinks you ought to have a horse," Spangler said to me. "We can go on down to Al Johnson's place this afternoon, and see what he's got," Spangler said to Jed. Jed grunted.

"He should not wear those clothes," Jed said. I had taken the chest protector off before I came into Betty's, but the shin guards were still shining through the rips in my jeans.

"How much do horses cost?" I asked.

"Get a good one for three hundred. Maybe five hundred. You got three hundred?" Spangler asked.

"Yes. What about the rest of the stuff? How much will a saddle cost? And I'll need a halter and bit." Jed grunted, and ran his fork through the last piece of liver with a jab.

"Not halters. Bridle and bit," said Spangler, trying not to laugh.

"I'm sorry." I didn't want to make Jed look like a fool for suggesting that I needed a horse. That was quite a step on his part.

"We've got an old McClellan saddle around the barns you can have. But if you want your own, you'll be out another two or three hundred—when it all comes together." I had saved some money during the year, partly because there wasn't much in Gorham to spend it on. I was trying to be cool about all this horse buying, but I was excited as a kid. I was determined to drink my beer slowly and ask questions one at a time.

"I can carry you against your wages," Spangler said, thinking, I suppose, that my silence was due to the fact that I was trying to figure out where the money would come from.

"I got enough," I said.

"Sure?"

"Yes." Jed finished off his milk and reached under his chair and got his hat, which he put on his lap. It was the sign that he was done and that he would wait impatiently for the two of us. Spangler had grown used to it over the years, but in the months ahead I never did.

"What kind of horses will Al Johnson have?" I asked.

"Quarter horses," Spangler said. "That's all anybody's got around here. I hear there's a girl schoolteacher who keeps an American Saddle breed out at Sullivan's. But they're not horses, and I don't believe Sullivan would let one on his place."

I was finished with my meal and beer, in spite of my deliberate slowness. I looked at my fork. I stared at the red nap inside my glass.

"You want another beer?" Spangler asked, as he ordered one.

"No. I mean O.K. Sure." Jed stirred on his elbows. After the second beer, we left Betty's and drove south to Al Johnson's place. I had taken my shin guards off in Betty's restroom before I left. There seemed to be a moment of silence in the place as I walked between the tables, shin guards under my arm. I tossed them in the back of the truck and we were off.

At Johnson's, I made a series of blunders, most of which resulted in a grunt from Jed and a weak grin from Spangler.

"Don't get on a horse, boy, without 'a having reins in your hands. See," said Al Johnson, an old leather pouch of a man.

"Now, you'll bust your arm clean off, clean off, 'a riding with your hand on the horn. You'll see. You'll stop sudden and it'll try to vault you over frontwards. But most arms don't hold the weight. They bust. See?"

What I couldn't see was how I was going to stay in the saddle unless I held on to something.

"Spring into the saddle, don't pull it down on you, you dumb son-of-a-bitch. A horse can't like that. Having a saddle twisted round him so it's upside down. Where the hell did he get those boots, Spangler?" Spangler said he didn't know where I got my official Explorer Scout hiking boots.

Spangler told me I ought to buy the last horse I tried, Chief Lightfoot. Johnson wanted three hundred dollars for him and agreed to throw in some worm medicine. The horse didn't have worms bad, but he had them, Al Johnson said. Spangler said we'd borrow one of Johnson's trailers and take the horse right then, if that was all right with him. I'd be by the next day to square with Johnson. Spangler gave his word on it.

It was dusk when we unloaded my horse at Spangler's ranch. The land in the west was making a clean black line against the red sky. There was no wind. I could hear cattle moving and bawling in the pasture near the barn. A pheasant called from the hedge row that circled the house, then flew, climbing above the cedars for an instant, from where it could see me leading my horse to the water tank, stroking it along its long neck.

The next day, I settled up with Al Johnson, who was careful to explain to me that I had bought a "horse," not a mare, and not a stallion, both worthless for work. Later in the day, I bought a good used saddle from the enormous salesman who runs the Chap and Spur Western Shop (branches in Goodland, Dodge, and Garden City). I also bought a hat, a shirt with snaps for buttons and three snaps on the sleeves, some Hyer cowboy boots, and at Spangler's suggestion, a bull whip. It gives you range on a horse, he said.

Before I went back to work (I had the morning off to settle affairs), I drove back to my place in Gorham to store my new stuff. I wasn't going to show up wearing shiny boots and a pressed shirt.

I'd break the clothes in, along with my saddle and my horse (and my ass). By the time I got back to the ranch, Spangler and Jed had moved the cattle. I gave Chief his worm medicine, and spent the rest of the afternoon fixing fence. A constant job.

I learned to ride by doing it after work (when we quit early) and on Sundays, when we didn't work. I wore my new clothes until they got dirty and old, and then snuck them into my outfit one piece at a time, boots first. My horse was good tempered and patient. The only time he got fed up with me was when I cinched the saddle wrong and wore a hole the size of a quarter in his side. When I went to saddle him up again, he reached back and bit me just above the kidney. I bellowed in pain; he turned loose after he gave the flesh he had between his teeth a good twist. Then he stepped on my right foot as he wheeled away and down the lane, his head high, the reins in the dirt. I didn't tell Spangler about any of this. Jed wanted to know if I was still wearing the shin guards, because I was walking crooked.

"How's the riding coming?" Spangler said to me after a couple of weeks. "We got some cattle to move the end of this week. Think you can help?"

"Sure." At nights I couldn't sit down; the insides of my thighs were raw, there was a large parenthesis of a horse bite turning blue on my back, there were strawberries on my ass, and the nail on my great toe was black with blood. By the time the end of the week came and we were ready to shift the cattle from one pasture to another, I was so stiff I couldn't get into the saddle without standing on a rock. I didn't want Jed or Spangler to see me, so I led the horse around the barn where there was an old limestone fencepost on its side. From it I'd swing my broken body into the saddle and ride around to the other side of the barn, all grins.

As I said, my horse was gentle, but not lazy. I rode him for nearly six months, pretty much every day. I rode him over two hundred miles in one stretch, and I learned a lot about avoiding pain and making things easy for myself and the horse. I've never asked Spangler if he knew how much I hurt that first time out.

Most of the work during the middle of the summer was getting the steers ready for selling. We'd put them in one pasture for a number of days and then move them on to another. We were also building calving pens and rebuilding the inside of an old barn to accommodate the cows that would be calving out that winter. Spangler figured he could cut down on the number of calves lost to the weather if he could run the cow inside the barn just before she gave birth.

We also built a cattle dip. That's a cement hole, shallow at one end and deep at the other, like the hole for a pole vault. At the deep end it was six feet; the shallow end rose level with the ground. It was filled with water and a pesticide solution that would kill the parasites on the cattle. One day we had to dip the heifers.

We set up the portable corrals and chutes and brought the heifers up through the pasture and into the run, and prodded them down the run and off the edge and into the dip. Down they'd go, in a swell of water and chemical foam, and up they'd come, swimming desperately and bellowing until they found their footing on the ramp that got them out.

I went out on my horse and brought up Tic-Tac-Toe, driving her from gully to gully and cow pile to cow pile. She always seemed oddly surprised that I could find her hidden behind a ten-inch clump of grass, or half-foot-high badger mounds. She wouldn't go down the run to the dip. Spangler and I carried her to the edge and together we swung her in. She hit the water on her back and came up feet first, kicking. She couldn't swim, or did it so poorly it amounted to the same thing.

Jed quickly tried to rope her when she bobbed up, but her head never got above the water, and the rope just played on the waves. I jumped in and grabbed her around her head and towed her to the shallow part. She was drooling and breathing like a broken accordion. She shook herself loose and started up the ramp, but slipped and slid back into the deep end.

I got her by a front hoof, and this time Jed roped her (he looped me too) and Spangler and Jed pulled us both out and onto the ground. She lay there, twitching. Then still. Then she coughed, her whole body shaking, and her eyes rolling around in her head. She shook like a dog when she got up. Then fell down. Up again, and this time she wobbled off to join the herd.

Spangler was running for the barn, and came back with a garden hose sputtering water at its end.

"Get naked, you dumb son-of-a-bitch. That stuff will rot you down to the bone." He began spraying water at me. He was right. My skin was beginning to sizzle.

I stripped off my shirt, but I couldn't get my jeans over my boots and I couldn't get my boots off because they were wet. Jed took a knife, cut my jean legs up both sides, and then pushed me in the chest, knocking me on my back. He gave a good tug at my jeans and pulled them off. All this time Spangler was spraying me with ice-cold well water, and I'm lying in the dust, naked except for my jock-strap and cowboy boots. My balls had burst into flame, I was sure.

"You better get that jock off," Spangler yelled. "I'll bet there's something there you don't want to rot off." He was right about that. A stream of ice water right in the crotch.

"Get on in the bunkhouse and get in that old tin tub," Spangler said. "Jed, you get some Comet or Ajax from the machine shop."

In a few minutes I was sitting in a tin tub of cold water thick with Spic and Span, Ajax, and Twenty Mule Team Borax. I scrubbed myself down with a horse brush. Spangler pulled my boots off by straddling my leg with his butt to me, and I'd push with the other foot.

That was the end of the day. Using gasoline, Jed burned my clothes and boots (if they'd only been the scout boots). I rode back to Hays in the truck, naked. Spangler loaned me some clothes for my trip to Gorham. Jed brought my jeep in, and as I drove it home, I thought about having my cowboy clothes burned and about my heifer almost dying, and I had to wonder. The radio was on and the merchants of Hays were advertising a full moon sale: *Moonlight Madness,* they called it. You could buy black wing tips at half the price between the hours of seven and nine. I thought that since I was going to have to buy some more clothes, I might call it quits as a cowboy and buy myself some of those wing tip shoes and maybe a seersucker jacket and yellow linen pants. Maybe I should give Heather a call. But it was only an idea in my mind.

That night I had a nightmare in which my heifer drove my jeep into the swimming pool where I had worked as a high school student. She floated to the top feet first, wearing black wing tips on all four hoofs. In the morning I wondered what it meant.

# The Weather

I read somewhere that weather is the first refuge of a sentimental writer. I suppose so.

There's an old joke in Hays about going out to the edge of town and watching the cold front come in. Things are pretty dull in a town whose theater plays *Hud* for thirty days, and whose students think Cornelia Otis Skinner is a contemporary playwright. But I've gone to the edge of Gorham to watch the cold front come in.

Once I walked up the railroad track that ran behind my apartment and, while tossing stones at fenceposts, watched the western horizon as thunderheads climbed past twenty thousand feet. I could see the tops of them glowing like hot glass in the afternoon sun. The bottoms were flat and dark, and as they got close, I could see that they made huge shadows on the ground, large circles of black that covered sections and sections of ranchland. Just at dusk these thunderheads would pulse with lightning and the whole inside would light up and then go dark, only to flash into life again a moment later. When it got dark, I could see bolts of lightning coming straight down out of the sky, long straight bolts, miles long, it seemed, and miles and miles away. Jed called these "gravediggers" and after he saw one, he would touch wood and not look at the sky again.

The ranchers were proud of the weather, as if it were a home-grown affair. They said it didn't take much to be a rancher in Texas or Oklahoma, where it was nice most of the time. They had greater respect for the ranchers to the north of them, especially the Montana ranchers, but then the cold weather there was pretty predictable. A fellow could plan on it. Spangler would say that the thing about Kansas weather was that it was "mercurial." I taught Spangler that word, and it pleased him so much that he'd use it like a teenager with a new car. He'd steer conversations to use it:

"How's that senile old judge down in Garden City?" he'd ask of a group of farmers and ranchers standing around the Co-Op.

"Just as always, I guess," a rancher would say. "One crook gets off and the next gets life. Just the same as always."

"He's a mercurial son-of-a-bitch," Spangler would say, just as he put his hat on to leave.

"The ballclub at the college is sure mercurial," he told the barber one day.

"Yes, I guess you're right about that. Hadn't thought of it myself, though."

"The price of beef in Kansas City has been awful mercurial this week," he said to his wife Opal one night when I was at dinner.

"You want another Coors here, or are you two going to the Palomino Bar?" Opal said.

Winter comes in bunches before Thanksgiving and then settles in for one hundred days of cold, broken at odd times (like New Year's day that year) by absurdly warm and gentle days. Blizzards are common through the first days of April. For every inch of snow, there is a foot drift; the land as much as the wind makes the drifts, the land that is flat save for the knolls and crevices and draws and creek bluffs scattered across the prairie.

The wind is vicious and people have been driven mad by its speed and constancy. It makes you paranoid, thinking there is something you didn't do, a gate you didn't close right, a barn door not latched properly that will beat itself to pieces in the wind. It unsettled me when I was by myself at night and there was nothing I could do about the nameless fear that haunted me.

When it all calmed down and there was still snow on the ground, the prairie was a study in brown and white. I became pretty personal about the snow I could see from my apartment windows on light nights. That's my snow you're trucking through. Stay off my snow.

"It all melts and turns the whole damn place into mud," Spangler said when I talked to him about it once.

In the late spring the whole western part of the state seems as soft as the feather pillows the ranchers' wives hang out on the clotheslines to air. Huge dandelions, with heads as big as cotton balls, come to seed in the fields. The grasses grow tall and seed out, bending over. The wheat moves like water in the wind. The cottonwoods set loose showers of flouncy white seeds that float lazily through the air: it is as if the pillows on the clotheslines had broken. Quail call for their mates. Doves sit in pairs on power lines.

# Spangler Gets in a Dark Mood

Spangler lived in a house in town; Jed lived in the old place on the ranch. Sometimes we'd meet in Gorham at Betty's (if we were going to work on some land Spangler had near there); other times we'd meet at the main ranch, but most often we'd meet at Spangler's house in Hays. There we'd have a cup of coffee and talk over what had to be done and who was going where. (Spangler not only had the main ranch and the land near Gorham; he had land south of Hays, in the irrigation district, and land way north of the ranch—a quarter section here and there—bought by his father in hopes of getting oil production off it.)

During these mornings Opal, Spangler's wife, would be scurrying from room to room getting herself ready for school (she was taking a summer course at the college and teaching public summer school in the afternoons). She was a tiny woman, friendly and alert. She checked with Spangler to see what he was going to do that day, looked to see if there was enough coffee made to hold us through our morning planning session, and asked if either Jed or myself would be at the house for dinner that night (we were most always welcome—she just wanted to know). There didn't seem to be any children around, though on a living room table there was a photograph of a boy. I recalled that when we had been talking about saddles and horses, Jed asked why didn't I use Harold's stuff. Spangler didn't answer.

After we decided what was to be done and who was to do it and who was riding with whom, we started off. Sometimes we planned to meet for lunch, other times it wouldn't work out. In the beginning I always went with Spangler; Jed didn't want to fool with me. But after the branding session, Jed warmed up a little, and sometimes he'd say that he needed me if he was to do such and such. Couldn't be expected to do it alone. Not that I'd be much help.

Sometimes we'd know in the morning it'd be a long day ahead of us, and Spangler'd leave a note to Opal saying not to wait dinner on us, we'd eat out.

It was July. Jed had changed into his "over hundred" outfit, very baggy bib overalls and an oversized armless workshirt that he wore inside the overalls, but which ballooned out through the straps whenever there was a breeze.

The price of cattle was going up. Spangler had over two hundred and fifty steers plus two hundred cows, a hundred or so heifers, and some bulls. I had a heifer. Spangler didn't want to sell the cows or the heifers. He planned to sell the steers when the price was right. It was getting close to right. It was higher that July than anybody could remember.

We had worked late one night, and Spangler and I were eating at Dirty Dan's, the Hays twenty-four hour restaurant where the farm and ranch hands and other working men take their meals when they're not eating at home, or at Betty's, or places like hers in other tiny towns. Spangler was using dinnertime to try to round up some trucks to move his steers.

He wasn't having much luck. He didn't like truck drivers and they knew it. He thought they were leeches on the ranchers, like the sale barn operators, the stockyard bidders, the future buyers and finally, the lowest class of leech, the traders in antique barbed wire. Spangler had no end of foul names for collectors of old barbed wire.

Spangler would take a few bites of his food, then get up and walk over to a table full of truckers and stand there talking to them a moment, then come back.

"Dumb sons-of-bitches. All the fences and loading pens of mine they've busted into kindling with their fucking trucks. I think I'd rather work with the railroads. They're dumb sons-of-bitches too, but at least they had to deal with me when I wanted them."

"Won't the truckers take your cattle? Money's money," I said.

"Oh, they'll take them all right. They might get to them by Christmas. Then they want an arm and a leg as pay. And a left nut as a bonus. Shiiiiiiit." Spangler always pronounced shit with seven syllables.

"Why don't we drive them to market?" I said.

"Shiiiiiiit." He ate his steak and eggs. In a moment he said, "You know, they built the Fort here to protect the railroad workers from the Indians. I'm not sure it was such a good idea. If there hadn't been a fort, then we'd have 'natural selection.' Right? You teach science. I mean, the ones that could keep from getting killed by the Indians would be better men than the dead ones. Right? If we'd had natural selection in this country back then, we'd have some real piss-cutters around here now. Instead of these candy-assed truck drivers and pussy barbed-wire traders." I made it a point of not commenting on Spangler's social theories. He seldom waxed philosophical unless he was about ready to do violence of some kind. I'd try to get us back talking about the main thing, whatever that was.

"Why can't you use the railroad?" I asked.

"It doesn't load cattle here anymore. I'm not sure it takes on people. You probably have to drive to Denver to get on a train. That's okay by me, though. Get that damn train out of here. The only people who need it are the suit and ironing board salesmen downtown. A merchant is just a goddamn housekeeper, as far as I can tell. Putting things on this shelf, hanging things up here, dusting a table. Fuck. They can stick that airport up their ass, too." He signaled for more coffee.

"Those eggs weren't fresh," he said to the waitress as she poured him some coffee. "What the hell happened? Did all the fucking chicken farmers start to raise cattle, and now we get our eggs shipped in by stagecoach from Arkansas?" The girl looked at him blankly. Spangler barked. A loud bark, just like a dog. She ran off.

"I wonder if I could drive my steers to Kansas City," he said, after he took a couple of gulps of coffee. "I might as well. By the time I sit around here for a month and then pay the price I'm going to have to pay, I might as well drive them down the road. What is it, two hundred miles?"

"Two fifty. Two seventy-five," I said.

"Twenty into two fifty. What's that?"

"Twelve and a half."

"Two weeks then. Hell, that's not bad. We could leave the middle of August and be home in time for you to be back teaching." He looked into his coffee cup. He could see himself frowning, pushing his facial skin toward the bridge of his nose. Then he could see himself clear the wrinkles from his face, save the ones from age and weather, and smile cautiously.

"Dad was once on a cattle drive," he said. "But I never was. Jed was, though." He finished off his coffee in sips.

"You ready?" he said.

"No. I think I'll have some pie."

"O.K."

He sat there, staring out the window. Every once in a while, he'd start to drink the coffee he'd already finished. He drank off his water. He drank my water. I ate my pie. Quickly.

"You ever been on a cattle drive?" he asked me absurdly.

"No."

"You finished yet?"

"One last bite."

"I'll pay the bill then. What'd you have?"

"It's right there on the check," I said.

"Right. I'll pay the bill and meet you out in the truck."

"I'm done."

"Oh. Well, I'll pay the bill then." We went to the cash register.

"Don't you curse at my girls like that, Spangler Tukle," said the old crone in a shiny black waitress dress at the cash register. "I heard what you said. Those eggs were fresh. We got them this morning from Harry Becker."

"Harry Becker. Harry's so fucking dumb he thinks you gotta let eggs ripen like tomatoes. Those eggs probably been sitting in the sun on his windowsills for a week."

"You get your ass out of here, Spangler. You don't need to bring it back in here again, either. Not unless you want it kicked." The woman grabbed Spangler's change as it rolled around in one of those change return cups, and threw it at him. He caught some coins, but others rolled out across the linoleum floor.

"Here's what's left for a tip, you black-eyed bitch," he said, and tossed the coins he had caught in her face. "Buy yourself some Virginia Slims. It's been a long time since you've come, Baby." We left.

"Mercurial old bitch, wasn't she?" Spangler said as we got into the truck. He drove me to my jeep, parked that day at his place in town. I drove home, wondering what he would do about driving the cattle to Kansas City.

Spangler brooded over the notion for more than a week (for most of summer, really). He didn't say much about it, but because I was there when he had considered it, I knew what he was thinking about. Not talking out the idea with other people was unusual for him. He'd usually say to Jed, didn't Jed think it was a good idea to plant Sudan grass on the Gorham section this year? And what the hell did I think about eating at Gorham today instead of driving twenty miles out of our way to eat at Dirty Dan's? I was consulted about the big stuff.

One morning, just as Opal was leaving the house to do some shopping, the three of us were gathered around the coffee pot in the kitchen, and Spangler said to her that he was thinking about driving a herd of steers to Kansas City the end of the summer.

Could she give us a hand? She paused at the door and looked at him straight on. Either she had married a fool, the look said, or she didn't hear right. She said she'd talk to him about it when she came back. And there wasn't enough food in the house to feed me or Jed.

# Harold

Spangler had a son, Harold. He was the boy in the photograph on the living room table. Harold went to the University in Lawrence. Sort of. Nobody knew, really. Nobody asked, that was the point. Each month Spangler would send a hundred-dollar check to Harold in Lawrence, and each month when Spangler'd thumb through his checks, he'd find Harold's check endorsed with some message scribbled under his name: Rich I'm not/But don't cop out/Got some pot/Not a lot/H.T. His ear wasn't good, but he was sensitive and loved plants. He could feel vibrations from all living things. I didn't like him.

The University is a big place and there was no reason why I should have ever seen him there, but I had—I thought. A friend of mine had dated a girl who believed in the Blue Spot, some mystical sign I was told. Not everyone can believe in it and fewer can see it. She saw it. I was over there once to drink some beer, and I remember the place being full of people I'd never met—thin men in madras shirts who wore long hair and were hollow-eyed. After a while they lit up some joints. I left because I didn't smoke and I didn't want to get busted. The University was pretty straight in those days and students like myself were in a landslide majority. Beer drunks is the worst we were—gregarious at taverns, trying to pick up girls.

The few potheads were odd and sad. But nobody disliked them much. In fact we all tried the stuff, but had better luck popping down capsules of ground-up Heavenly Blue Morning Glory seeds. I saw God under a stuffed chair one night, but went back to beer the next day anyway.

It seemed to me Harold was at the party given by the girl who saw the Blue Spot. I thought I'd seen him around campus, too. You get so you notice people in their places, and I thought he might be the one I'd see every once in a while walking across campus during the dinner lull—when I was coming back from a late Physics lab. Perhaps he was the one who used to sit near the door in the Quiet Room in the Student Union, and never seem to do anything but sit. I couldn't be sure. Just impressions.

Once the girl who saw the Blue Spot held a seance. It was a pretty famous event around campus. I wasn't there, but I heard she got Hemingway and John Milton to appear. Hemingway wouldn't talk to Milton, so the story went, and Milton wouldn't talk to the Milton professor who was present. The whole thing ended up with the Blue Spot girl running around the bell tower nude, saying that a white panther was chasing her. They put her away, but everytime I'd see Harold—or one of the students like him—I'd wonder if they had been at the seance. I hadn't thought about any of these things since I'd come west. Now they seemed farther away than a year—and something of a secret. I didn't ask Harold if he had been at the seance.

He drifted through Hays a couple of times during the summer, and I learned more about him—in bits and pieces. He was a vegetarian and a drama major. But he didn't act because that was all ego. He put up sets and took them down; he studied Japanese *No* plays. He had devised two sets of language: one for the philistines (I got lumped into that group pretty quickly), the other for pure folk. The language I got was a string of commercial messages strung to make a kind of comical sense. He thought Jed was pure folk and Jed got "breath units." The first time I met Harold, he was on his way to Denver to "relive and revitalize pure sensations recorded Kerouac's *On The Road* Neal and Sal Larimer Street." That's what he told Jed, anyway.

"There's a decent gun store on Larimer Street," Spangler said. "I bought that Winchester Model 70 there. Paid less than a hundred bucks for it. That was a buy, even five years ago."

We were sitting in the living room. Opal was cooking supper. Jed had been convinced to stay. Harold was in a half-lotus position under the window air conditioner, rocking back and forth. Spangler seemed at ease. I didn't think he would be. The only difference was that he seemed obliged to keep track of the conversation—or be in on it. I was the one who felt odd. I kept thinking Harold was going to say, "Aren't you the guy who was at what's her name's place a few years ago." / "Did you hear about the seance?" / "Don't I know you from somewhere?" I didn't want connections made.

"Leo went to the University," Spangler said to Harold.

"Harvard on the Kaw. I'm a Jay-Jay-Jay Hawk down at Lawrence on the Kaw." Harold stopped rocking. I looked away.

"I went right here to College," Spangler said, meaning Fort Hays Kansas State College. "All the Tukles have gone to college in Kansas. We've been in the state three generations, with me."

"Where the buffalo roam and the deer and the antelope play," Harold said, and started rocking again.

"Is Opal from Kansas?" I asked Spangler.

"She's a sunflower from the sunflower state. She's the one flower, she's the flower of my heart," Harold chanted.

Opal said from the kitchen that Harold had learned all those Kansas songs in grade school. And that he shouldn't be so smart. He should talk right to company. Dinner was ready.

"I hope you like duck," she said to me as I came into the kitchen. "Spangler shot these last year, and he shot so many of them we had to freeze some. They're pretty strong, but I soaked them in salt water to take some of the wild taste out."

"What the hell for?" said Spangler.

"Not everybody likes to taste every little worm and weed the duck's been eating, Spangler," Opal said. "We've got company."

Spangler looked at me and frowned. I sat down. Opal turned out of the kitchen and told Harold his rice was ready, she thought.

Harold claimed to own only one material object: his rice cooker. He didn't count his clothes, books, the McClellan saddle, and one-third share in a six-thousand-acre ranch. His rice cooker was electric because the world was electric.

"I don't think he'd bring even that with him," Opal said, "if I'd let him build a fire in the front room or on the lawn to boil water." I gathered he toted the rice cooker, which was a G.E. electric pot, everywhere he went. He seemed to have an inexhaustible supply of brown rice stored in small, firm paper bags hidden all through his knapsack and clothes. He said he liked brown rice. Spangler said saki was made from rice—at least it was when he was in Japan after the war. No telling what the little Nips were sending to the States these days.

"You only go around once," Harold said to me as he sat down at the table. "Give it all you got. Take your very best shot."

"Does Buddy Jenkins still teach in the drama department?" I asked, remembering the name of a popular teacher. It was my first try.

"When you've said Bud, you've said a lot," Harold said as he fiddled in his rice with red and black chopsticks. Jed gnawed on a duck carcass.

"I think these are gadwalls," Spangler said. "You know, I don't know much about ducks. I know a mallard when I kill one—and a red-head, but all this other stuff that flies around when you jump a pond, I don't know what they are. Some people call those small ducks butterballs, but then I know some Army Colonels down at Junction City that call them dumb-dumbs." Harold hummed softly to himself as Spangler spoke. I couldn't make out the tune.

The ducks were strong, rich, and oily in an odd way. I ate lots of bread. But Spangler and Opal ate theirs with great relish, and in total oblivion of the powerful odors and tastes. Jed grunted with pleasure every now and then, and Opal seemed to be able to distinguish a pleasure grunt from one that meant Jed was in search of, say salt, or butter, or another one of the four glasses of milk he drank. Spangler and I drank Coors.

After dinner Opal cleared the table. I helped and she didn't protest. Spangler and Jed sat still, Spangler bending over his beer, Jed in a polite trance. Harold helped himself to more rice, and began to talk to Jed.

"Summer SunHot EarthWarmth NewGrow ReLive Breath Hot-Hot MeadowLark SunFlower Prairie PrairiePrairie PrettyPrairie PrairieMan PrairieMan Well?"

Jed made a small noise and ran his upper lip down his black and yellow teeth a couple of times. Opal brought him a toothpick.

"Yeah," said Spangler, "Old Jed's in good shape this year. Right, Jed?" By then, I knew he wasn't, and I thought that Spangler was no use in telling a lie. His voice changed, and it was full of made-up gentleness. I'd have rather heard him say that Jed was rotting from the inside out, like an old turtle, and we should leave him alone about it. But he didn't say anything like that, and I couldn't tell who the lie was told for.

"How's Duke?" Harold asked in a straightforward way, as if to say he could cut the crap when he wanted to. He turned to me. "That was my horse when I was a kid. Jed's horse too, but I learned to ride on him."

"He's all right," Spangler said. "Duke and Jed know how to get along with each other."

"I thought he came up lame this winter," Opal said, "and Pratt said we should put him away."

"Pratt's a killer," Spangler said. "If I put everything away that Pratt says to, I'd have my pasture covered with leather."

I finished my beer. I caught Harold looking at me.

"You working for us this summer," he said.

"Yes." He stared. "I like it," I said.

"You get a lot to like with a Marlboro. Filter. Flavor. Flip-top Box." I should have hit him then.

There was an awkward silence.

"How about some beer, Opal?" said Spangler. "Give us a couple more beers." She said we were out.

"When you're out of Coors, you're out of . . ." Spangler cut him off by pushing the table back into his lap as he got up.

"I'm going to the Palomino Bar," he said. "You come along," he said to me. I did.

"Two for the road," Harold said as we went out the door.

When we got back around midnight, Harold had left for as little reason as he had come. We had not talked about him at the bar, and we seldom talked about him any other time, either. Only sometimes, Spangler would mention him in connection with something else.

# We Have a Conference

All through the summer, the idea of the cattle drive grew in my head. Any chance I'd get, I let Spangler know what a good notion I thought he had to drive his cattle to market. I worked hard in hopes that he would see there would be no problem with my taking care of my end of the deal. And I'd play to prejudices about the matter, too.

"I see the price of gas is going up. Bet the truckers pass that and then some on to the cattlemen," I said.

"Dumbfuckers."

"I wonder if there's a law against driving cattle to market."

"Probably. Some ass-hole Wichita dentist who spends a week a year as a state legislator no-fucking-doubt got some law passed so his golf courses won't get shit on."

"What if Opal puts her foot down and says no go?"

"Shiiiiiiit."

I was getting anxious. I could see myself, straw cowboy hat set straight and level on my head, back straight in the saddle, with a bull whip in my right hand, the reins in my left, riding in my faded jeans and Levi's workshirt—riding back into the part of the state from where I had come. I could never get the dream of the drive to go through the particular suburb where I had lived. It was much too far out of the way, for one thing. Plus the vision of two hundred and fifty steers scattered throughout my lawn and hedge and pin oak suburb was more than my mind's eye could see. But I could get the girls I had ogled at the swimming pool to stand in lines along Central Avenue and say, "Yes, yes, that's the same Leo Murdock who used to guard at the pool. The very same one." They'd wave and I wouldn't remember them, but I'd wave back. I left Heather out of the whole thing.

When it came right down to it, though, I didn't see how we'd ever make it. I thought we'd get across the western part of the state without much trouble. Most everybody drives their cattle a few miles down the road from one pasture to another, or even a day's drive from one ranch to another. It was just a matter of stringing a number of one-day drives together. But I didn't see how we'd ever get through Kansas City. I grew up there. I knew what it was like. We'd either have to come through the suburbs to the south and down the Southwest Expressway, or come straight through Kansas City, Kansas, and then over the Central Street Bridge. Going through the heart of the city was shorter. But that didn't make it possible.

I got to thinking. These weren't my cattle. This wasn't my ranch. I had nothing to lose if the Tukles got two hundred and fifty steers into the middle of Kansas City and they scattered all over the place. That's why I could afford to bait and push Spangler into the drive. I got to ride high in the saddle and have all those guys I drank with back home at Kelly's offer to buy me a beer and ask what it was like before the herd went berserk. Any way I'd cut it, though, it seemed wrong not to tell Spangler I didn't think he had a chance to make it through the city.

"We can't get through the city," I said to him one morning as we were drinking coffee at the house in town and waiting for Jed. Opal was upstairs getting Harold's room ready for a possible visit. (He arrived a week later.)

"What?"

"You'll never get the steers through the city. If you're still thinking about driving the herd to Kansas City at all, I think I better tell you that there's no way you're going to get them into the stockyards."

"Why the hell not?" he said.

"Have you ever been to Kansas City?" I asked.

"I guess I have. In fact, every time I go there I get lost and wind up in the stockyards." He grinned. "Never fails. We tried to go to the Starlight Theater one year to see *Oklahoma* and wound up in the stinking stockyards. I think I can get there by now."

"That's not what I meant," I said.

"What did you *meant,* then?"

"How you going to keep the herd together in all that traffic? How you going to keep them from running up every alley along Central Avenue? What makes you think traffic is going to come to a grinding halt, so you can drive down the middle of streets that are so crowded now everybody wishes his horn was a gun? What makes you think some shoe clerk who keeps a thirty-two pistol under his cash register to shoot niggers isn't going to go ape-shit when he sees two hundred and fifty steers coming down the street at him and pull off a few rounds at you?"

"That's your problem," he said, just as Jed drove up.

"What?"

"I'm not keeping you on 'cause you're the best steer roper in three counties. And the last time you tried to pull a calf, Jed and I were thinking the mother was winning. Jed figured we'd have to pull you and the calf out, if we left it to you. Do you know how high your ass bounces off the saddle when you get to galloping?" He frowned. "I'm keeping you on as a specialist. A 'city specialist.'"

I was hurt then. And now. But I shot back: "Fine. My first act is to tell the both of you (Jed was beating the dust out of various parts of his body with that frayed hat of his) that you better hire the trucks to pick up the cattle at Bonner Springs. That's twenty miles up the road. You'll be lucky to get that close to the city without a major mess."

"I could get a woman to tell me that," Spangler said.

"What?" said Opal, coming into the kitchen from upstairs. Jed sat down at the table. Spangler passed him the coffee. "He thinks we ought to truck them in from twenty miles out." Opal looked at me.

"I don't think you can make it into the city," I said. Jed had poured out the last of the coffee. Opal took the empty pot and began making some more.

"What do you think, Spangler?" Opal said.

"I think he can figure it out," he said, pointing to me. Jed grunted into his coffee hard. He must have produced foam.

"You don't just 'figure out' how to get two hundred and fifty steers down Central Avenue in the middle of the day."

"It's not like we're going through Kansas City, Missouri," Spangler said. "That's the big town. Big doings in that place."

"It's not like the Kansas side is a village," I said. "Any way you go, you've got to come down a main street. I grew up down there. Those streets are packed. It's a regular, full-sized city. It doesn't make any difference how much bigger it is on the Missouri side."

"That's your problem," Spangler insisted.

"Then my solution," I announced firmly, "is to have them trucked in from Bonner Springs."

"That's like jacking-off on your wedding night," Spangler said. Opal sat down with a cup of coffee. I was glum.

"How do you think the shopkeepers would feel about coming through there?" Opal asked me.

"Pissed," I said.

"Fuck 'em."

"So pissed they'll get out an injunction before we get there. The cops will shut down the drive around Bonner Springs and we'll have to truck them in." I looked at Spangler. He growled. Just the same way he "barked" at the waitress in Dirty Dan's.

"What happens if we beat the injunction?" Opal said.

"I'm not a fortune teller," I said. "It's not like I know these people personally. I just drank beer with them when I was growing up. I don't know what they'll do. But I imagine they'll shoot a few steers for openers. Block off the street with trash. Set fires. Shoot out our tires. Gather in a mob. Throw bricks and bottles. With gas in the bottles. Snipe at us from rooftops. And then lynch us from a streetlight."

"I see," she said.

"That's his problem, Opal," Spangler said.

"How about some help?" I said. Spangler wasn't in the mood to be reasonable.

"Why don't you find something to do while Leo and I figure it out," Opal said to Spangler.

"Like what?" he demanded.

"Fix the riding mower," she said.

"What the fuck for?" he said.

"Harold might be home today. He might mow the lawn if the mower works."

"I'd have to cement his ass in the seat." He frowned, his nose and lips pursing toward each other. "Is the tool box in the truck?" Spangler said to Jed. Jed nodded. They went outside. Opal drank her coffee.

"I'm sorry," I said. "I don't want to screw things up. It just won't work."

"That's all right" she said. "But he'll never drive those cattle two hundred and fifty miles just to have them trucked the last twenty." Outside we could hear the lawn mower start and die. Start and die. Not start.

"Maybe we could get the cops to escort us through the city," I said. "We might have to pay them, though."

"A bribe?" she asked.

"No. I was thinking maybe they'd have a way of renting themselves out for special services like that. I don't know. Only we can't get that last five miles—maybe not even the last twenty—without cops everywhere." They were pulling at the lawn mower again. Spangler was swearing. Opal stared out the window for a moment, then said:

"I better get it organized. I think the thing to do is to drive the route first. All the way to Kansas City. Then, while I'm there, talk to the cops. Spangler's not too good at talking with people like that. Besides, he might say there's no need to get their help. That wouldn't be doing it right."

There was more swearing now from outside and what sounded like a banzai-bellow followed by a large thud. We went to the window. Spangler had thrown the mower on its side. Its up wheels were spinning, and gas was leaking out of its tank. Spangler was standing there, peering down at it, hissing through his teeth. Jed had backed off. Spangler turned and stalked toward the truck.

"Spangler. Spangler Tukle. Don't you dare!" Opal screamed through the window. He had gotten to the truck and was pulling the shotgun off the window rack. Opal ran out of the kitchen and down the stairs into the garage, which would lead her outside to the driveway. I followed. We were both still in the garage when we heard the first shot. We were just outside, as Spangler pumped the shotgun and fired it again, blowing the plastic seat away into shreds. There was a large ragged hole through the bottom from the first shot, and the blade was bent back and up through the hole. While we stood there, Spangler methodically pumped the gun again and, as we moved out of the way, went around to the other side and shot the lawn mower straight on, into the engine's tangle of wires and metal lines. The machine shuddered. Small pieces flew across the lawn. We ducked. A large piece (the carburetor?) clanked to the driveway.

"You want a shot?" Spangler said to me from across the way, holding out the gun.

"No," I said.

"I didn't think so," he said.

"That wasn't necessary," Opal said.

"Yes, it was," he said, shucking the smoking empty shell out of the shotgun and leaving the breech open. He walked back to the truck and put the gun away.

"You," he said to me.

"Yes."

"Set fire to that son-of-a-bitch and then tow it to the rendering plant with that jeep of yours. Tell me what they say to you when you bring a dead riding mower in." He stalked back into the house. Jed followed him.

"What should I do?" I asked Opal as we stood there looking at the mower.

"Burn it. Tow it to the rendering plant. Tell him what they say. Once he shot a radio that told him the government was going to regulate cattle prices. He sent it to Ezra Taft Benson." Opal went back inside.

I threw some gas on the mower and tossed a match into the machine. It burst into flame with an explosion, singeing my hair. I could see the curtains of the kitchen window part and faces looking out. I stayed outside until the mower stopped burning, and then backed the jeep up close to the charred hulk and, using a chain from the truck, towed the mess through the streets of Hays (it left an ugly black stripe as well as various charred parts all along the way) and a mile south to the rendering plant.

"What the fuck's that?" said the man in the pearl-snap red western shirt who ran the rendering plant.

"One of Spangler's bulls got hit by lightning," I said.

"Get that piece of shit out of here," he said.

"Grind it up fine and you can sell it to the burger shack in town," I said as I unhooked the chain.

"I mean it," he said. "What kind of fucking deal is this anyway?" I got back in my jeep and drove away, quickly. Men were gathering around the mower. The man in the pearl-snap shirt scooped up a handful of gravel from the driveway and threw it at the machine. The other men circled it.

# The Palomino Bar

The summer was closing off. There was little more talk of the drive. I was beginning to worry; I had school to teach starting the third week in September. Opal had made the trip to Kansas City. It had taken her the better part of a week. She didn't say much about it—only that she had worked out the details, except for Bonner Springs (Spangler had it in his head to put the herd up at the Farmers Hall of Fame. Opal said they were mulling it over). If she talked to Spangler in any more detail about her trip, he didn't say anything about it. Only that I was still in charge of the "CITY." Still, it didn't seem to me that we were going for sure.

At times I'd wonder if Opal was trying to talk Spangler out of the drive, but she wasn't (or hadn't succeeded) and I guess I began to add up little things to that conclusion. Spangler bought new tires for the truck and horse trailer (they were on sale, he said.) He drove the steers into the big pasture, the one with the best grass. He bought another horse (a good buy—he could always use another horse). He bought extra ropes, saddle blankets, flashlight batteries, and rain slickers. He had the horses shod (mine too). We got so that we assumed we were going, but we didn't talk about it, and we didn't know when we'd be leaving. Opal was working out the plan.

It was late in August and we were sitting in the Palomino Bar after dinner, just me and Spangler. I had done well this summer, Spangler said. I had caught on fast. Aside from what he'd said a few weeks ago. Such speeches usually preceded an invitation to do something with Spangler he'd normally do without me. Like the time just the week before, when he asked me if I wanted to fly down to Texas with him and McCormick in McCormick's Bonanza to look at a herd of Angus that was for sale. I did. We went. A fine trip.

"Monday's the first day of dove season," he said. "You want to go?" It was a cautious invitation. I had the feeling he wasn't too pleased he'd made it.

"Sure. I'll have to buy a gun, though."

"You don't have a gun?" Spangler frowned at me. I wanted to go hunting badly, or I would have let him out of it.

" No. I've never owned a gun. Never been hunting." He drank his beer off.

"Well," he said after a moment, "I've got a gun you can use. No use buying one." He stopped and looked at the pitcher of red beer between us. "Only, you've probably never shot a gun before. If you don't have a gun. Maybe we ought to . . ."

I told him I'd shot a gun a few times at Boy Scout camp and that I didn't think I'd blow his head clean off, if that was what he was worried about. He looked at me wearily. I thought the reserve of respect that had been building in him for me was being drained at about the same rate the level in our pitcher of beer was going down. Didn't I know by the way he drank his beer off that he wanted out of the invitation? Of course. But I had done well this summer.

"What time do we get going on this dove shoot?" I asked.

"I don't know if Harold's old Model 12 works or not," he said.

"That's all right. I'm going to buy my own gun anyway. I've been saving for it. I might as well do it now. What would you recommend?"

"A single shot," he said quickly, while nodding his head in an affirmative way. "It's best to learn on a single shot. Especially when you shoot doves. That way when you miss the first shot you . . . I mean, when you're out there swinging around on a bird and you miss . . . you miss. You can't take another shot. For instance. There isn't another shell in the gun." He drummed his fingers. "I'd get a single shot. I've got a good one I'll sell you. Five dollars."

"How about an automatic? A five-shot Browning automatic," I said, watching him shift around on the bench seat in the booth.

"Oh no." He filled up his half-empty glass. "I wouldn't do that. They cost a shit pot full of money, and then an automatic always jams. Besides," he said with growing conviction, "that's what those damn Kansas City dentists are always bringing out here to shoot pheasants, and sure enough, one of them shoots the other and then says he didn't realize all you had to do was keep pulling the trigger and the damn thing would keep shooting. I think a single shot is just the gun for you." He looked at me, wanting to know what I'd thought of what he'd said.

"There's a Winchester pump, a Model 12, down at Red's," I said. "He wants a hundred and fifty for it. Jed told me it was a good buy. If it's still there, I guess I'll buy it."

"That's good enough," Spangler said. "I think that's better than an automatic." In his mind I could see that he was calculating just how much more dangerous a pump was than a single shot, but then on the other hand, how much safer it was than an automatic. Maybe we could shoot some beer cans early in the afternoon, he suggested, and then after that we could go stand by a pond the hour before sundown and shoot the doves as they came in for a drink. Fine, I agreed. The talk turned then to women.

"Do you have a woman?" Spangler said to me directly.

"Sort of," I said.

"What the hell does that mean? That you take her to the movies, but you don't get the job done?"

"Not really. I mean . . . well, I mean I don't take her to the movies," I said. This wasn't any of Spangler's business, but I didn't lie—and I didn't tell him not to pry. It wasn't that I minded that he knew about Heather—if it just hadn't been Heather. I had been doing a pretty good job of not answering the letters I got from her. Not even the one I got that morning made me think of her once all day.

"She the girl that spent some time with you at the first of the summer?" Spangler asked, and drank from his beer.

"How'd you know?" I said.

"Gorham is a small town. They say you were bouncing around so much in bed you set off the crossing lights ten minutes before the train got there."

"I don't think so," I said.

"Hear you get some mail in purple stationery."

"That might be a federal offense, you knowing about that," I said.

"Nobody reads the letters. It's just that everybody knows about them. She poked around town after you one day. Asked was it true you'd gone to Idaho."

"I had a long lunch hour that first day," I said.

"I take it you're only in love with her now and then," Spangler said.

"She's a mercurial woman," I said. Spangler nodded.

"Opal's mercurial too," Spangler said. "Only she's not as mercurial as she is stubborn." He signaled for another beer.

"I don't like women," I said.

"You queer?" Spangler asked.

"No."

"Good. You don't go after goats or cows do you?" he persisted.

"No."

"Good. They say in Missouri that you aren't a man unless you've put the hindlegs of a cow into your boots. That's not true out here. But then they've got ugly women in Missouri."

"I like to screw women," I said. "I just don't like them."

"You ever hear about the sheep herder who committed suicide?" Spangler asked. "He heard the song 'There Will Never Be Another You.'" I told Spangler that was a terrible joke, but he didn't hear me he was laughing so hard.

"I like that one," he said. He drank some beer to end his laughing. "I know what you mean about not liking women," he said. "But that's a slim attitude. It's partly their fault, though. A lot of them fall in love with you just because you fall in love with them. That's not right. It makes things unpleasant when what got you moving after her was the idea of her in the rack. What do you notice first about a woman?" he inquired.

"Her boobs," I said.

"You won't change your notion about women until you notice the face first," he said. "That's when you'll get to like them. You won't like them all. Not even most of them. But then most men are turkeys anyway." I said maybe he was right.

After some silence for drinking, we started talking about the cattle drive: "I guess we'll leave the middle of September," Spangler said. "That's when I'd take them off grass, anyway. By the way, that heifer of yours got through the fence again."

"I'll cut her back tomorrow."

"Just leave her. She's no problem."

"I guess I can't make the drive," I said. "School starts late this year, but not that late."

"I've fixed that. Opal's going, too. I had to talk to the school board about her and so I talked to them about you. You'll get docked pay, though. I'll make it up."

"O.K.," I said. I got scared at being left behind, and relieved at being included so fast, I looked cool. "No better offers from the truckers?" I said.

"Haven't asked. I'm not going to deal with those shit-heads until I'm dead and come back to haunt them as a rusty spike in the bottom of a pothole on Highway 40."

"You going to drive cattle every year?" I asked.

"I don't know. The bottom's going to fall out of the market any time now. By next year we may all be broke." He paused. "I'm going to get the Green Gables out of the truck and make me a boilermaker." He left, but was back in a moment with the bottle in a paper bag. I turned down his offer of Scotch in my beer. He poured himself a hefty drink, about one-third Green Gables, the rest beer. I told him he'd get pretty drunk pretty fast that way, even if it was right after dinner. He said he wanted to get drunk.

"You know," he said, putting his finger in the rising foam of the beer in order to stop it from topping over, "we're going to do this cattle drive just like we knew what we were doing. Just like the real thing. What do you think?"

"Pour me a little of that whiskey," I said. I wasn't going to take care of him. "What do you mean 'like the real thing?'" I had my doubts too (if that's what he meant), but I couldn't name them.

"I mean, I've never been on one of these deals before. I've driven cattle. From one pasture to the next. Everybody has. Even the fucking barbers. They drive them from one backyard to another. The other day I saw a steer in a college teacher's yard. Tied to a cement block. The guy was hauling grass clippings to him. I don't know who's worse, the barbers or the Kansas City dentists or the college teachers." He paused to drink. I left to take a piss. He was talking when I came back.

"Those bastards up to the college have lost it, too." I said I didn't know what "it" was. "Only they don't care. They used to be poor and they didn't mind it, because nobody'd be a professor unless he wanted to. There wasn't any money in it. Only lots of time to read. Summers off. Always a job. And people like them doing the same thing. But not now." I still didn't know what "it" was. That didn't matter. "Not from what I read in *Time*. They make twenty thousand a year and spend their afternoons riding lawn mowers and their evenings playing bridge, and their summers visiting Disneyland. Right up here at the college, they've got a professor who peddles real estate and a dean who runs for mayor."

"They're involved," I said.

"Goddamn right they're involved. They're involved in the fiberglass and plastic middle class. Do you see them sitting in the sun playing chess like the pictures of them in Europe in the *National Geographic*? I wouldn't mind if they played poker. But bridge!" He was beginning to yell. Some people at the bar had swung around on their stools. Spangler had gone off the deep end in this bar more than once. He continued in a quieter voice.

"The guy down the block comes up to me the other day and wants to know, since I'm a farmer, if I know anything about his yard tractor. It's stopped. Shiiiiiiit. I know enough to put a match to that toy tool. That's about as low as you can go in this country. If you can't be a rancher, then you ought to mow professors' lawns on toy tractors and sell old barbed wire on weekends." He stopped. He was through another boilermaker. I wasn't, but I could feel myself slipping over the edge into drunkenness.

Two men were playing a clumsy game of pool on the quarter-coin-slot pool table in the middle of the bar. The juke box was playing. A Coors beer clock, with the time on one side and a pheasant on the other, was turning slowly above us. I couldn't tell the time.

Eddy came over and told us he had to tell us that we couldn't have the bottle in here. Spangler asked him if he wanted a shot and Eddy said he did, pulling it from the bottle, the bag wrapped around its neck. The pheasant was making me dizzy.

I tried to look outside, but the window I thought was to my right was up the street at Dirty Dan's, and here there was only a cinderblock wall, out of which I stared into the quiet night until Spangler said, "It's them that lost the tradition. Not me." I looked at him, and decided that we were in a conversation and that I had some obligations, but I was getting too drunk to make them out.

"Nobody said you lost your transition," I said.

"We never had it," he said. "They talk about the torch being passed from one generation to the other, and how the war broke all that up out here. Bullshit. This country doesn't have tradition. It's like instant coffee. You know how goddamn long the pony express lasted?" I didn't. "Fourteen months. That's all. And now you look around and you see every mailman from Maryland to Los Angeles wearing a pony express patch on his uniform. The west hasn't had four generations go through it. The twentieth century swamped us before we had a chance. Like that movie company that's coming out here. It's all thin."

Spangler got up to take a piss and waved the empty pitcher at Eddy. I dove into the bottom of my boilermaker and took it in.

"You want another shot?" I asked Eddy as he took a pull from the bottle Spangler had left on the seat. Eddy said thanks and that this pitcher was on him. Was it true that Spangler was driving his steers to Kansas City? Goddamn right.

Eddy left and Spangler stopped by the juke box to play some songs. I remember thinking it looked absurd, Spangler bending over the juke box, digging into his jean pockets for quarters, and peering down into the lit glass. A cowboy on a horse chasing a calf was neoned in blue light on the front. First the cowboy and the horse would light up, then the rope, finally the calf. Spangler played "Country Roads" and both versions of "Bojangles." He was grinning when he came back to the table and seemed not as drunk as he should be. But he quickly turned sour.

"You see, I've been thinking about it a long time," he said, easing himself into the bench seat, then stretching out, leaning against the wall and putting his feet up on the rest of the seat. "In 1886 we had a blizzard that froze the state solid for a month and killed off half the people and all the cattle. That wiped the ranchers out, and the dirt farmers moved in, and the cowboys didn't have work. They took to drinking and brooding about their low way of life. Then Carrie Nation came through the state with all the dirt farmers' wives wanting the place safe for their children. Out went the bars and the cowboys. All that's left is the fucking rodeo. What a bunch of turkeys. Everything that's work gets turned into a game. That's how you know when you've been fucked over. So we got the rodeo and the Marlboro ads and a few piss-cutters like Jed. The whole place has become a T.V. museum. Nobody's had a chance in this country since the war." He paused. His eyes narrowed. "The truth is, I've been a cunt hair away from driving a riding lawn mower all my life."

He broke the beer glass in his hand, over the table, and beer foamed in thin, separate pools among shiny glass. Spangler looked at his hand; it bled a bit, but he wasn't cut badly. He sucked some blood away from between his forefinger and his thumb and wiped the rest on his jean leg. Eddy brought a bar rag. Somewhere it sounded like a dog was trying to sing. Spangler looked at me and got up and walked out the door.

I stayed at the table for a few minutes before I left and walked the five blocks through the town to Spangler's home to get my jeep. The red truck was there; its parking lights were on and I turned them off. The house was dark. As I drove home, I remember thinking I needed to buy a gun, but I couldn't figure out why. I slept in my clothes.

# We Get Entangled
# with a Cat

I bought my gun and went hunting. I didn't do badly: I didn't shoot any birds, but I didn't shoot Spangler, either. We couldn't hunt much this fall, Spangler said. We had to get the drive organized. Opal was working on a travel plan; we had to begin to get the gear in shape. We also had to get odds and ends around the ranch tied up, so we could leave it for a couple of weeks. That took most of our time: checking and mending fences, fixing gates, taking the wells off the gasoline pumps and hooking them back to the windmills, and fixing the lane so that the two or three people Spangler had asked to check on the place could get in without a four-wheel drive truck.

It was cooling off. The days were in the eighties, the nights in the fifties. We could work harder and longer than in July and August. I was put on my own more. I spent whole days by myself, only seeing Spangler and Jed in the morning and Spangler in the evening when I ate dinner. I was a regular guest by now. Opal wouldn't let me go home. I'd bring dessert or a bottle of wine. During the meal we'd talk about the drive. Afterwards Spangler and I would either have a Coors in the living room while Opal drank some port wine, or we'd leave Opal and go by ourselves down to the Palomino Bar, where we'd drink beer until about ten.

I think Spangler liked to go to the tavern because news of his drive was getting around, and people there would ask him about it. He liked that, even if he was embarrassed by not being too sure what he was doing.

Two days before we left, we stopped by the Palomino Bar one last time, promising ourselves not to stay long and not to get drunk. We arrived just in time to give Eddy a hand in trying to kill a stray cat that had been turning his trash cans over.

"I got the little shit trapped now," Eddy said. "I turned the trash can over on him. You ought to hear him bang around. Got a gun in the truck, Spangler?"

"Yes, why?"

"Why? Why, I figure what I'll do is kill the goddamn cat. He only turns my trash over every night."

"You going to shoot him through the trash can?"

"I'm not that dumb, Spangler. I may run a tavern and let you come in here and bust up my glasses, but I don't think I'm going to fill my good trash can full of buckshot just to kill a cat."

"How you going to do it, then?"

"I'm going to lift the can off the ground, and when the cat runs, you're going to blow the piss out of him. You can kill a pheasant from here to Hill City, you tell me. Well, you can kill a cat in the alley."

"No." Spangler said.

"No? What the hell do you mean, 'no'?"

"I mean, draw us a pitcher."

"You don't trust yourself with a gun unless you've got a little beer in you?"

"No. I don't see any reason to kill the cat. Why not just catch him and take him out to the country and let him go? I could use a good cat around the ranch. I shot most of them off last year when I thought they were killing the quail."

"You catch the cat, Spangler. Not me. I'm asking the next guy who comes in here to kill the cat for me. I'll kill him myself, if you'll loan me your gun."

"Let's catch this cat," Spangler said to me. "It's been around this bar too long to have Eddy go and kill it. What the hell you going to have to bitch about, Eddy, if this cat's dead? If we keep it alive, at least you can worry about it coming back."

We went out into the alley. Spangler asked Eddy which trash can it was under. The one turned upside down, Eddy said in a level, patient tone. Spangler said that made sense. There was plenty of light; the sun had an hour yet to go.

"You lift the can up, and I'll grab him," Spangler said. I lifted the can, tipping the top toward me, the opening his way. He reached and grabbed the cat. The cat howled. Spangler bellowed as his hand came out of the trash can holding the cat by the neck. Not by the scruff of the neck. It was doing a job on Spangler with its back claws, scratching all down his forearm. Spangler shifted his grip and held it by its scruff. It drew up tight, feet up like a baby.

"Your cat bit me," Spangler said, looking at Eddy.

"It's not my cat. It's your cat," Eddy said.

The cat was grey with narrow yellow eyes and a thin tail. Its teeth showed because its face was drawn back. It hung from Spangler's fist like a possum.

"You can castrate a big male like him, holding him that way," Eddy said. "That's what the vet said."

"Have you got a box to put him in?" Spangler asked Eddy, clearly not the least bit worried about castrating the cat. Eddy went and got a cardboard beer case carton. He brought some silver refrigerator tape, too. Spangler dropped the cat in the box. I shut the lid and Eddy and I held it down while Spangler taped it. When that was done, we put the box in the back of the truck. Spangler went back inside, cursing.

"How bad are you bit?" I asked.

"To the bone, by the way it feels. He tore my wrist up, too."

"I see he did. Maybe you better have that looked at," I said. "There's such a thing as cat-scratch fever."

"And rabies," said Eddy from behind the bar, getting us a pitcher of Coors.

"No rabies in cats," said Spangler.

"The hell you say. Ray Pratt was in here the other night, saying that they got a notice from the vet school, or wherever they get them, that says Kansas is a rabies quarantine area and that you can't move dogs or cats in and out without a shot of some kind. He was telling us because some of these movie people wanted to bring their dogs and cats in and they were raising a fuss." He paused and wiped the bar. "That cat could have rabies, Spangler. Then you could have rabies, too. See." Eddy brought us our beer. Spangler told him to put it on the tab.

"Has Ray come in tonight?" Spangler asked, then sucked his hand again, although he wasn't bleeding.

"No."

"Well, then, we'll just drink our beer slow and wait for him."

Ray came in about an hour later and just naturally joined us.

"How's business, Ray?" Spangler asked, and indicated to Eddy that he wanted another glass so that Ray could share our pitcher. "You guys barbering a lot of poodles with these movie people here?"

"I guess," said Ray. "I haven't been outside the office for a week. It's not just the movie people. It's people going away on vacation."

"You guys work on cows and horses anymore? Or is it all gold-fish and gerbils?" Spangler said.

"It's getting to be that way. I think we ought to move out of town. Get away from all this crap. You know what I got today? An iguana. That's right. Now what the fuck do I know about an iguana? A long-haired back-to-nature type brings it in and says it's got a boil on its back. A girl all dressed in black is standing in back of him, jiggling all over."

"What did you do to the iguana, Ray?" asked Spangler. "You didn't flush it down the toilet, like you do the goldfish?"

"That's not true," Ray said.

"The hell it isn't," Spangler said. "I know that's what you guys do. You got a whole tank of them back there, and when somebody brings you one in sick, you flush it down the toilet. When they come back, you get one out of the tank and tell them it's theirs and all well. Right, Ray?"

"Nooo. We watch them for a while to see if they'll get well first."

"Shiiiiiiit. Maybe the twenty seconds it takes them to go round and round down the toilet bowl." Ray grinned and drank his beer to keep from laughing.

"What did you do with the iguana, Ray?" Spangler said.

"It died," Ray said. "They took it home to feed it to their python. That's what they said, anyway."

"How'd you kill it?" Spangler said. "On purpose?"

"Not really. But what the hell am I supposed to do? I never saw an iguana in school. There was some Jew in my class who studied snakes as a special project. He went back east. It's not a zoo out here, Spangler. I've got enough trouble with cat-hair balls and poodle anal worms. What am I going to do with an iguana?" He stopped and drank his beer. "I gave it a shot of penicillin and it curled up and died. Right on the table. The girl said to the boy, 'See, I told you.' The boy whistled. I didn't even charge them."

"That was the Christian thing to do, Ray," Spangler said. He ordered another pitcher, our last, he said to me. We were silent for a moment.

"Ray, what do you know about rabies in cats?" Spangler looked at him. Ray poured us all a beer. Eddy hung around.

"Cats can get rabies. We got rabies in this part of the country." He took a drink. "You get bit by a cat, Spangler?"

"Yes. Just before you came."

"Got the cat?"

"Yes."

"Chop off its head, and we'll send it into the state and see what we got. It's a pretty slim deal. Not much chance he'll have them. But then you die a pretty nasty death with rabies."

"I gotta chop its head off?" Spangler said.

"Either that, or keep it penned up for twenty-one days to see if it dies. Then you chop the head off and send it to the state. It'll have rabies then."

"Is there somebody from the state that watches cats like this?" Spangler asked.

"Are you kidding, Spangler? The only time we see those state public health boys is during pheasant season, and then they're drunk on their butts. No, you got to watch him yourself. Just chop the head off, and I'll send it in for you." He lit a cigar. "Give me the cat; I'll chop his head off, if it's a cat you like or something."

"Not much of a chance of me having rabies, is there, Ray?"

"Not much at all." Spangler looked into the bottom of his empty glass, and then up at the clock turning into a pheasant.

"I guess we'll keep the cat," Spangler said. "But you can finish off this pitcher, Ray. See you later. We got to go. Big doings." Ray shrugged.

"You moving your cattle like they say?" Ray said as we stood up.
"Yes."

"That's a nice herd. Same one I worked last year about this time?"

"That's the one."

"Good luck," Ray said.

We were leaving before the regulars got there, so the parking lot was near empty, and we slanted across it to the exit onto Vine Street. I could hear the cat howling when we stopped at the light.

# Opal's Plan

O pal had spent the weeks since she visited Kansas City working on a plan. She wrote it out, ran off Xerox copies at the college, and gave one each to me and Spangler and Jed (who lined his hat with it). She also taped one to the inside of the back window of the truck. Throughout the drive you could see her checking the back truck window, matching up our progress against the itinerary.

She hadn't said much as she worked through August, preparing for the drive. She didn't tell much about her trip to Kansas City. I had the impression she thought quiet efficiency would be the only way to success. She took up smoking, again, after a two-year vacation from it. Spangler didn't like that, but there wasn't much he could do to retaliate, since he did pretty much everything he wanted to do in the first place. He bitched a lot about it, though.

We all had our work: Spangler's was getting gear together, a job he didn't seem to be getting done, except in a random way. Of course, he had to run the ranch. He also had to contact his friends who lived along or near the route we proposed to take. We needed their help.

Jed was responsible for the animals, cattle and horses alike. He put the horses on high-protein feed and began to feed the steers cattle cubes (compressed meal, with sugar added). He'd put the cubes in the back of the red pickup and drive around the pasture until the whole herd would follow. When the drive began, we would use the truck in back of the herd, but we wanted them to know how to follow it, if that became necessary. We also wanted them to begin to act like a herd.

I had a part of everybody's job, and because of that, I wound up as an errand boy. But I didn't mind. During the last few days before the drive, there was a scattered quality about what we were doing. We didn't meet for coffee at Spangler's; we left notes for one another on the front door or on gates or car windshields: Pick up maps at the Texaco station./ Cigarettes are on sale at the A&P, get me two cartons. Don't you dare./ What dumb shit broke the gate lock?/ Somebody tell Jed to fix the gate at Gorham and make his mark when it's done. X./ Tell S. the cat's got a runny nose./ Eat at Dan's tonight. I've gone home to Gorham./ Your fucking heifer is in with the steers again./ Everybody to be at dinner tonight—Opal. The night before we left we all ate dinner at Spangler's.

"What's that?" I said, pointing to a plywood box Spangler was painting metallic red in the garage.

"Rabies' box." The cat that had bitten Spangler, and had been fed scraps through holes cut in the beer box, had come to be called "Rabies."

"What for?" I asked.

"Taking him with us. If he dies, I'd like to know about it. That cardboard box would rot through after the first rain. We'd spend two days finding him."

"You got a point."

Spangler finished up and we went inside for dinner. Jed came in late; he had had to cut out two poor steers. Put them back in the pasture with the heifers. We had steak and potatoes.

It was after dinner that Opal handed out copies of her plan.

"What the hell is this?" Spangler said. "You declaring independence or something?"

"Read it," she said.

"I guess I will," he said.

Jed looked at it blankly for a moment. He squinted his eyes and then began to move his head back and forth, like a typewriter across the page. He was finished with this process before I'd begun. He put it in his hat. I've saved my copy.

ONE CATTLE DRIVE (September 15 to October 1)
Spangler and Opal Tukle's herd.
Jed Wilson Adams and Leo Murdock, hands.
The Plan:

1st Day:    From ranch to schoolyard, Paradise, Kansas. Dairy King for dinner. Motel in Natoma for Opal. Boys sleep with herd. Cross Saline three times. Keep watchful.

2nd Day:    Paradise to Lucas. Along Route 18. Cut south three miles before Lucas. Ed Dreiling's pasture. See Garden of Eden. Say hello to Ed for Phil and Judy. Say hello to Ed from Cindy. Eat at Ed's. Stay there too.

3rd Day:    Lucas to Blackwolf. Cut across Wilson Dam. Under Interstate. Larry Holmes at Blackwolf. I haven't seen him since Kansas City. Eat at Larry's. Stay in Wilson at motel (Opal).

4th Day:    Blackwolf to Brookville. Dinner at Hotel. Finally. After twenty years of bitching at Spangler. Herd in schoolyard. Phone home in case Harold's there. Buy chicken for next day. Don't let full meal be cause of late start.

5th Day:    Brookville to Holland. Long drive. Under Interstate 35. Cousin Ted's place. Tell him about mother and that man from Chile. Ask about Tammy.

6th Day:    Holland to Woodbine. Short drive. Take a break at lunch. Schoolyard. We don't know anybody.

7th Day:    Woodbine to White City. Short drive. White City Cafe and Tavern. Make sure Spangler calls his brother at the home in Council Grove. No place to sleep. I get truck front seat.

| 8th Day: | White City to Alta Vista. Stay with Sally and George. Rest up a day. Drive Jed up to see relations in home in Junction City. Spangler keeps away from those drunks at Army base. Come home early. |
|---|---|
| 9th Day: | Rest as said above. |
| 10th Day: | Alta Vista to Eskridge. Flint Hills. A Ted Wiggins just this side of town. We don't know him. Ed Dreiling worked it out. White house with red barns and milk can mail box. Call him from Alta Vista. |
| 11th Day: | Eskridge to Wakarusa. Under turnpike. I go into Topeka and see *Midnight Cowboy* which is playing there now for three weeks. We stay on Little League baseball field if we keep to the outfield. Don't have to clean up shit unless in infield. Leo knows difference. Stay with herd. Or can use jail. As we wish. Our man in Wakarusa is Jody Warner. |
| 12th Day: | Wakarusa to Clinton. Field behind gas station store. Leo worked it out. Try to call Harold. I sleep in Lawrence. Boys can sleep in store. |
| 13th Day: | Don't tell Jed. Clinton to Eudora. Big field by post office. Tom at P.O. made arrangements. Says it's illegal but he's got a Mr. Welty to agree. Call him before we leave Clinton so he can meet us. |
| 14th Day: | Eudora to field beside trailer park on Highway 7. Owned by guy (forgot name) whose brother sold Spangler this horse trailer. Gets them from this nameless guy and tows them west. Tell him last trailer was better. Spangler won't tell his brother. We can stay in demo-trailers. Highways ahead. Plans made with cops. |
| 15th Day: | Trailer part pasture to AGRICULTURAL HALL OF FAME, Bonner Springs, Kansas. No answer from them at time of writing. Not open when I went down. Harvest vacation. My letter requests permission to put herd on well-advertised Original Prairie Sod Pasture. Five Acres. Spangler says they can't refuse us. I have his |

opinion in writing now. We taxpayers own the land. Call home to tell friends we are going to Kansas City tomorrow.

Last Day: Ag. Hall of Fame to Stock Yards. Kansas City. Long Drive. Leave early. Work hard. Meet Becker of Highway Patrol. They are unhappy but will help. Hope we change our minds. This is Leo's home. Sell herd. Eat at Golden Ox. Sleep in Mulebach. Celebrate but don't gloat. Rest a day to sleep off hangovers. Drive home to here by three. Put money in bank.

(signed)
Opal Pearl Tukle

# The First Day

I hadn't slept, except fitfully. I was glad when four came around, and I turned the alarm off even before it rang. I had set my clothes and gear out too neatly the night before, so after I got dressed and out the door, I was haunted by the impression that I had forgotten something. I stood in the darkness in the street in Gorham and tried to think of what I'd left. Finally I reasoned that we'd be coming this way anyway and I could drive down and pick it up, whatever it was. Of course I'd forgotten nothing. I drove to Hays.

Spangler's front-porch light was on; the truck (with the horse trailer behind it) was idling in the driveway. Spangler came out the front door, disappeared into the dark around the side of the house, came back, and threw something that made a loud crash into the back of the truck. Opal was in the kitchen and handed me a coffee mug when I came in.

"Ready to go?" she said.

"Why not?" I said. "I haven't got anything else to do this fall."

"What did they say down at the school?"

"Mrs. Dreiling needed a little extra money, so it all worked out, after a fashion."

She poured herself a cup of coffee, and poured another for Spangler, who was just coming in the front door.

"Let's get this fucking show on the road," he said. "We can drink coffee all day long in two weeks. What the hell are we doing sitting around a kitchen? Jesus-Larry." He drank his coffee and sat down with a thud.

He had been up all night finding tools and lights and saddle gear that the last twenty years of helter-skelter ranching had scattered throughout his properties. Around midnight he was in the irrigation section looking for a good scissor jack that Bobby Layher had traded him for an old International truck that hadn't run for seven years. He found it. An hour before he had been north of Gorham looking for the spare tire to the horse trailer. He found it, and driving through Gorham he had stopped by my place to see if I was up. He waited for a few minutes, but the light wasn't on, and he didn't want to wake me. The house was a mess, Opal said, because Spangler had rummaged through everything looking for special shirts and pants and his World War II bayonet. He was sure she had finally thrown out his pheasant feather hatband after all these years. She found it in the bottom of the gun case. Now she calmly picked up her cigarettes, drank the rest of her coffee down, tucked a copy of *Woman and Madness* under her arm, and walked out of the kitchen and out the front door and got into the truck and honked the horn. Spangler and I joined her, leaving a light in the house on and not locking the door. Harold might come home, Spangler said. Opal drove.

The back of the truck was piled high with cattle cubes, rolls of wire, posts, 3' × 3' cardboard signs reading CATTLE DRIVE IN PROGRESS, and at least two cases of Green Gables Scotch. Jammed in between the spare tire and a Coleman cooler was Rabies' box. I remembered I hadn't seen him since that night, but now I could hear him howl when I got out to readjust the signs, which were threatening to blow away.

Jed was waiting for us when we drove through the south gate of the ranch. Light was cracking the clear eastern sky. We didn't know what time it was—all watches had been stowed deep in the glove box for safekeeping. It would be daylight that counted.

Jed was ready to go. Opal was ready to go. Therefore Spangler and I were ready to go. The horses were saddled; the steers were up in the pasture by the south gate. Jed loaded Angel, the spare horse. Opal turned the truck and trailer around and pulled out into the road. She stopped, got out, and looked at Jed and Spangler and me as we mounted and rode to the back of the pasture. The steers stirred. The east was alive with light, brimming over the horizon. The west was starry, but bluing up, save for the black line down low.

"What the fuck's that bingy heifer doing in here?" Spangler roared, as he spotted the black-eared heifer backing into a fencepost.

"We'll never be able to cut her out now," I said.

"I'll shoot her. We aren't taking that black-eared bitch to Kansas City. I should have shot her a long time ago. Opal, get me the pistol." Opal said that if Spangler shot the heifer all the steers would go bats and we'd have a fine mess right here at the start. She opened the gate, got back in the truck, and lit up a cigarette. The spare horse whinnied.

"Shiiiiiiit."

Some steers ambled out the gate, and started the wrong way. Opal got out of the truck and turned them. They jogged down the road a bit and mooed. Others followed. We stirred in the saddles, coaxed, whistled, began to talk to them, at first feeling silly, but finally deciding it was for real. We were on our way. Spangler said to Opal as he rode past her, the last steer in front of him, that she should stop smoking those fucking cigarettes. She waved. Jed rode to the head of the herd. I took one side, Spangler the other. Opal came behind in the truck.

Our beginning system was simple: When we got to a crossroad, Spangler and I would ride up on the sides and block the side roads off, stringing a rope from one corner fencepost across the road to another, and putting out our signs. Opal would keep pushing the herd with the truck. Jed would lead them with the horse. Opal or one of us would pick up the ropes and the signs after we passed the side roads. We changed the system after a while. But that's how we started.

As long as the fields were fenced, the stretch between roads was easy, like driving them down a chute. We took it slow and let them grab mouthfuls of high grass from the road ditches as they went along. The idea was not to run too much weight off them; drive them from sunup to sundown; don't break for lunch; and let them gain back the weight at nights. Slow and steady.

We crossed the Hays-to-Plainville highway just as the suit was a clear round ball sitting above the ground haze of the rising dew of the night. There were no cars, although Jed rode on ahead and put out the signs and red flags. I picked them up and put them back in the truck. There was a stretch of hills in front of us.

For all the noise of the moving cattle, the truck in low gear behind us, our own chatter, I remembered the silence that seemed to surround us. It was as if we were a cell of light and sounds moving down the road, and if you'd back off a mile or so, the world would seem too quiet to explain.

Ahead, we could see the dust of a truck coming at us, then the truck itself, rising to the top of a hill and then dipping out of sight. Three hills away, it took him longer to get out of the draw. He was slowing down. Jed moved out ahead. The cattle at the front slowed; we pushed harder from the back, dropping toward the rear, as there were no crossroads coming. We kept moving. The truck came into view, slowed, and stopped. Jed rode up on the driver's side. The driver got out and looked down the road. He reached back in and turned off the engine, then climbed onto the truck's hood and waited and watched. That was the best thing to do; we could drive the steers around him. Good for him, I thought; that's a good sign, the first guy we meet doesn't give us a bunch of shit about how the roads are for trucks and how he's got to be at Dirty Dan's right away or he'll miss his coffee with a bunch of other clowns who haven't got anything to do till lunch.

"Where you going, Spangler? Down to Gorham?"

"Kansas City, George."

"I didn't think you were going to Gorham. You put that in milo this year, didn't you?" said George, not taking Spangler seriously. "You rent some of the Schmidt stuff, did you?"

"No," said Spangler, and stopped beside the truck, holding the horse steady by grabbing the mirror.

"Dennis Teems said you were going to drive some cattle to Kansas City," George said, as if when he first heard about it he'd bet a hundred dollars it wasn't true.

"That's right, George. I've had it with these pig-fuckers who take some hide off my ass coming and going."

"I'll be damned. That was the first time Teems ever got anything straight in his life," George said with a half-assed grin on his face. "Well," he said, grinning and looking around at two-hundred and fifty-nine steers easing down the road, "goddamnit, Spangler, I hope you make it. Here, have a pull." He jumped off the truck and got out a pint of Green Gables.

"Thanks, George," Spangler said, and sent bubbles to the top as he tipped it up. George took a pull. Opal honked.

By noon we had gone eleven miles, had crossed the Saline twice, met dozens of trucks and cars, some from as far away as McCracken, who just happened to be heading for Paradise that day to pick up something for the wife. Most of them would watch from a side road. Some, not knowing where we were, had come onto us from the front and had stopped and let us drive around them. The ones that were hardest to handle were the ones coming up from behind. All but one of those just backed up after a while, or followed us until we hit a section road and then went around.

One "bots-ridden horse-turd of a son-of-a-bitch with a limestone fencepost for a brain and stale marshmallows for guts" had to drive on through. A steer panicked and jumped through a fence into a wheatfield. It cost us ten minutes, while Jed roped it and led it up to a gate and back into the herd. The fence wasn't broken, though, only the staples popped. We fixed it.

Most people were happy to see us on the road. They'd call Spangler over and reach under the seat of their pickups, and he'd lift his arm (with his back turned to Opal) and tilt his head back. Then the man in the truck would do likewise. If I was close by, Spangler would wave me over. Afterward, I'd look back and through the dusty windshield I'd see Opal, smoking a cigarette that she'd let hang out the window in her left hand. Honk. Honk.

Later she passed out some sandwiches and apples. We took turns riding back to the truck and tying our horse to the tail gate and climbing in and eating a quick lunch and drinking some water while the horse walked along behind. It was hot in the truck, hotter than out on the horse, and dustier. Opal's blond hair was brown; the dust swirled into the truck from the side vents and from the mat-covered holes in the floorboards. Ahead, all you could see were the horses and the top of the steers; all the rest was dust. Sometimes Opal'd back off a little, and the dust would settle before it got to the truck and you could see the puffs of it coming off the steers' hooves as they jogged down the road.

The radio was playing, telling us that we were three inches short in rainfall against our average. Then it played, on special request, "Tie Me Kangaroo Down, Sport."

"How's it going back here?" I asked.

"Not bad. I have to keep one foot near the brake in case you bastards fall off your horses from drinking so goddamn much."

"It doesn't have much effect when you're working."

"Or in the hot sun either, I suppose," Opal said.

"Well, everybody is wishing us well," I said.

"I think I'll run the next well-wisher down. Only you'd all have a belt over his death. When you finish, tell Spangler to come back here. I want to give him his lunch."

"O.K."

"Your heifer's doing well. I'm surprised."

"So am I. I guess Spangler will run her down with the truck if she messes things up."

"*I* will," Opal said.

"I'll get Spangler."

As I left, the radio announcer told us: Now are the "gentle hours," until three o'clock, when it would be the "golden hours." Frank Sinatra sang "Old Man River." I took my apple with me and after one last gulp of water, jumped out of the slow-moving truck and walked along in back, untying my horse. I rode up to Spangler. No doubt Opal could see me pointing to the truck, and see Spangler nod and ride back toward her. I fed my apple core to my horse, who ate it as we rode. The sun was crossing behind us.

The morning of the first day was taken up with well-wishers and gawkers, Opal chewing on Spangler for drinking, and Jed working his ass off seeing that everything was going well. I was getting on all right. About an hour after lunch I worked a steer out of a culvert, all by myself. Spangler had the toughest one: A steer broke out of the herd just as the road was crossing a little creek, one that the highway department had taken care of by putting one of those big galvanized tubes under the road. The steer got in the tube, and so did Spangler and Canyon-Snip, his horse. I could hear them thrashing around down in there like he was in a sewer trying to kill an alligator. Every time Spangler'd curse, it'd echo and echo. You couldn't exactly hear what it was he was saying; it'd come out in bits and pieces.

"Worth _____ son _____ bitch. Shit _____ fuck _____ dick _____ piss _____." Finally, as they came out onto the highway, he said to me:

"I told that grubby bag of fat and hamburger that if he didn't get his wormy ass out of that pipe, I was going to turn him into a pussy little lamb and have my way with him right there in the tube. Dumb son-of-a-bitch." Spangler's hat was crumpled where he had hit it on the top of the pipe.

# The Afternoon of the First Day

We ran into the film company just south of Natoma. They had been making their movie in and out of Gorham and Hays for a couple of months now. The star lived in a big limestone house a couple of blocks from the Tukles. We saw him once, with his daughter. Anyway, the movie people had brought quite a change to the town. One we pretty much ignored—or didn't have time for. Opal had tried out for one of the parts they filled with locals, but they said she wouldn't do. I'm not sure how you would tell Opal she didn't get a part, but I don't think I'd say "you won't do." She was pissed.

All around town you'd see sunglassed men and women—earnest young men with moustaches, who always turned out to be in their forties when they took their sunglasses off or when the wind blew their hair so the bald spots showed. The women were younger, blond, halter-topped, and could be seen wandering through town in absurdly big shoes out of which peeked tiny painted toenails. Purple toes, green toes, black toes.

"Did you see Miss Blue Toes in the hardware store this afternoon?" the man who ran the Co-Op said to Spangler one day. "Her crotch hair is coming out her shorts, they're so tiny. They said she was heading this way. She never got here, though. The one I like is, Black Toes."

"I hear she screws if you ask her," said Spangler.

"I heard that too. Heard she can put her feet on her ears. I'd like to get some of that," the man who ran the Co-Op said.

"Maybe," said Spangler. "They all look a little bingy to me."

During the winter, Gallo Port was the best wine you could buy at the Saddle Blanket Liquor Store. That summer, there were cases of Rothschild Mouton-Cadet that the movie people and the social whizzes drank like Kool-Aid. The whole town seemed to be drinking Mouton-Cadet. The men at the Country Club were discussing the virtues of 1967 Mouton-Cadet as opposed, say, to 1969 Mouton-Cadet. It was mixed with Seven-Up and called a Dandy. They poured the red and white together and said it was a Rosé (you could eat anything you wanted to with a Rosé). They mixed it with tonic water and called it a Cooler. Spangler called it all Turtle Piss. And he called everybody who drank the stuff turkey turds.

"Any turkey turd who wears a golf hat deserves to pay four dollars a bottle for that turtle piss. It's all grapes mashed by feet, isn't it?" he said to Eddy one night when Eddy offered Spangler a pull on the house bottle of Mouton-Cadet.

"I keep it around for special customers. Like you," Eddy said. "And then you shit on it. The state boys wouldn't be any nicer about this bottle of wine in here than about the bottle of Green Gables I keep back there for some of you."

"Then bring on the Green Gables. No use having your wife shoot at you just cause you got your hand in another woman's pants. You might as well be full in the saddle."

"It's more civilized to drink wine," Eddy said.

"What the fuck does that mean?" retorted Spangler. "That a map of Paris is going to pop out on my head when I take a pull? Or that the juke box is going to start playing opera? Maybe that chicken-farmer-brother-in-law-of-yours will start hitting the pisser if he drinks Mouton-Cadet. You guys would drink whiskey sours if those movie people told you it was civilized." Eddy said nobody he knew ever drank a whiskey sour. Maybe the queer piano player in Hill City, but nobody who drank in his tavern.

We saw them filming a couple of times when we were working. "I hope they leave the place the way they found it," Spangler had said to me one day, when we saw them setting up south of Hays. "Nothing's the same after you take a picture of it." He looked out through the windshield at prairie that began to gather into hills and bluffs down by the Smoky Hill.

Now it looked as though we had happened onto their set.

"What the hell we got here?" Spangler said as he leaned over his saddle horn and looked down the road.

"It's the Movie," I said. "Maybe they'll take our picture." We had made pretty good time after we had gotten out of our territory and the well-wishers had thinned out. We were pretty lit, though. Spangler figured that unless we kept nipping at the bottle, we'd get an early hangover. The best thing to do was to keep a little tight. With Opal behind us, that required some sneaking. She'd just stop and not bring up the rear if she thought we were pulling at the bottle. Spangler would ride ahead to a dip in the road, and pull a pint out from under this flap or that flap of his saddle and take a shot. Every once in a while, I'd see an empty shining like an emerald in the ditch. I'd get mine by dropping behind the horse trailer where Spangler had stored a quart in a sack hanging from the trailer divider. For Spangler, this drinking was a matter of keeping things as they were—a little buzz on. But by the time we came upon the movie people, I was in the trees.

"Take our picture," I said, and waved my hand madly in the air.

"We don't need this," Spangler said.

Ahead, and down a slight hill, the road was full of cameras and trucks and old cars and a herd of people. There was a husky bald man yelling at everybody else. And everybody else was wearing sunglasses and moustaches—or halter tops and tan arms and legs. I had seen these people pretty much one at a time during the summer, and thought there couldn't be more than four or five of them—I must have been seeing the same people over and over again, I thought. But here they all were together and the place seemed littered with them. Jed came up to the left of us and stopped and beat his hat against his leg. I beat my hat against my leg, but lost my grip after the first whap and my hat flew behind me and into the herd. The bald man stopped yelling and looked up the road at us. So did the rest of the movie people.

They must have been a hundred yards away, but I could still tell they were looking at us like we were queers. One of them pointed a telephoto camera our way and began taking stills. His lens must have bunched us all toward the front so we seemed poised on the hilltop ready to fall down upon them: two hundred and fifty steers, all tossing their heads with worry. A tall cowboy with a bottle in one hand and a bull whip in another. His good-looking young sidekick holding a taut rein on a powerful horse. An old man trying to keep the herd together, and through the dust coming off the road a truck looming into view, as if it was in the middle of the herd, riding up on their backs. Honk. Honk.

"Take our picture!" I yelled, and reached for my head to wave my hat at them.

"You threw your hat away, you stupid jack-ass," Spangler said.

"What's holding us up?" Opal yelled out the window of the truck.

"The movies, the movies," I said.

"Back off, Opal," Spangler said, and cracked the whip in her direction. The cattle turned in on themselves and began to mill around. Jed took Duke back and forth across the front of the herd, pushing back the bulges. Down the road I could see the stars sitting in a car. The bald man said something to them, and they got out of the car and went into one of the Winnebagoes parked nearby. There were other trucks and campers and cables and lines all over the road. The bald man was talking with a circle of moustached men.

"Let's put up ropes front and back," Spangler said. "You dump some cattle cubes down the middle of the road going the other way," he said to Jed. "We'll see if they'll feed. Tell Opal to hold the back line. You stay in front," he said to me. "I'm going down there to see what we got." He didn't have to.

One of the Winnebagoes (not the one the stars went into) was coming up the road toward us. The guy who had been shooting us with a telephoto lens was now perched on top, snapping away. There were some moustached sunglassed men riding on the back bumpers, hanging out to one side like they do on fire trucks. The bald man was riding in the door way. The Winnebago stopped about ten yards from the herd and swung across the road. The bald man stepped from the doorway.

"What you got here, boy?" the bald man asked Spangler.

"Cattle, you Cue Ball. What you got there?" Spangler pointed down the hill.

"Don't be testy, boy. We got a movie here. We're the movie people and we got a deal for you."

A tall woman came out of the Winnebago. She was carrying a bottle of wine in one hand and some wine glasses in the other. She was wearing tight blue-jean shorts and a red bandanna top. You could see her nipples through the bandanna. She had blue toenails. Spangler stared. I got off my horse, but my foot got caught in the stirrup. I wound up hopping backward to keep up with Chief, who decided to walk through the herd toward the truck where he hoped to get some cattle cubes.

"What's with him?" I heard Cue Ball say to Spangler as I hopped away. I couldn't hear what Spangler said.

"What's going on?" Opal said to me as I hopped by her.

"The movie people got a deal for us. I'm going to be in the movies." I got my foot loose and fell on the ground.

"What's the matter with you?" Opal asked.

"I'm acting like a rookie for the movie people."

"Jesus Christ."

I tied up Chief, and Opal and I walked back up through the herd to where Blue Toes and a couple of moustached men were standing. Spangler and Cue Ball were down the road a bit talking.

"What's going on here?" said Opal. She stared at Blue Toes.

"They're making a deal together. The two of them down there," Blue Toes pointed toward Spangler and Cue Ball.

"Who are you?" I said. It seemed as if it took me a week to speak the whole sentence.

"I'm Honey."

"Hi Honey." If Spangler had not returned just then, I might have gotten somewhere. I was making great progress.

"They want to put us in a movie," said Spangler to Opal. "We get a hundred bucks apiece. Even Jed."

"Plus a case of Mouton-Cadet," said Cue Ball. Honey held up her bottle so we could all see. One of her breasts started to sneak out of the bandanna, but she adjusted herself.

"You can keep the wine," Spangler said. "Buy us some Green Gables and leave it with Eddy at the Palomino Bar."

"I don't like the deal," said Opal.

"Let's get going," I said. "Do I get to ride my horse?" Everybody stated at me. I sat down on the road and listened from there.

"They want to take a film of us, Opal. They don't think they'll use it in this movie, though."

"We might," said Cue Ball. "You never know. We thought we'd just film this cattle drive. You never can tell when you need some footage of a cattle drive. Right, boy." Cue Ball turned to Spangler.

"Why does he call you 'boy'"? I said from the ground.

"Shut up, pistol," Spangler said.

"It's the way he talks to all of us," Honey said. "To me and George and all of us."

"It smells, Spangler," said Opal.

"All we want to do is film you," said Cue Ball. "Look at it this way, ma'am, we cleared using this road on this day, all this day, sunup to sundown—we cleared that with the city people, the country people, the state people, and the Knights of Columbus. We laid a few cases of Mouton-Cadet on a couple of biggies in the Highway Office and we got ourselves one Kansas Road. We can stay here until sundown. Now all you got to do is let us film you, and everything will be good. I'll take lots of shots of you ma'am." Opal told him to shove his camera up his ass, and walked back to the truck, where she lit up a cigarette.

"We still got a deal?" Cue Ball asked Spangler.

"You lay four hundred big ones in my palm at the start, and I'll collect on the other end of the deal tonight," Spangler said.

"Give him four hundred dollars," said Cue Ball to one of the sunglassed men, who peeled off four stiff one-hundred-dollar bills. Spangler and Cue Ball talked a bit more, and I got off my ass and went back to the truck. I was playing politics. I figured I was in dutch with Spangler, so I better go back and let Opal vent a little steam on me.

"You don't like this deal," I said.

"You been drinking?" she said.

"Well . . ."

"I hope you've been drinking. Because if you haven't, you're going spastic on us on the first day."

"I've been drinking the send-off drinks," I said.

"Why the hell did Spangler let these movie people make a deal?" she said.

"Don't you want to be in the movies?" I asked.

"No." Spangler was coming our way, with Jed. Spangler had the four hundred-dollar bills fanned out like cards. He held out his hand as he got to the truck.

"Take the first one, Jed." Then I took mine. "Now you, Opal," Spangler said.

"No."

"What's the matter? That hundred dollar's yours. You'll be in a movie after all. I thought you'd like being in a movie." She blew out a stream of smoke, but wouldn't say anything.

"Opal, goddamnit. Quit smoking. Here I get a movie deal for us, and you turn nasty bitch." He turned to me. "You drive the truck. I don't want you falling off your horse during a movie of my cattle drive. Opal, you get on his horse. They want a woman in the middle of all this. We haven't got time to beat up on each other. We've got to get this thing going." He walked back through the herd to where he had tied Canyon Snip to the Winnebago. Jed folded his hundred-dollar bill lengthwise and tucked it in the inside band of his hat. I could see the white edge of Opal's plan along the band. Opal slid out of the truck and I slid in. I was downcast. She went back by the horse trailer. I looked in the mirror and could see her untie Chief. She swung into the saddle with the cigarette between her lips. Spangler looked back across the herd at Opal coming his way and told her not to smoke during the movie. She gave him the finger.

Jed had taken down the ropes, and the cattle were beginning to stir. I started the engine. Out of the windshield I could see the movie trucks getting into place. Blue Toes was sitting atop the Winnebago with the man who had been taking stills. I honked and waved at her. Some of the cattle startled. Jed cut back against them and kept them in the herd. Spangler looked around at me and glared. The trucks were flat beds on pickup frames. They had tracks down the beds and the cameras were mounted on the tracks so they could slide back and forth. There were three trucks, two coming along the side of the herd, and one up front, taking pictures off the back. Far ahead, I could see the Winnebago where the Stars had gone, parked up a section road on a slight hill.

We edged forward, Spangler and Opal up front, Jed back of the herd with me. It didn't seem the same. We were boxed in. Even at the tail end of my drunk, I knew this didn't seem right. A man on the front truck began writing signs on a chalk board: BACKS STRAIGHT / DON'T SMOKE / KEEP HORSE HEADS HIGH / WHISTLE THROUGH YOUR TEETH, LADY. Opal flipped her cigarette at the truck camera nearest her.

GO FASTER / POP THE WHIP / FASTER.

"No. Goddamnit!" Spangler yelled. "We aren't going any faster. These cattle are spooked as it is." DON'T TALK. "Fuck off." FASTER.

The truck near Opal had Cue Ball on it, and they let up a bit and the herd passed them by. Then they were back with me and Jed, getting shots from behind. I waved out the window. They came full behind me and then up on my left, even with me. They were shooting over the cab. Cue Ball leaned forward and said something in the window to the driver. He honked and spooked the cattle right in front of him. Jed cut into the herd to settle them. The truck honked again and pulled ahead of me.

"Hey you!" I shouted. "Slow down."

"We need some film of these babies running," Cue Ball yelled at me. He said something to the driver. In the mirror, I could see Blue Toes' Winnebago coming along. She held her hair with one hand and her breast bandanna with the other. The camera truck beside me honked again, and then went into neutral and raced the engine. The steers in front of it plunged forward, past Jed and into the herd in front of them. It was like a car pileup: the steers near the truck jumped into those in front of them, and they crashed on into others further up. Spangler and Opal both looked back at the same time. The camera truck shifted into gear again and made a quick start toward the herd. Dust spurted out from behind its wheels and it jumped forward and then stopped abruptly, its horn blaring. Cue Ball lost his balance and fell off. The whole back of the herd went past Jed in bolt. All I could see were the tops of Spangler's and Opal's heads as the dust rose. The camera truck pulled ahead, keeping with the herd and driving them faster. Jed beat Duke with his hat, but they fell behind. I saw Cue Ball pick himself out of the dust. He was on my left. I swung the truck his way and took aim, but he saw me coming and ran for the ditch. He made it, and hustled up the bank and dove through the barbed wire fence into the pasture. I had to cut away to keep the horse trailer from tipping over. The spare horse whinnied. Rabies' box toppled out. I could see my heifer had been left behind in the stampede. She was on her side in the road in front of me, her legs thrashing. Cue Ball was standing far into the pasture. The herd was a storm of dust two hills away. I drove after them.

We were lucky. Most of the herd went straight. The ones that had peeled off on the side roads, or through the fences, stayed close to our road and we could pick them up as we went back along. The main herd went through a fence, where the road made a T, and wound up in a small pasture. The film trucks cut away a mile after they started the run, and when we got back to where they had been shooting, there was no sign of them. Only Rabies, who was unhurt—but had pissed all over himself. My heifer was a mile west. She had started walking home, I guess. We had left Opal with the herd, and the three of us (I was still in the truck; we loaded Rabies and my heifer) worked the road. We probably lost four or five steers out of the deal.

"I think I'll go back to Hays tonight and see if I can't find Cue Ball," said Spangler in an even voice. "I think I'll nail him by his nuts to the north quarter-section barn and then set it on fire. I'll toss him a knife and stand back and take some pictures." Opal told him he could not go back to Hays to kill Cue Ball. He could beat him up when we got back, if he wanted to, but if Spangler was going back to Hays, so was she. And she'd stay there.

"I tried to run him over," I said. Spangler looked at me. I had tried, I thought, and now that I thought about it again, I realized I hadn't been faking. Spangler didn't know that. He knew the difference was that had he been driving the truck, Cue Ball would have been a dead bug on the grill. I knew that too. We had plenty of day left. We started again.

We got to Paradise around sundown, with just enough light to see that the schoolyard was fenced off, and that somebody had been good enough to set a drift fence from the edge of one post clear across the street, with little red strips of cloth hanging from the fence. We drove the steers right down the street, coming in on the dirt road that runs parallel to the main highway. When they saw that fence, they came up short for a moment and then eased on, looking both ways for a way out. The lead steer saw it to the left and broke into the schoolyard like he was getting away. There was a big tank of water and the grass hadn't been cut, so there was feed enough for one night. The other steers followed in a rush, and Jed got out of their way, pulling to the right of the drift fence. After the last steer went in, Jed took off his hat and beat it against his leg and got off his horse. Jed wobbled a bit. Then steadied. Twenty miles for an old man. I wondered how old he really was. I wondered how he'd do.

We checked the fence all around and hooked up our electric wire and battery. Everything looked good. The steers were drinking water, pushing and shoving and climbing on each other's backs to get to it. They wouldn't be crowded here; the yard was big. Spangler had ordered some cattle cubes, which were in small piles all over the playground. The basketball goalposts at one end stood up in the fading sunlight like the raised arms of tall boys, wanting to know from somebody what the hell all these cattle were doing on their court.

There were some local people there, including the principal of the school and his children. They asked us to dinner. Spangler agreed. But Opal said we were all too dirty to sit down in anybody's home. We'd eat at the Dairy King. No, said Spangler. So we went with the principal, and Spangler sent one of the boys out to get a case of Coors to bring to the house as a gift. He had learned somewhere that it was "civilized" to bring a gift when you're invited to dinner. He had been there before, he said, as we walked through the streets to the edge of town to the principal's house. The boys and girls would hang around the herd and let us know if anything went wrong. Jed and Opal fell behind. I was hungry.

Later, after dinner, we walked back to the schoolyard. Opal had been convinced by the principal's wife to spend the night at their house, where she could take a bath and pretty up. We had run the horses in with the cattle and hung the saddle pads on the fence to dry. You could smell them clearly, even though there was so much else to smell.

We could sleep in the gym if we wanted to. We had a key. Or we could go down the road ten miles and rent a room at the boarding house. But we decided to sleep right there, on the hill behind the schoolyard. This was the end of the first day of the drive. We had done it and we hadn't. It had been sunny, and people had been friendly and curious. And we had been taken. The night was dark, but not ominous. I realized just before I went to sleep how different our fears of failure were from those of the men who had done all this a hundred years before.

# The Garden of Eden

The second day was different from the first. Right off we had a little rain, but that only settled the dust. Then we had some wind, but with the dust down that didn't do anything to harm us, though it did keep us from hearing one another. By the afternoon it was clear and calm. We had gotten out of our territory. Things would be different.

In the morning one Officer Stiltson of the Highway Patrol wanted to know just what the hell we thought we were doing.

"We'll, we're going to be rounding up cattle from all over the fucking country unless you let us keep going," Spangler said.

"May I see your driver's license?" Stiltson said.

"I don't have it with me," Spangler said.

"I'm sorry, sir. It's a law that you must carry your license with you whenever you operate a motor vehicle," Stiltson recited.

"I'm on a horse. Well, right now I'm off a horse. Wasting time. But before that I was on a horse. The very horse that I'm holding. Right here."

"Who's driving?" Stiltson demanded.

"We all are. All except me. I'm standing here wasting my fucking time explaining the obvious to a pig farmer of a cop."

"I'll have to take you in, Mr. Tukle."

"What the fuck for?"

"Obscenity."

"This is a private conversation, you ass-hole. Besides, if you take me in, I'll tell your wife."

"About what?" Stiltson said.

"You know what. I've seen you in Hays."

"I don't know what you're talking about."

"O.K. Let's go." Spangler gave me Canyon Snip's reins. "Let's take your car."

"What are you talking about Hays for? I'm stationed in Russell," Stiltson said.

"Well, now, sometimes you are, and sometimes you're not. I'll tell your wife about when you're not. O.K.?"

"Well, the next officer that comes along might not be so nice about all this," Stiltson said. "I'd get on some back roads if I were you."

"Thank you, Officer Stiltson. I expect we'll do just that," Spangler said. Officer Stiltson could not drive away because there was a herd of cattle around him. He sat there for awhile until we had driven them all past him, then he turned around and drove off toward Hays.

"Opal," said Spangler, "is it illegal to drive cattle on a state highway?"

"Only on the interstate," she said. "We're all right."

"That son-of-a-bluffing-bitch. Twenty minutes down the drain while that clown makes up laws. Shiiiiiiit."

"Lucky you knew about that guy's affair in Hays," I said.

"No such luck. I just took a chance. Most of those guys got something going. Most everybody does." An hour later we had more trouble.

About five miles outside of Lucas, we were greeted by a barricade. Behind it were pickup trucks and in between the pickup trucks were about twenty men and women standing in small groups. They had fenced off all the roads. It looked like they were giving us just enough room to turn around. We held up about a hundred yards down the road. Jed strung a rope across the road in front of the herd, and I stretched one behind it. Opal stayed in the truck, and the three of us rode to the intersection to see about the trouble.

"I guess you're Spangler Tukle," a tall man said from the front of the pack.

"That's who I am. What's the trouble here?"

"Well, we've talked to Ed Dreiling, and he's changed his mind about letting you put this herd up. So we just thought we'd tell you that, so you wouldn't have to go through Lucas."

"We were going a mile south of Lucas."

"Well, now you won't have to do even that."

"Where's Ed?" said Spangler.

"Well, now, he wasn't feeling too well this morning. Maybe that's why he decided you better not put your herd there on his place. His back has been giving him trouble, you know."

"No."

"Well, it has. Now, we figure if you take this road south for about ten miles, you can catch 176 over to the dam. That ought to be about six of one, half a dozen of the other for you."

"No," Spangler said.

"Well, that's the way it's going to be." Somebody in a truck started an engine. Some of the crowd was pulling in tighter around the tall man.

"That's not the way it's going to be," Spangler said. "First, we've made no provisions to stay anywhere along that route. Second, we got a plan and it says we're going one mile south of Lucas, that we're putting up the herd on Ed Dreiling's pasture, and that we're going to get in early so we can see the Garden of Eden, right there in Lucas. My wife made up the plan. That's how I know we're going to do all these things." Somebody in the crowd laughed, then so did some others.

"There's a lot of people hereabouts that don't want you taking that herd through," said the tall man. "Now, we got milo up, and we don't want that herd busting in there."

"I'm insured; you're insured."

"And we both know what kind of bastards insurance agents are," said the tall man. He had Spangler there. Spangler thought insurance agents were right in there with Kansas City dentists and barbed-wire traders.

"You take my check?" Spangler said.

"For what? We got a nice town, too. We don't want those cattle in that town. What if they get into the Garden of Eden and bust up all those statues? What the hell we got then?" said the tall man. "S. P. Dinsmoor don't look like he's about to come back from the grave and fix them up."

"I'll put five thousand dollars up against damages. I'll let you hold the check," Spangler said.

"I don't know about that," the man said. There were some women behind him shaking their heads no.

"I don't think that's what we have in mind," the tall man said, after looking over the crowd behind him. "We don't think you ought to take that herd this way. Dreiling hasn't got a place for you to stay, anyway."

"Then let him tell me that, you pig-fucker!" Spangler yelled. People moved about. Some got into trucks. "Now, I've been nice about all this. You pussy vigilantes come out here and hold up this whole deal for about an hour. Cost me my time. I stand around and be nice and offer to put up some money, and you come up with a wormy pile of horse shit about Ed Dreiling not wanting me to keep the herd on his place. Your milo, my ass. It's your wives that got to you, and you know it. I got a right to go down these roads, and if you don't get out of my way, we'll have cattle all over these fields." He stopped.

A woman said something from the back that I couldn't hear. Another truck motor started. The tall man stood there, looking at his boots.

"You take the road south, Spangler," he said. "We don't like that kind of talk in front of women."

"Then I've got another kind of talk. I'll just give Officer Stiltson a call. Now, he works out of Russell and he knows about this drive. And he's going to know that all of you are outside the law. That you *constitute* a mob and that you are *depriving* me of my *civil rights*. You just think that has to do with niggers, those *civil rights*, but all of you standing in this road are guilty of a *Federal crime*. Unless you plan to secede Russell County from the United States, you'll all wind up in jail. In Leavenworth."

He stopped again and looked back at his truck and the herd milling impatiently. "Now there," he said softly, "there wasn't a nasty word in all that. Not one. Now, how do you want it? You want me to drive through this country real careful-like and all you people go home and catch the football game? Or shall we stay around here for another hour while my good friend, Officer Stiltson, loads you up? Then, of course, I'll have to drive these cattle pretty fast to make up the time." The tall man said he'd see what the others said, and went back to some trucks with a group of about ten.

"How about the five thousand?" he said when he came back.

"Well, now you've cost me about an hour. And the wife (you know how they are), she's been living in this country for thirty years, and she's never seen the Garden of Eden. Or eaten at Brookville. You know how it is. I promised her we'd get in early and see the Garden of Eden. The deal is this: I'll put up the five thousand if at least ten of you'll give me a hand moving this herd, now that we've got to move them fast enough to get to Ed's with some daylight left."

The tall man talked it over with the others.

"We don't have that many with horses," he said.

"We'll take the ones who do. The rest can fence off roads."

"You write out the check now?" asked the tall man.

"Go back and get a checkbook from Opal," Spangler said to me. A moment later he was writing a check out on the hood of a pickup.

"Its date ain't right," the tall man said.

"That's the day after tomorrow," Spangler said. "You come around in the morning with that check, and we'll talk about any damages. You won't need it till then. My word's good. But I don't trust you."

"Don't push it, Spangler," the tall man said.

"I got one other thing I want to add to this deal," said Spangler.

"What's that?" the tall man said quickly.

"I don't care who helps us as long as they aren't retards, politicians, queers, chicken fuckers, Texans, or you."

"Kiss my ass."

"I don't stand in lines." Spangler turned away. We went back to the truck.

"What's the problem?" Opal asked.

"They wanted us to take a detour by way of Dallas. Jed here talked them out of it." Jed grunted.

In about five minutes we were going up the road. It was easy not having to tie off the crossroads. Some of the men had stayed behind to help, while others had driven off to get their horses.

In about twenty minutes horse trailers came up behind us, and men got out and helped us push the herd along at a fast clip. The new guys seemed to enjoy the job. After a while they started talking to us, asking where we were going from Lucas, and how many miles we'd make a day, and why in the hell were we doing it. They said Ed Dreiling was in Kansas City, because his brother had died, and the tall guy (who was running for mayor) was supposed to tell us that Ed was sorry he couldn't be there, but to go ahead anyway. Spangler was right, too, about the wives. They thought the herd would get into the town and bust things up. I learned all that, and we still moved the herd faster than we would ever move it, except when it stampeded.

We got to Ed's pasture a mile south of Lucas a good hour before dark. We drove the cattle right in. Ed had water all ready for them and cattle cubes everywhere and a big pile of good prairie hay right in the middle. We closed the gate on ourselves, took the saddles off the horses, and turned the horses loose with the steers. We let the spare horse out of the horse trailer, tossed the saddles in the saddle compartment, and hung the blankets out to dry. I checked on my heifer. We passed a bottle with the men who had helped us. Opal fed the cat some leftover lunch meat, putting it through air holes in the box. In fifteen minutes we were on our way to the Garden of Eden. Jed said he had seen it. Opal was driving and Spangler was fishing around under the seat, looking for the bottle. It was crowded with four of us in the truck.

**II**

The Garden of Eden was a local tourist spot where there were seldom any tourists. It was the yard garden of S. P. Dinsmoor. Apparently Dinsmoor was a mad, tiny man who got it in his head to build a replica of the Garden of Eden. He made his garden out of cement. It was one of those places that everybody for a hundred miles around knows about, but for some reason never visits. Like New Yorkers never get to the Statue of Liberty. Only nobody outside Kansas ever heard of the Garden of Eden. Spangler had been promising to take Opal to the Garden of Eden ever since they were married.

There was plenty of light left when we got there. It was smaller than I had imagined. As we walked through, we pushed small white buttons that started records, the voice of a Lucas housewife reading from *The Cabin Home in the Garden of Eden* by S. P. Dinsmoor.

"This is my sign," writes S. P. Dinsmoor, who was a Civil War veteran and because of a clerical error received two pension checks every month of his life. "GARDEN OF EDEN—I could see so many, as they go by, sing out, 'What is this?' so I put this sign up. Now they can read it, stop or go in, just as they please." Behind the sign was a rather large cabin and in the yard, cement statues and a network of serpents and birds and trees and vines forming a canopy over the whole thing:

"This is the tree of life. The angel is guarding the apples so we can't live forever. That is tough, but it is according to Moses, and when I put the braces across to the devil's elbow and tree, I noticed he had his fork poised on a little kid. He is always after the kids. I thought if it was my God he would throw up his hand and save the kid. My God would not let him get all the kids, but Moses did not give God credit for any kindness toward the human family, so I don't give him credit for that hand. That is my idea of God, but all the rest is Moses." Vines had grown over the devil since Dinsmoor wrote his pamphlet, and now the loudspeakers were hidden among them.

"Two snakes form the grape arbor. One is giving Eve the apple. The Bible tells all about that. The other snake didn't have any apple, so Adam got hot about it, grabbed it, and is smashing its head with his heel. That shows the disposition of man. If he doesn't get the apple, there is something doing. And the Bible says, the heel of the seed of the woman shall smash the serpent's head, or something to that effect." We moved on.

"The devil was in the Garden of Eden. He is in the background here. He has got glass back of his eyes, ears, nose and mouth, a bulb inside, and at night, when he is lit up, he looks like the devil, and the darker the night the more like the devil he looks. Here are the storks. Moses never said a word about them. He just wrote up enough to bring down the fall of man. All the preachers talk about is the original sin. There must have been many things in the Garden of Eden that Moses didn't mention. I have substituted some things that I know were there. The storks were there, because the kids were there: Cain and Abel. The storks always bring the kids. Nowadays they bring them in baskets in their mouths, but the Bible says, 'There was darkness on the face of the earth' and these storks had to have lights in their mouths to see which way to go, so they carried the babies under their wings."

We went in a few more steps, and another speaker said: "Moses says, 'Cain was a tiller of the soil,' and he raised great big pumpkins. He is offering a pumpkin. Got hold of the vine pulling it up, but he is trying to hide a hole in the pumpkin with his foot. You see, it's a rotten pumpkin. The Lord didn't like rotten pumpkins. I don't blame Him. Abel was a shepherd and he raised sheep. The Lord liked good mutton, so Abel has a crown on his shepherd hook, above the light up there. Now this made Cain mad at Abel, because Abel's good mutton was more acceptable to God than his rotten pumpkin, and he killed him. He couldn't have killed him with a gun: they did not have any such implements of warfare in those times, but Cain was a tiller of the soil. I just imagine he got Abel out in the 'tater patch and brained him with his hoe. He gave him an awful lick with his hoe handle, spoiled his face, and broke his hoe handle. He has it on his shoulder on the next tree." We walked on to the next tree.

"Poor Abel is dead and the angel is coming down after him. That is the way they used to bury the dead. Nowadays, we tote them off to the bone yard. Times have changed since Moses' day. Here are Abel's wife and shepherd dog, just discovered him dead." Ahead of us there was a stone-grey statue of a woman and a dog. "Here is the eye and the hand looking and pointing towards Cain and his wife on the next tree." We went to the next tree. Opal pushed one white button on the speaker, and it said:

"Do you know what the mark of Cain was? The Bible don't tell. Preachers didn't tell. A kid playing will always try to do things right. You see kids making a mud pie, they will try to get the lid on right, and when I was mixing mud putting up Cain here, I wanted the mark of Cain. I happened to look down in the Garden of Eden and think, there was the fall of man. The redemption of man is the crucifixion, so I imagined the mark of Cain must be a little red cross placed in his forehead, typical of the future crucifixion that was to come. Now I don't know whether that is right or not, but it connects things in dandy shape. You see Cain and his wife are scared. Now, when people are standing around here on the sidewalk as we are, and I am in the house, and feel all right, they will hear voices away over there where that angel is, saying, 'Cain, you son of a gun, where is your brother Abel?' Cain's answer nowadays would be, 'Damned if I know. Am I my brother's keeper?' Now that is all Scripture except the flourishes. I put them in, because when I was building this they accused me of being bughouse on religion. I am bughouse good and proper, but not on religion, perpetual motion or any other fool thing that I cannot find one thing about."

There was more to the place, and we wandered around for a while. Jed went back to the truck. He said he had seen it all when it was being built and that Dinsmoor was a kook. I figured Jed would catch a nap.

We went around to one side of the house, where the crypt was, and noticed a row of old beer bottles forming a fringe above the porch. Opal pushed the white button.

"This is the southeast view of the Cabin Home. You can't drink booze anymore. You can only use the contents of beer bottles on those shelves, jugs and mugs on the corner posts to look at. If you can't drink it, look at it; it will help some. It's waste that makes people poor."

Spangler said he wanted to go over to the crypt and see the old fart. He had heard you could look right into the coffin. We listened to the recording on the outside first:

"The coffin is made over a screen-reinforced Number 6 wire and half-inch iron. The handles have five-eight iron running full length, fastened to coffin with Number 6 wire. The plate glass (under the little lid with the square, compass, and trowel) is fastened to screen with Number 6 wire. All cemented over with white cement and sand. When I quit breathing, my body will be embalmed and placed in the coffin, the large lid cemented down by running cement around in the groove, the little lid (with square, compass, and trowel) placed on coffin near the foot, then put in a niche in the wall inside my mausoleum, and a plate glass placed in a groove in front and sealed up. This is where and the way I expect to go. I never joke, but if it were not for jokes, life would be dull. I like a joke. It seems to me that people buried in iron and wooden boxes will be frying and burning up in the resurrection morn.

How will they get out when this world is on fire? Cement will not stand fire, the glass will break. This cement lid will fly open and I will sail out like a locust. Some people know they are going to heaven and those they do not like are going to hell. I am going where the Boss puts me. He knows where I belong better than I do. If I get to go up, I have a cement angel outside, above the door, to take me up.

We went inside and there he was, tiny and shriveled. You could see him from about his waist up. There was a flashlight on a ledge, and we closed the door and shone the light in his face. I found the white button on a two-by-four by the door. I pushed it, and we heard what Dinsmoor had to say by way of good-bye.

"Visitors have asked me many questions about myself, some of which I'll answer here. I served three years in the Civil War. I was in eighteen big battles besides skirmishes, saw the capture of Lee, and every fight I was in we either captured or run the Johnnies. About half the time we were in the lead and outrunned them. I came to Illinois in the fall of 1866. Taught school five terms. Married Mrs. Frances A. Journey, on horseback, near Grafton, August 24, 1870. Farmer by occupation. Moved to Lucas, Kansas, in the fall of '88. Moved to Nebraska in the fall of '90. Back to Lucas, Kansas, in the fall of '91. Built the Cabin Home in 1907 and later on, the Garden of Eden. My wife died in the spring of '17. Married Emilie Brozek in the spring of '24. She was born January 17, 1904, in Podlusky, Czechoslovakia. I am the ninth generation from England, seventh from Scotland, sixth from Ireland, fourth from France. I have a record of twenty-three of my ancestors. Their average life was over seventy-six years. But one died under fifty and one lived to be a hundred. So far as I know, not one of my ancestors died in infancy."

By the time we got out of the mausoleum, the light had faded so that the houses to the west of us had no color but were only silhouettes. Down the street one of those yard lights that turns on at dusk blazed absurdly. Jed was asleep. Through the truck window I could see the top half of his body slumped against the door. For the first time in weeks, I remembered that he was an old man, a quiet cranky old man. The only one among us who knew what he was doing.

Opal was picking up some literature that was kept in a cedar box on a post by the gate. Spangler went up to the back of the truck and asked Rabies if he still had his ass in gear. The cat stirred in the box. We drove to Ed Dreiling's (he lived in town), where there was a note on the door telling us the key was in the mailbox and to come on in. We cooked up some steaks we found in the kitchen and went to bed early, though Spangler watched *All in the Family* on T. V.

# The Motor Home

During the middle of the third day we had the accident. We were trying to get to Blackwolf, but we'd settle for the other side of Wilson if we had to. We had come out of Lucas in good shape; we were on the road so early that Opal kept her headlights on as we started south. To our left the sun was turning the high cirrus clouds over the eastern part of the state red, then pink, then, oddly, bright yellow. In an hour the clouds were gone altogether, and the sun lit the third clear day in the three days of the drive. We were going to try to make it to Wilson Lake by noon. We did.

It happened right after we made our usual rounds to Opal's truck for lunch. I was the last to eat, and as usual I took my apple with me so I could feed the core to my horse. We had a difficult stretch ahead of us, and just as I was back riding again, we came down out of the hills east of Wilson Lake and began crossing the bridge.

We had let the cattle run to edges of the road, which had wide, grassy shoulders there and were well fenced. Some of them grabbed mouthfuls of grass as we moved them along. We had two rows of steers going forward, one on each side, with Jed in the middle looking for trouble. When we came down the hill to the bridge, we had to bunch them up again, and they acted up. A pair got behind the truck, but Spangler went back with the bull whip and pretty soon they were running ahead of him at a trot. We got them all across the bridge.

The children of the tourists who had camped at the lake the night before came up and waited just outside the fence on the other side. Husbands/fathers came from their campers with cameras and took pictures of us. Some people from New Jersey sent their children across the fence to catch up with Jed, who accidentally spat absurdly close to them as they came up by his horse. The parents waved the kids along; the father always took three pictures of everything, just to make sure.

The ones who took pictures took them of Jed and the front of the drive. I'll bet that there are living rooms in Newark and Hoboken where balding men are showing slides of their trip west to friends (who stayed home and played golf), and Opal's truck and horse trailer are left out, just as the Dodge and Winnebago campers that brought the cameraman west are left out. The west is pretty much the same, they are saying over Beefeater martinis to their buddies.

After we crossed the bridge we bent south again, toward the upper end of the lake and eventually the Interstate. We had gone about four miles along the main road. The grassy shoulders were wide, but cars came more frequently. We crossed the southern boundary road of the lake. A pink and white GM motor home came down the road to our left, took a bend behind a large rock outcropping, and then entered our road. As it did, it plowed into the middle of the herd, behind Jed, who was waving his arms, and in front of Opal, who was honking her horn.

Spangler and I cut to the left where the cattle had bunched as if they were being pushed in front of a plow. The motor home tried to turn into the road, slid sideways, tottered on its left wheels, but righted itself and stopped. Five steers were down, although Spangler and I couldn't see that because we were below the level of the hill trying to keep ahead of the herd. We met Jed coming down the other side in front of us, waving his hat at the steers, turning them in. I was surprised how quickly we drove them against a far fence and held them there. Jed and Spangler rode back to the road, up the incline, and onto the road. I stayed with the herd.

The driver of the motor home, his wife, an older woman, and some children had spilled out of the camper and were looking at their bumper. The man walked around it, pushing the sides with his hands, as if testing its strength. Opal had stayed in the truck; the hazard blinkers were pulsing. I could see some steers on their sides, one thrashing around, unable to get up, his feet kicking in the air. The herd was easing away from me, down the fence the wrong way. Spangler rode back to the truck and leaned in Opal's window. She handed him something, and a moment later, when he had gotten off his horse, I saw small puffs of smoke from his hand and then the far-off sound of a shot in the wind. He walked around, sometimes pointing at something I couldn't see. Once he was out of sight, but I saw him again before I heard the shot. He had killed the twitching steer first.

I saw Opal walking down the slope toward me, and out across the field; she waved me toward her. When I got there, she told me to go up on the road—they needed help—she had the bull whip, she'd watch the herd. I bunched it for her, then rode up on the highway. When I got there, I looked back and saw Opal cracking the bull whip as she walked across the field, getting some practice, I supposed. The herd looked at her but didn't move; she stayed well clear of them, and they began to graze. I watched all this before I dismounted and tied my horse to the motor home.

"Well, we've got a goddamn mess here now," Spangler said. "Any hurt down there?" He pointed toward Opal.

"I don't know," I said.

"Well, if you don't know, just who the fuck is going to know? You were down there. Any of them thrashing on the ground?"

"No."

"Any bleeding or limping around?"

"I don't know."

"Shit. We'll check that out later. What the fuck are we going to do with five dead steers?" The driver of the motor home came up.

"Could I have your license number, please?" he said, his ball-point pen poised over a yellow note pad.

"No," Spangler said.

"Look, I'm sorry about your cows, but the roads are for cars, fellow. I can get the number myself," he said, and went back to the truck. People were beginning to gather.

"There isn't room in the pickup for them, and I hate to put them in the horse trailer," Spangler said. Jed had climbed into the saddle and was watching Opal and the herd.

"Look," said the man with the note pad as he came back, "it turns out it didn't hurt my home any. I won't push the matter if you won't. Only the bumper bent a little, and the wheels are probably out of line. Why don't you come on in for a drink? It's air conditioned. We can start it up and have a drink. Call it even." He smiled. Spangler looked at him. He had put the gun on the hood of the truck.

"I haven't got time to fuck with them," Spangler said to Jed. The man from New Jersey looked at Spangler, then at Jed.

"It wasn't my fault. There isn't even a stop sign there. I don't think we need to call the police. I only lost a little paint. Of course, as I said, the bumper is pretty bent in, but I'll call it even. Look, Ethel's got the home going again." The home's engine started. "We can have a little nip. It's cool inside."

It was cool outside. Jed rode back to the truck and took the pistol off the hood and put it through the window on the driver's side. He got off his horse and tied him to the tailgate. I did the same. Spangler turned to the man from New Jersey and said, "Move that house out of here." And then to us: "We'll roll them into the ditch and call the dead wagon from Blackwolf. We haven't got time to fuck around." With the three of us pulling on each steer, we dragged them to the side of the road and down a ways into the ditch. Ethel had pulled the motor home off on the road, and the man and some friends watched us from the picture window, the engine idling. There was blood all over the road.

When we got done, Spangler and Jed got back on their horses. I pulled the truck off to one side first and rode down to Opal. The cattle were grazing easily, although they had begun to fan out. Spangler pulled Opal up behind him and took her back to the truck. Jed pointed for me to go to the north end of the fence. When I got there, Jed held his hand in the air, telling me to stay. Jed went to the other end of the herd and began cutting in between the steers and the fence, slowly, gently, as if he had nothing better to do. They eased out of his way but did not drive. When he got to the middle, he stopped. By this time Spangler was coming back down the hill, and Jed held him up by raising his hand and pointing Spangler to the end of the herd opposite me. When Spangler got in place, Jed motioned us both toward the middle, along the fence, shaking his hands to tell us to take it easy.

The steers were jittery; they bellowed, they turned circles, the ones in front stopped grazing and looked toward the road where they did not want to go. Spangler and I were in a little ways on each side when Jed stopped us. The cattle settled back a little. On Jed's signal we moved ahead slowly, cutting gently to the left and right as soon as we got our backs away from the fence. The herd was in a pancake bunch and spilled over on the edges, and it took nearly half an hour to drive them two hundred yards up the draw, angling away from where the accident had happened and joining the road at a forty-five degree angle.

I remember when we got to the top of a little rise, I looked back. Past the truck I could see the lake and the shallow valley that led to it. I could see the spot in the road where the accident happened, and I could see people standing around there and more coming up the road out of the valley on foot and in campers. They were parking just off the access road and getting out and looking at the dead steers in the ditch and talking with the man from New Jersey. I could see behind and to the left of the man from New Jersey, and see that many more people were coming out of the picnic area around the lake to talk to him and to see what had happened and to look at the dead steers in the ditch.

We did not go back up on the road but stayed in the east ditch, which was wide and fenced on one side, until we had to cross the underpass at Interstate 70 into Wilson. When we did that, some cars pulled over and people got out and leaned over the bridge railing and took more pictures. The accident had cost us nearly two hours, and the sun, although high in the west, was beginning to get that strong yellow color that tells you it will soon be sinking fast. We were going to get to Wilson too early, but we might not make it to Blackwolf before dark. There was no place to stop in between. After we crossed through the underpass, Spangler joined Jed in front and they talked for a while and Jed kept shaking his head, but Spangler had made up his mind to go to Blackwolf.

Ted Rooks, Spangler's friend at Wilson, greeted him outside of town and using his truck, helped push the herd through Wilson with no trouble. Spangler told him we were pushing on to Blackwolf. Ted said he'd help, and kept his truck behind the herd, along with Opal.

The sun was low enough that I could see the sun and the horizon at the same time. It was getting orange and pretty. With two trucks behind us, three men on horses, and a narrow, well-fenced road to work, we picked up the pace a little and set the herd into a faster walk, sometimes a trot. We'd trot a mile and ease off a mile. I could feel the sun burning on my neck as we turned east out of Wilson. The shadows of one fencepost were stretching to reach the next fencepost. The trucks came up tight behind the herd and cast their shadows over the backs of the stragglers. Spangler and I rode the ditches, and Jed didn't stop at crossroads to put out the signs or rope them off; Spangler and I'd have to pick up the stragglers when we went by.

It got a little raggedy once, with nearly twenty steers behind the trucks after one crossroad, but the trucks slowed down and Spangler and I brought them back into the herd. It was an hour or so before we found the fastest pace. Once we did, it was smooth riding, although we had to hustle to pick up the steers that cut out at the crossroads, and that was hard work. Two miles out of Blackwolf, three who had cut away to the south jumped a fence into a pasture, and we left them there; we could see the pasture was a fenced forty with a couple of horses in it. We could come back that night with the horse trailer and load them up. I could see my heifer beginning to fall off. I wondered if she could keep up.

This side of Blackwolf, Larry Holmes had set up a drift fence across the road, and we turned a corner to the south and drove them another mile and made a left to the east. Ahead, the road was fenced off and the gate to the pasture to the south open. The sun had gone below the horizon, but I didn't realize that until we turned them in, and in turning around in the pasture, I came face to face with the western sky, black up high where I had last noticed the sun and red along a line where the sun had melted out onto the prairie.

I stayed with the herd. Jed and Spangler and Opal went right away back up the road to fetch the three steers. All was black when they brought them back.

We drove back to Wilson to the motel for dinner. Afterwards we drank in our rooms where Larry Holmes, Ted Rooks, and another fellow who was in the restaurant joined us. The last fellow said he had heard that some people up at the lake had butchered the dead steers and that they'd had quite a picnic up there this afternoon. Cooking the meat over open fires. It turned out to be true. We drank until midnight.

# Opal Pearl Tukle

Now that I am looking back at it, I see I was taking some things for granted. I had gotten pretty close to the Tukles and Jed without much knowing it. I ate at the Tukle house nearly every night from around July until we started the drive. I drove their cars and trucks, ran their errands, offered up suggestions to solve their problems. Jed and I had not begun well. He resented me, I guess. He didn't think anybody could do a cowboy's job who had not been doing it all his life. Spangler once told me that if we could pry Jed's mouth open, and mind apart, we'd find he didn't much care for anybody, not even Spangler, who he thought was a thin version of old man Tukle. But I'm not sure Spangler was right.

Anyway, I got pretty close to them all, got to be one of them. That makes it more difficult to tell stories on them. Only I learned a lot about Spangler just by being with him all the time. And most of what he is, is what he does. Opal was different. There were certain things she wanted out of this trip—simple things, like the Garden of Eden visit, and the Brookville visit coming up. She wasn't as silent about herself as Jed, but still it took a while to get to know anything about her. She'd confide in me now and then, but they weren't important confidences, and she never played me off against Spangler. But that went without saying, once you knew her.

Opal had it in her mind to marry Spangler before the war, but he got away from her and didn't write all the time he was overseas. She was waiting for him when he came back.

She told him he had to marry her within the year, or she'd marry Harry Beeker, whom Spangler hated because of something Harry did to Spangler when they were boys. Nobody knew what it was, because Spangler had never talked about it. Neither did Harry Beeker, who ran away from home a week after it had happened. Spangler said that if she didn't bother him about the matter for a year, he'd marry her. On second thought, Opal said, they'd have to get married in six months.

They were married in the farmhouse on the ranch, where they lived until Harold was ready for school. Then they moved into town. When he is drunk, Spangler says that is what he did wrong with the boy.

According to Spangler, Opal was stoic and fierce. She didn't like other women. She declined the sewing circle set when she was a young bride. She didn't bake cookies for the Methodist Youth Fellowship. She wasn't a den mother; she wasn't asked to be, come to think of it. Later, when they moved to town, she didn't learn to play bridge or golf. She didn't have a daughter.

Opal kept the books for the ranch and looked after the house in town and the one on the ranch. She ran errands Spangler didn't know he needed run until they were done—and there, in the bed of the pickup, was the tire that had gone flat two days ago, now fixed. She knew what needed to be done because she was smart, and she listened to what was being said at the dinner table while she was putting the meal together. I suspect she was convinced that Spangler could never make ends meet without her, although she never said so, and her silence on that matter was her greatest weapon.

She didn't mind his drinking, not the way he minded her smoking: he'd rip them out of her mouth, burning the palm of his hand once in awhile. She didn't even mind his "pussy possing," as he called it. Just as long as she didn't know about it. And nobody else did either. She didn't want to be made the fool in front of a community she didn't give a damn about.

When she heard about the cattle drive, she began to plan things out. Not that she knew Spangler would do it, or that he wouldn't. She just wanted to plan out what she'd have to do if he did do it. She was trying to measure the possibility of success: given that what she would have to do would be done perfectly, and holding that against the half-botched job we would do, could we still get the cattle to Kansas City? She figured we could. But she'd have to take on more than her share.

She was five feet tall, weighed one hundred pounds (just as she had in high school). She was blond and pretty and seldom drank water.

# I Choose My Horse over a Woman (Blackwolf to Ellsworth)

I like the country between Blackwolf and Ellsworth. Some people prefer the Flint Hills, where we would be in a week or so. There, in the spring, the short blue grass covers the battered old hills so that everywhere you look it's like the grass is thin wires of slate. Thunderheads pocket the sky. Old windmills creak in the canyons, and cattle gather in herds at the water troughs. Other people like the land even farther west than Hays, where it is flat everywhere you look—both the land and the sky—and you know you can see farther than you are supposed to. In towns like Goodland, Sharon Springs, Whitelaw, and Shallow Water, you wonder why you can't see the Rocky Mountains you know are climbing out of Colorado, behind Denver. But I like the stretch through the creek and bluff land that converges on the Smoky Hill River as she ambles through the country from south of Wilson to near Kanopolis. We had been down here before, during the summer, to see about buying some cows.

"You like this country?" Spangler had asked me as he noticed that I was silent and looking out the window of the big red pickup.

"Yes. I don't know why."

"It's the rocks in the grass. I like it, too. When I think about it."

He was right about the rocks. It was not only that there were outcroppings of rock along the edges of modest bluffs, but salted all through the land were rocks as if they were growing like the wild pasture flowers that grew out of the land and the cracks in rocks as well.

"I like the way you can't look far enough to see a house or a barn," I said.

"Some of my people came from here," Spangler said. "They traded land along the Smoky Hill for a house in Wichita. I don't let many people in on that bit of family stupidity." He grinned.

As you travel this country, you are always aware of the Smoky Hill, even though you seldom see it—unless you cut off Highway 140 and go down one of the dirt roads until you reach a snubby old wooden bridge made out of railroad ties and oddly warping thick planks. Beneath you is the Smoky Hill River, shallow and yellow in the west, and deep and brown in the east before she becomes the Kansas River. You don't see her often during the stretch between Wilson and Ellsworth—and yet you know she is there, beyond a bluff, at the edge of a pasture where the cattle are gathered along a line of cottonwoods. You can see doves and red-wing blackbirds darting toward the dents and dips in the landscape where—you suppose—there are pools and backwaters of the river. All along this stretch the Smoky hid in the bluffs and hills and draws, listening to us as we took our herd along.

"Think Indians used to hide along that river?" I asked.

"In movies," Spangler replied. "The only place I ever heard about their hiding was at Pawnee Rock. Near Victoria, too. Where they killed all those railroad workers. They should have got more of them. The rest is T.V. ads and movies." I stood up in the stirrups and looked around me.

"Just as pretty now as it was a few months ago," I said.

"Don't turn runny on me," Spangler said. "It's good enough country. I like it better out near Atwood." Just then a trio of hen pheasants sprang out of the road ditch and into the early afternoon sunlight. The horses startled a bit, but we held them. Spangler raised his hand for me to stop and be quiet. The herd was a little ways behind us.

"There's a cock-bird in there," he said. "I saw his tail. Let's get him to pop out." Spangler edged forward on Snip, but before he could get to the ditch, the pheasant was in the air in a whirr—a big, nearly black bird whose gold and red seemed brazed on his dark body. Spangler took imaginary shots. Bang. Bang. The bird flew hard for about fifty yards, beating his wings like a quail, then set into a glide and banked first to the left and then to the right, and dipped toward the ground and out of sight along a section road that was running from the north toward our road. Far to the north on that road I could see the faint trail of dust against the sky that might mean a car coming our way—or perhaps only a wind funneled along a draw until it kicked up the dust from the road. Spangler saw it, too.

"I hope that's a home on wheels. I'll put a few rounds in it just to get the species flinching," Spangler said.

"It's a long way off," I noted. I looked back at the herd. Opal had the truck off to the left and Jed was bringing up the right. We had had no trouble all day. The cattle drove as a herd and we just walked along with them. It occurred to me we hadn't met a car since early in the morning—that was good even for this part of the country.

"I think it's the wind," I said. "I wonder how far up that section road cuts in on us." Spangler studied the thin sprout of dust, then looked up our road, then back north. We could see the road going north for miles, dipping, bounding back on top of a hill and then down again, until finally it seemed to go over the hill of the horizon. From the other side the dust began to rise into a plume. It was a car, for sure, and going fast.

"You get some signs out of the truck and take them up the road until you get where it cuts in," Spangler said. "I'll keep the herd down to a walk until I see you got that bastard stopped. I'd rather not have Barney Oldfield tear up my herd." I did as he told me.

One of the changes we'd made after the motor home mess was to have one of us go way ahead and check for bad intersections—or intersections like this one, where we could see the road would join us but because of the hill we couldn't tell where. Most of the time it was my job. We had kind of settled into jobs. Opal always kept the truck behind and became a general commentator on how things were going.

"The herd seems too tightly packed this morning. Let them string out a little bit," she said to me just that morning. She could see the patterns of things from where she was. Spangler rode in front and sent me off to do my jobs. Two of my jobs turned out to be taking care of Rabies and my heifer. We'd start the morning with Tic-Tac-Toe in the herd—otherwise she'd bawl in a high-pitched cracking whine and finally lean so far out of the truck she'd fall to the ground. For most of the morning she'd do pretty well in the herd—she'd start up front, and when I'd look back over the cattle, I could see her oddly cocked head and her shriveled black ears bobbing among the leaders. But by noon she was tired and had begun to fall back. When she came out the rear end Opal would let me know and we'd stop and put her in the truck. She'd look over the edge, but she didn't have the strength to fall out, and most often she'd rest, leaning against Rabies' box. He'd hiss like a snake, which would make her jump, and the box would rattle around even more before everything got settled down. All I had to do with Rabies was feed him leftovers and tell Spangler if the cat was dead or not. He didn't want to look for himself, but he wanted to know, and if I forgot to tell him, he'd ask.

"That cat gone to bird heaven yet?" he said that morning.

"No. Still alive. It stinks pretty bad within about a block of his box," I said.

"I won't get rabies before he does, will I?"

"I don't think so," I said.

"If you see me start twitching and drooling, you do something."

"I'll cut your head off and send it to the state," I said. Some things didn't strike Spangler as funny.

If taking care of Rabies was a bad job, being kind of a scout for the herd was a good job. I'd ride ahead by myself a couple of miles and see what was up there, and then come back. It was a change from the easy walk Chief and I had gotten into. Except to chase a steer now and then, I seldom got to run the horse. But when I'd scout out the road, I'd dig my heels into Chief's flanks and off we'd go in a gallop. It was just a matter of a couple of hills and I'd feel completely separated from the herd. It was good to be alone. Sometimes I'd meet a truck on the road and I'd flag them down and tell them about the drive. If there was a dangerous intersection, I'd nail up one of our cardboard signs on a fencepost. I did a little daydreaming, too. I could never get used to the idea that I was a real scout for a real cattle drive, and I'd find myself imagining doing pretty much what I was doing. There weren't any Indians, though. Only cars. Like the one whose plume of dust was growing bigger as I galloped Chief up the road to where I thought the section road from the north would intersect us. You can see a long ways in Kansas, and even with a car going as fast as this one was, it takes quite a while for it to come on you. I didn't beat it to the junction, though. It was Heather in the MG.

She had turned the corner and was heading my way as I came down a slight hill. I pulled up hard and the horse reared slightly. She had stopped.

"How dramatic," she said, shading her eyes from the sun. The top was down and the wind had blown her hair into tangles. Women never look as bad as they think they do when their hair is messed up like that. "Where did you learn to ride a horse?" There was an edge to her voice that told me she had been driving for hours, looking for me—up one section road and then down another. She wasn't happy to see me. At least not on a horse.

"I'm working," I said. "I thought we had seen the last of each other."

"I didn't," she said. She turned off the car's engine. The cattle were too far behind me to be heard.

"There will be a cattle drive coming through here pretty soon," I said. I reached behind me to the back of my saddle where I had tied on some signs, rolled up and attached with the saddle thongs. I showed her one.

"Very nice," she said.

"I think you better get the car out of the way."

"I'm out of gas."

"It was running a minute ago."

"Not out of gas this moment," she said. "I've been looking everywhere for you. All these roads look the same. The gauge is on empty. I know I don't have enough to get back to a town."

I was pretty sure I didn't want Spangler and Jed and Opal to meet up with Heather. I had told him some about her. How she'd take off her clothes.

"Bless her little heart," Spangler had said. "Drops those pants without a fuss, does she?"

"It's better and worse than you make it sound," I said.

"There's no such thing as free love," Spangler said. "You think it's free, but that's because you don't know what the price is."

"I don't think you'd like her," I said.

"I might," said Spangler. "A pretty girl who takes her pants off like that means there's a God. Irish whiskey is proof of God, too."

I guess I didn't want Spangler to meet up with a proof of God in an MGTC. I was embarrassed, too. It had been more than a year since I met Spangler and here I was again, the MG out of gas, stuck miles from nowhere, not knowing what to do. I felt like my life was snapping back at me, like the bull whip Spangler used that would snake out over the cattle and then curl back. If you didn't watch it, you'd pop yourself. I thought I could hear the herd over the hill behind me.

"There's a station up the road," I said to Heather, not all that sure there was one, but I thought I had seen a town on the map we had looked at that morning. "I think you can get some gas there."

"When can we talk?" she said.

"Why don't you get some gas?" I said, "and you can meet me tonight in Ellsworth. After work."

"You're always putting me off," she said. I looked west down the road. I could see the dust in the air from the herd on the other side of the hill.

"We better get that car out of here. Those cattle will be here pretty soon." She started the engine and turned around in the road and drove back to the section road she'd come in on, and parked. I followed. In a moment Spangler crested the hill, and behind him the cattle. When he saw me, he waved his hat. He leaned forward on Canyon Snip and took a good long look at the MG and Heather sitting in it. I thought I could see him laugh. He uncoiled the bull whip from his saddle and popped it ahead of him. Nothing seemed to please him more than adventure, unless it was coincidence. The chance meeting with a woman who took off her clothes filled him with joy. Perhaps ambition.

"I've got to get back to work," I said. "I'll get you a can of gas from the truck, and you can get as far as Ellsworth."

"I need to talk to you now," she said. I thought it might be less trouble to deal with her there. I could see the whole evening gone if I got into it with her in Ellsworth. I had begun to need my sleep for a day's work, and the thought of spending hours on end talking to Heather—popping buttons and sliding zippers aside—didn't look too good.

"I'll get you the gas," I said. "I'll ask Spangler if he can spare me for a few moments."

"That would be nice," she said.

Spangler said he'd had to talk to a few women in his time. I could take some time off—not long though—and see what she had to offer.

"Make it a quick one," he said. I told him it wasn't like that. Spangler didn't seem to hear me—he said no two women were alike, some twitched and some popped. From a distance, he guessed Heather was a twitcher.

"That car looks familiar," he said.

"It used to be mine."

"I thought you sold it to a Kansas City dentist," Spangler said. I said I didn't know about that—I'd sold it to a dealer in Hays and Heather bought it from him. It was a long story.

"She's the one who takes her pants off, isn't she?" said Spangler. I nodded. "Make it a short one," he said and rode back through the herd to talk to Jed and Opal. I helped until we got the cattle past the section road. Heather had gotten out and was sitting on a fender as we went by. She waved. Spangler waved. Opal looked. Jed worked the cattle on the side away from her. He wouldn't look at me when I rode up to the truck to get a gas can.

I tied Chief to a fencepost off the road, and then poured the can of gas into the MG.

"You can keep the can," I said. "We have plenty."

"I'll bring it back to you," she said.

"What do you want?" I said.

"I don't know. I just felt it might have been long enough since we last saw each other that things might have changed. You didn't tell me about this cattle drive. Did they come from Idaho?"

"I told you I was a cowboy and cowboys drive cattle."

"You're filthy," she said, looking me over. "Can't you find some clean clothes? Do you ever take a shower?"

"How did you find me?" I asked.

"I read about it in the papers. Hays papers. It's the weekend. I came out to see you and you weren't at home. I read the paper that was on your porch, and it said you were one of the hands on a cattle drive. I've been looking for you all day."

The herd was well past us now, and the dust it scattered into the air was thinning out. It drifted by us in wisps. The sounds of the cattle and horses followed one another into the afternoon. I caught myself looking up the road and feeling anxious. I could see my heifer in the back of the truck looking over the tailgate at the ground. Spangler was bringing Jed up the right side to block off a section road that would be coming up from the south. Maybe Jed would go ahead and scout. Opal was alone in the back. I didn't think it would work. You need someone on a horse in the back of the herd to push along the slow ones. Jed wouldn't make a good scout because Duke couldn't run as fast as Chief. Everything seemed to be working, though. The sounds were fading—the bawling of the steers blended together like the dust coming off their hooves. A dip in the road cut me away from the drive. My horse whinnied after Canyon Snip, but we couldn't hear the response.

"I've been talking to you," she said.

"Yes."

"I said why don't we have dinner tonight."

"I'm not hungry," I said.

"Don't you think you'll be hungry by tonight? Wouldn't it be nice to have a clean dinner? I can pick you up after you . . . you get off work." She looked at my horse, who was stomping the ground and moving against the fencepost impatiently. "We could find a nice restaurant," she said.

I looked at her and I looked at my horse. I thought to myself that something was going badly wrong here. Chief whinnied. Perhaps a mile down the road, Duke or Canyon Snip or Angel had called out and he had heard.

"We need to talk to settle some things before the fall. I can't go on like this," she said. I was looking at my horse. I felt pretty silly when I realized I was stuck in a choice between a girl and a horse. It was getting hard to tell the movies from the life. A certain giddiness of absurdity rushed across me, like when you can't keep a straight face while you tell someone about a ridiculous tragedy.

"I don't think so," I said. I had kind of forgotten what the question was, but my guess was that a gentle "no" would be the best answer.

"Why not?" She swung her leg, twitching her foot in the air. "If you give me a chance, I can be good to you," she said. I took a step backward. She noticed that and put out her hand.

"Give me a hug," she said. "Even if you are dirty, it would be nice to have a big hug from a cowboy." I looked at my feet and then at my horse.

"I'd prefer not to," I said. She took off her sorority ring and put it on the hood of the MG. It made a slight click when she set it down and we both looked at it, startled at the noise.

"I'm leaving," I said. I turned and walked across the road to Chief. Heather threw a shoe at me as I rode past and screamed something I couldn't understand. My horse was eager to get back to the herd and I had to hold him a little, because I didn't want him to be winded for the rest of the day's work. I could see the dust of the drive. I hoped they'd need me.

# The Brookville Hotel

I

The rest of the drive to Ellsworth was uneventful. Spangler wanted to know how I'd made out.

"You didn't have to make it *that* short," he said. "She must have been a popper." I told him it was too short a story to tell. Opal asked me who the girl was. I told her a friend. Jed dropped back by the truck without saying a word to me, but then whole days would go by without our speaking. I was glad to be back, but felt a little melodramatic about it. I'd only been gone fifteen minutes.

My short rest aside, we were tired on the stretch from Blackwolf to Ellsworth. It took us until night to make the shortest drive so far. Toward the end, Jed's legs began to cramp and Spangler told him to ride in the truck awhile. But he wouldn't do it. We were stiff and sore from the first three days. The excitement was wearing thin and we were getting down to work. We went to sleep right after dinner and got an early start for Brookville in the morning.

About midmorning, Spangler remembered that he'd forgotten to make reservations at the Brookville Hotel Restaurant and we had to stop the herd while we rode up a slight hill to a filling station that had an outside phone booth. The highway came close to the road we were using, which for some reason reminded Spangler that he'd forgotten to call the night before.

"Opal Pearl always wanted me to take her to the Brookville Hotel for dinner," Spangler said with one hand covering the phone receiver. He wanted to know how late they were open.

"Think we can make it by 8:30?" he said to me.

"No."

"There will be four of us," he said into the phone. "We might be a little late. Just a little. But we'll be there. Don't shut down on us." He hung up and turned to me. "Let's get going. How far have we got? Fifteen miles?"

"More like twenty."

"No," he said, and swung into the saddle and rode at a run toward the herd.

Jed had ridden about fifty yards up the road to get to the top of a hill. Opal sat in the pickup, the engine idling. Between them were the two hundred and fifty steers and one bingy heifer. It looked good. The cattle were standing easy, the sky was clear everywhere you looked. A light breeze from the west would keep us cool. Maybe the worst was over. Twenty miles to Brookville on a morning like this didn't seem impossible.

"I got a surprise for you," Spangler said to Opal as he walked up. "You know how you always bitched at me 'cause we lived in this country thirty years and we've never gone to the Brookville Hotel to eat? Well, guess where we're eating tonight?" He grinned.

"You sure know how to ask a woman to dinner," she said.

"What the hell you talking about? You know goddamn good and well you want to go to dinner at Brookville. The only thing might piss you off is that after thirty years of bitching about it, you'll have one less shot in your gun." He grinned at me. I went around the other side of the truck. I know a crossfire when I see one.

"We better get going," I said. Opal put the truck in gear. Spangler looked at her.

"Opal, goddamnit. Why the hell aren't you happy?"

She looked straight ahead. "I'm happy. But it was on the plan, Spangler. It's not like you thought of it all yourself."

"That's the trouble with plans. They don't give you any room to be good," Spangler said.

Opal eased up on the clutch, and the truck and the horse trailer moved ahead. The spare horse whinnied sharply. Far up the road, Jed's horse whinnied back. Spangler was disgruntled. "For years she said we were just like the Jews in New York, who all live on one block and work on another, and never see the Statue of Liberty or Yankee Stadium. Two things she always bitches about: one was the Garden of Eden, and the other is Brookville. So we're going to Brookville and she's pissed."

By now we were ahead of the truck. I looked back. Opal was lighting a cigarette. Ahead, she could see the cattle beginning to move up the road. The ones in front balked for a moment, bellowed in protest, then moved ahead. Jed waved us forward. In the distance we could hear the whine of cars on the Interstate. Dust drifted back into our faces. When that happens, you don't hear the Interstate anymore. It all still looked good.

By noon we had gone seven miles without a hitch. We had modified our system a little. When Jed hit a crossroad, he would block off one side; then I'd ride up to the point and Spangler would block off the other side. I'd stay on point until the next crossroad, and then I'd block off the right side road and Spangler would come to point. It wasn't much of a change, but it helped, because then Jed didn't have to ride through the whole herd to get back to the point. Small things like that make a big difference in keeping the cattle quiet.

Our map showed the road crossed a stream about ten miles west of Brookville. With things going well, we decided to push ahead and wait on lunch. Opal agreed with a silent nod. I don't think she was mad; it was just that nobody wanted to make any quick moves of any kind. Just keep it steady and quiet.

I rotated back with Jed just after we decided to go on. Cars had been few that morning, and Jed was thankful.

"It's pretty good today," I said.

He grunted and turned his horse back toward the truck, coming alongside the stock rack, which he rapped with his fist. He came back up. Opal stared at me. Jed was superstitious for all of us.

"I'm sorry," I said. We rode on. We had come onto a flat stretch, and as far as I could see, no section roads cut across us. Jed was stuck with me for at least an hour.

"Do you know any people in this country?" I asked.

"No." He swung away from me and into the ditch to move a straggler along. When he came back up, he said, "Your stirrups are too long."

"I like them that way," I said, determined not to be obliging just because Jed had made a rare move to start a conversation.

"You will get prostatitis," he said. "You will get it anyway, but you will get it sooner with your stirrups too long. You cannot stand up in them." He spat. I cut away to push the right side along, not that they needed it, but just that Jed gave me the feeling that I should be doing something. The feeling was stronger when he wasn't doing much himself. When I came back he said, "You should ride on your toes. If you don't, you'll rip the heels off your boots. You will get prostatitis, too." He spat again. I looked down the road and spotted a coyote in a field below a ridge. He was thin and brown and he watched us coming.

"Is that a coyote or a dog?" I said to Jed.

"I rode to the Dakotas with two niggers who wouldn't ride on their toes. It jostled them till they got hernias. A coyote."

Spangler saw the coyote before he moved and pointed him out. I looked back at Opal, but by now the windshield of the truck was covered with a layer of gray dust, and while you could see her, you couldn't see if she was looking.

The coyote went up the ridge, stopping every hundred yards or so to look us over again. Near the top he stopped for quite awhile, and from there he could see back behind us where our tail of dust plumed out and then was scattered by the wind. In front he could see road clear to the river. He could see that there were no crossroads, that there was an open space on the other side where the cattle could stand while we ate lunch, and that the river was sparkling in the midday sun. In between the silver water to the east and the white dust plume dissipating in the west, he could see a tidy knot of men and horses and cattle, and Opal and her truck, moving easily down the road. He loped up to the top of the ridge and over, without stopping to watch us make a slight bend in the road and go on down a low, gentle hill to the river.

Spangler rode ahead across the bridge and found an open place where the county had fenced a section road off catty-corner to the bridge. Jed got some rope from the truck, and we roped off the road on the right (it didn't go on through) and the road ahead. I roped off the bridge and put out our signs down the road behind the truck. Jed and Spangler did the same. We had gotten used to all this by now and it was easy to do. We thought of it as a ritual. Jed wouldn't carry a sign on horseback, though, and so it took awhile for him to walk up the road and back again. By that time we were into the sandwiches and apples, sitting on the tailgate of the pickup, drinking Coors.

"Jed talking to you, is he?" said Spangler.

"Not really," I said. "He says I should ride differently."

"He's talking to you," Opal said. "If he bothers to tell you how to do anything, he likes you."

"It's only been three months," I said.

Jed was walking back down the road toward us, looking sideways at the fence. As he came up to us, he said, "This county builds fences like the garden club. The bottom wire is too high for the little calves. The corner post is not braced. They used steel posts. The wire is loose. Government." He tossed his hat onto the truck hood.

"Here's your sandwich," said Opal. He took it and went back by the horse trailer and sat down, leaning against the wheel.

"Opal, goddamnit, don't smoke if you want to go to dinner."

She looked at him and, cocking her lower lip, blew the smoke up in the air. Jed came back from the horse trailer.

"You ready?" Spangler said to Jed.

"Yes."

"How about you starting out in front again. Unless you want to rest and drive the truck." Jed walked past him and untied his horse and led him off through the cattle. When he got to the other side, he looked back. Opal got into the truck. I led Chief back and undid the wire across the bridge and rode back down the road to get the sign. By the time I got back, we were underway, with Jed up front and Spangler behind. I tossed the sign in the bed of the truck as I rode by. Opal smiled at me in the outside mirror. We still looked good, I thought.

"We'll get there," I said as I rode by.

"You might be right," she said. "I wonder if they still rent rooms. I could clean myself up if they'd rent us a room. I packed a skirt and I've got a clean blouse. Not much I could do with my hair unless I had an hour." She took a last drag on her cigarette and tossed it into the dust. I rode up and joined Spangler.

"Good day. Right?" he said.

"Jed would go back and knock on wood if he heard you say that," I said.

"It's not luck that makes things work out. It's pushing them around until they go your way."

Jed whistled. There was a road coming up and a blue truck on the road coming from the right. We could see its dust kicking up behind it. Then it slowed. Spangler rode up one side to hold the herd back, so the truck could cross before we got to the section road. The truck eased on through the intersection, and a man and his wife stared at us. They stopped. Spangler rode on up to the intersection, tied up Canyon Snip, and began stretching a rope across the road. Jed was doing the same. Opal and I held our ground. The man in the truck got out; so did his wife. Both were as old as Jed.

The wife had a large red mark across her face. It looked like the sliver of a moon cut in red, from just over her right eye down through her nose and across the left part of her mouth. She was talking to her husband and her mouth opened the moon, and when she blinked her eyes the other end of the moon wrinkled up. He nodded and then went up to Spangler. The herd was just getting to the crossroads. I rode up on Spangler's side. Opal could push them on through in the truck.

"This fart says we can't go down this road," Spangler said as I rode up.

"Why not?"

"Says he hasn't got his wheat fenced off in the next quarter." The man stood there looking at the ground.

"There's nothing he can do about it, far as I can figure, unless he gets the sheriff out. By then we'll be on by. Right? And if we haven't done any damage, have we broken the law?"

"I'm not a lawyer."

"Maybe not. But you got yourself one hell of a fancy education. Now, unless we fuck up old fart's wheat here, have we broken the law? I want an instant judicial opinion." The old man walked back to his wife, where they stood together.

"I guess not. It's a public road," I said.

"It's a public road," Spangler said to the couple as he walked up to them. "Don't worry about your wheat. We'll keep them off. Don't you see, it would cost us three miles to go around your place."

"Two," the moon-faced woman said, as she turned to get back in the truck. Her husband joined her and they drove off slowly, going straight for a mile, then turning right toward Brookville.

"Get those steers back on the other side of the rope," Spangler yelled at me. Opal started up again, and we took the herd across the road with no trouble and eased them down the hill toward the unfenced quarter-sections, one on each side. Jed eased ahead, not riding out in front, but high on one side. Spangler copied him on the other side. I rode on Spangler's side, figuring that Opal and the truck could handle the rear. Now I could see that the fields surrounded the farmhouses, the one on the right in a clump of trees with a long, barren drive going straight to it, the other a new house with no trees and close to the road.

"How are we going to work this?" I called to Spangler.

"Come on up."

Down the section road a mile away we could see the blue pickup coming from left to right, heading toward our road.

"You know I don't think that old man wanted to cause us any trouble," Spangler said. "I lay it all on the woman. She gave him an earful as he was driving through. It's not the wheat, it's her clothes hanging on the line to dry that gets her."

The truck was coming up the road. I figured it would turn into the drive leading to the old house, but it kept on coming, slowing down, but still coming.

"He's going to stand his ground," I said.

"Shit. That's all we need is a truck in the middle of the road and these goddamn bingy steers will scatter all over his wheat."

Spangler rode on ahead. The truck stopped, but no one got out. Behind us Opal had stopped. Jed had cut in front of the herd. I joined him. The cattle seemed edgy. A few of them crowded into the ditches and began eating the grass. Others were easing up on our side, eyeing the fenceless fields and the thin layer of green wheat that covered them. Spangler and the old man talked, Spangler leaning over and down. The woman looked straight ahead.

"What do you think?" I asked Jed.

"He should have fenced his wheat in," Jed said.

Ahead, I could see the old woman lean over in the truck and shake a finger at Spangler. The old man pushed her back, and she took a quick swing at him and hit him in his chest. Then she sat up straight and looked out the other window. The old man put the truck in reverse and backed slowly down the road. Spangler rode back to where we were.

"He's going to help," Spangler said. "He said he used to work cattle in Wyoming. He likes the looks of what we're doing. The old lady is pissed. Let's hold the herd here until he gets ready. Says he still has an old bear-trap saddle. Wife says he doesn't and that the horse is lame anyway. I'll bet he gets out here." Spangler went back and talked to Opal.

Elwood Dunn, the man whose wife had a red quartermoon on her face, came riding down the lane on a horse who threw his left hind-leg a little to the side when he trotted and who whinnied, shaking his head as if to get rid of the bridle. Dunn wore a baseball cap with the emblem of his Grange on it. Jed, who had been back with me, told me to move up on the right, and Elwood joined Jed in the back. His wife, in an apron, was taking her laundry off the line as we passed Elwood's place a moment later, but he didn't notice; he was talking to Jed. Spangler and I put out signs and left Jed and Elwood in back. To the south and west there were clouds. It wasn't an hour before it began to rain.

Opal passed out slickers as we rode back to the truck. She gave Elwood hers. It wasn't raining hard, but by the looks of the western sky, a warm front was moving in, and that would mean a couple of days of slow, dreary rain. It was slowing us down. The sky had turned gray, there was little color in the land. The dust was turning to mud and the mud was caking on the hoofs of the horses and the cattle. It seemed as if we traveled every mile twice. We could see a paved road to our left, but Spangler wouldn't go up there. There was no way to tell what time it was by the color of the sky; it seemed as if it had been evening all afternoon. The rain cleared the windshield, and in between the sweep of the wipers I could see Opal, grim, not smoking, leaning forward against the steering wheel, which she held near the top with both hands. She had turned the headlights on, and her four-way flashers were blinking silently. The herd was quiet, too. Perhaps they had gotten used to going about twenty miles in a day and knew they would go that far today, too, in spite of the rain and the mud.

The bingy heifer couldn't keep her feet. She would fall down and lie in the mud with steers going around her until the herd passed, and then she'd get to her feet again and catch up and work into the herd and fall down again. Elwood and Jed loaded her into the horse trailer. That brought us to a stop, but it was either that or shoot her.

Opal said she'd kill the cat if Spangler shot the heifer. I was left out of it. Spangler said that we'd be late to Brookville. Opal said she figured as much. If it hadn't been for Jed and Elwood starting up the drive again, there might have been a scrap between them.

We drove past the Kanopolis road and could see to the south a field full of campers and mobile homes. It looked like the early stages of a junkyard, with grey hulks of trucks and campers and buses scattered over a sad field.

I figured we had about six miles to go. It was getting darker and raining harder, not pouring like a cloudburst, just raining harder all the time. My straw hat leaked on my head and my boots soaked through the tops. My horse shook his head against the rain, then lowered it and plodded on. We passed a quart of Green Gables among Opal, Elwood, Spangler, and me (Jed took it once). It went around five times before Spangler threw it empty into the ditch. It helped. Spangler and I rotated to the back.

"This is what it's all about," he said. "All that fucking fair weather is fine, but if we can get these sons-of-bitches in tonight, we can make it all the way. How you doing?"

"My hat leaks," I said.

"A little water won't rot that schoolteacher's brain away."

"I guess not. I wonder how Rabies is doing."

"Standing right in the middle of his box, I'll bet. We got to figure a better way to let him shit. Did you smell that truck this morning? I feel a little sorry for anybody who's got to sleep in the same room they shit in, but cats got special problems."

"I don't know how you're going to do it," I said.

"Maybe I could take him for a walk. On a leash."

"I don't think so."

"What time do you figure it's getting to be? Six?"

"More like seven," I said. "Want me to check?"

"No. We just got to push. We can't miss the Brookville deal or my ass is in a vise. She's been pretty good about all this. I guess I give her too much shit sometimes."

I didn't say anything.

"I'm out here with two hundred fifty steers, it's pouring down rain, I got some Green Gables in my gut, and I know I'm going to get to Brookville. All this is mine and Opal's. We put it together, and I'll take it right now. None of that posterity shit." I thought he might be thinking about Harold. He laughed again. "God, this feels good. I'm wet from the waist down and cold as a witch's tit." He broke away to cover a side road. I went the other way. I didn't think we'd make it to Brookville in time. We did and we didn't.

## III

It was pitch dark when we crossed the little bridge just south of Brookville and came up by the gas station that is a tavern. We took the herd east again and then jogged to the north into the school-yard, which had been lit up for us. We didn't know if we had lost any of the herd during the last hour, but we had.

Against the playground lights you could see the rain coming straight down. It seemed as if the rain didn't exist until it got into the light, but then it disappeared again into puddles on the asphalt and the mud.

"This is sure going to tear hell out of this playground," the principal said when we finally got unsaddled and walked over to talk to him. "I'm afraid I'll have to ask you to pay to have it leveled. If it comes to that, Spangler," he said.

"That's all right, George. Send me the bill. I'm glad to have the place. join us for dinner," Spangler said as the six of us walked toward the pickup, Jed and Elwood behind.

"Where are you going to eat?"

"The hotel. Come on, I'll buy yours."

"Hotel's closed. It's past eight-thirty."

"Not much. We called ahead and told them to wait. Come on."

"I don't think they're still there. But I'll go over with you." Spangler and the principal got in the truck and I caught a ride on the bumper. Jed and Elwood rode the running board on the horse

145

trailer. There was a light in the back of the restaurant, but the front was dark and the sign was out.

Spangler banged on the door. A fat young man with a moustache finally answered. All of us stood in the rain.

"We're here," Spangler said. "I called this morning and told you we'd be along. Maybe a little late."

"We're closed."

"The fuck you are," Spangler said, and grabbed him by his bib apron and picked him up and moved into the lobby. "Now you get your ass back in that kitchen and fix us a chicken dinner with everything that goes with it. Just like it was the middle of mealtime."

Opal and the principal yelled at Spangler when he grabbed the fat boy.

"I'm not the cook. The cooks have gone home."

"The hell you say." He marched the boy backward across the lobby into one of the dark dining rooms, past the automatic coffee maker, and through the swinging double doors into the kitchen. We all followed, Opal and the principal trying to intercede. But Opal was giving up, and the principal was too timid to do any real harm.

The kitchen was bright with electric light. There were about six people back there, including a pretty redheaded waitress sitting on a counter eating a chicken wing. They all stared when we came through the door.

"O.K., O.K.," said the fat man. "I can get you a picnic basket. Stuff we got left over."

"Shiiiiiiit. We're going to have a regular dinner. Now, how about that, shit-for-brains?" He pushed him against a stove.

"These people want to go home," the kid whined. "They just did all the dishes. They'd have to do them all over again."

"You cook the dinner and I'll do the dishes," Spangler said. Opal swore.

"I said, I'd do the dishes. Not you, bitch. You go sit down and get ready to eat. All of you, except you." He pointed at me. "You get the bottle."

146

"Oh, you can't drink here," said the fat kid. "There's no drinking here."

"Consider this a private party, just like the Knights of Columbus. Now light a dining room. I think we want to eat in the Bank Room. All of us at one table. I'll just stand here and watch this chicken-cooking process."

I went to get the bottle. The redheaded waitress led the rest of them out of the kitchen to the Bank Room. She was lighting the candles when I came back in with the scotch. I poured straight drinks all around, offered her one, which she took, and brought the bottle back to Spangler, who was asking questions of the fat boy.

"How long you had these frying pans?"

"I don't know."

"Are you cooking enough chicken for all of us?"

"Oh yes." There were four or five silent, husky women busy over the stove and digging into large refrigerators. Some of them were grinning to themselves. I think we had their main pain in the ass by the nuts, and they were getting a kick out of it.

"Cook up enough for yourselves, girls, if you haven't eaten. I'll pay." They smiled.

"We've all eaten," the fat boy said.

"I'll bet you have," said Spangler, and poked the fat boy in the belly with the Green Gables bottle. Spangler took a pull and passed it to me.

"It looks like these girls are doing a bang-up job. I think we can go on into the Bank Room. You come along, fat boy." Spangler steered him by his neck out of the kitchen. I caught the cooks looking and laughing.

In the lobby Elwood was calling his wife to tell her to come to Brookville for dinner and to pick him up. She had already eaten dinner. She'd wait for him in the truck if he wasn't done when she got there. The redheaded waitress had another drink. I went to the truck for a second bottle.

Dinner came. The cooks served us; the waitress was getting drunk and decided she'd better sit down. We pulled another table against ours and poured the cooks a round. The fat boy said he wouldn't mind a beer if we had one. Spangler poured him a scotch and asked him to pass the creamed corn.

"Too bad we don't have some wine," Spangler said, "That's what they have in the East when they sit down to a meal. Wine. Red wine with beef and beer with fish. You've got your choice with chicken."

"I've got wine. I've got wine at my place," the waitress said. "Just wait here." She got up, knocking her chair over. "I'll get the wine at my place." She was back in five minutes with a gallon of Gallo burgundy. We poured it into water glasses and Spangler made a toast.

> "Friendships wane and friendships grow,
> Some friendships peter out, you know.
> But we'll be friends through thick or thin,
> Peters out or peters in."

Opal's grin was so big I wondered all through the toast if Spangler hadn't proposed to her with it. Everybody was drunk. Even Jed.

"Let's not eat to sobriety," Spangler said. The cooks talked among themselves, unless Opal asked them questions. Sissy, the redhead, asked me where I lived and what I did. Elwood and Jed giggled like girls about something. We tossed the chicken bones on a plate in the middle of the table—to save for Rabies. The pile grew high, the wine bottle grew light, the Green Gables was gone. Fat boy said we didn't have to do the dishes; they'd do them in the morning. A pickup honked in the road outside.

I remember seeing Spangler with fat boy's apron pulled around him and soap suds dripping from his elbows. I remember some discussion about whether the rooms upstairs were for rent or not. They weren't. They had been turned into a museum of turn-of-the-century decor. By the end of the discussion the rooms were for rent. Opal went upstairs. I took the chicken bones to the cat. Sissy went with me. We pushed some bones through the holes in Rabies' box. He hissed and growled once he got the bones, as if some other cat might take them away. I don't remember Elwood's leaving. There was no one outside when we were out there. Sissy showed me to my room. She went in ahead of me, but didn't turn on the light. Neither did I. The door clicked closed, and by the time I found her on the bed she had opened her dress, which buttoned all the way down the front. She sat up in bed to let me push it off her arms. Only the faint gleam from the lone Brookville streetlight let me see patches of her body. The edge of a breast. The inside of a thigh. Shoulder strap marks. She arched her back to make it easy for me to roll her panties off.

Spangler bashed the door with his fist the next morning. First once. I heard it, but did not move. Then he bashed the door hard a number of times. The door bowed where he hit it. That got me up. Sissy rolled over and took deep breaths. I said I had to leave. She said she'd make the beds so the manager wouldn't know.

Spangler left a movie hundred-dollar bill, the face of Franklin staring at the chandelier in the Bank Room from the table where we ate.

"It's enough, don't you think?"

"I hope it gets split up right," I said.

The morning was mean. We had to go back down the road to get a few steers. We had the drive to Holland to make. We were all sick and sore and silent. The drive to Holland was no trouble. Just long. The horses seemed to take singular pleasure in bouncing our bodies. By noon it seemed as if my head had fallen off, and it seemed to my stomach as if I had swallowed it.

# I Get a Lecture on
# Medicinal Sex and
# Undiscriminate Screwing

The stretch between Holland and Woodbine was an easy drive on a clear day. We had been working hard and playing hard and that was beginning to bruise us up a bit. Jed worked harder than any of us. He was always picking up after our mistakes: bringing steers back up a road that I had let out because I was too slow in getting to the section line. Getting steers out of a pasture where they had gone through a fence because Spangler had pushed them too hard and they'd panicked. Jed's legs would cramp on him from time to time, and he'd get off Duke and stand in the road until the cramp let go. It was good to get an easy day. It gave Jed a break and Spangler and I talked.

"You ever wonder about that deal with the movie people?" he asked me as we began the morning.

"Yes."

"I was about to commit Undiscriminate Screwing. That's not as low as you can get. It might be better if it was. If you live doing half-bad things, you'll never work up any character. Like lawyers.

Those buzzards are always about half-assed bad. But any way you cut it, Undiscriminate Screwing is not to be admired."

"Will it grow hair on your palms?" I asked.

"On the inside of your head. That's where it grows. Your hair bends around and grows through your head into your brain, so you can't tell what's good and what's wrong. Which makes it tough when you're out to do something strongly bad. I think it's good to do a few bad things. But it's no good getting the candy-assed bad things like Undiscriminate Screwing mixed up with a good pussy posse."

"What happened with the movie people?"

"A lot of bad things are worth something besides building character. Like the time I shot Al Schmidt's black rooster because he'd crow undiscriminately through the night. Used my .30–06. You should have seen him pop open. Made pillow feathers and soup of him. Whap."

"You were going to tell me about the movie people."

"Cue Ball said he'd fix me up with Blue Toes. He'd park the camper up the section road that night and Blue Toes would be there."

"I didn't think she was your type," I said.

"You might rot before you're dead, if you turn away a chance at a woman," Spangler said.

"You were pretty down on those movie girls all summer. She didn't seem any different."

"I know. I'm not telling you I was right about the whole thing. I'm telling you I was wrong. I just figured Blue Toes was a nasty woman. I figured she knew how to do things that were crimes against nature and illegal in Puerto Rico. I haven't had a woman like that in a long time. I got myself a stainless steel hard-on just imagining. A cat couldn't scratch it. But it would have been an Undiscriminate Screw if there ever was one."

"How's that?"

"I would have done it, except Cue Ball double-crossed us. That's a pimp for you."

"Why would it have been an Undiscriminate Screw?"

"She wasn't my type."

"What?"

"The deal wasn't mine, either. It wasn't like a whore deal, where you know where you are. This was one of those mushy deals. Like lawyers get set up."

"Didn't you think Opal might catch you?"

"Maybe. Getting caught is one thing. Flaunting it, that's another thing. That's part of Undiscriminate Screwing, when everybody knows about it. It's all right if everybody knows you bird dog. But it's no good if they know about it bird by bird."

"I had my eye on Blue Toes, too," I said.

" 'You were pretty loose, as I remember," Spangler said.

"My eyes were bigger than anything else, that's for sure."

"You got a lot to learn, pistol." I said I knew that, but I also knew that learning wasn't any guarantee. We rode on that morning, the sky blue and flat like a pond, no wind, and the herd gentle in front of us. We stopped for lunch near a creek south of Navarre. When we started up again, Spangler asked me about Sissy.

"What about her?" I said.

"Do you think you'll ever see her again?"

"No. Does that make me an indiscriminate screwer?"

"Hell, no. There's no law against falling in love for a short time." He paused. "But then there's no law against keeping up a good thing."

"You want to give me a day off? I could catch a bus back to Brookville. I'll trade you a day off for a graphic account of sex in the afternoon."

"Shiiiiiit. I need you around for yuks. I don't need any stories about women. I need to see your ass bounce all over that saddle when you finally get that horse out of a trot. Besides, Jed would know we were in trouble for sure if you left. The only reason I look like a million dollars on this deal is because you look like a nickel." Spangler didn't feel it was important to praise his help.

"I don't need to go back there anyway. I got something waiting in Kansas City for me," I said.

"The girl in the MG?"

"Yes."

"That's medicinal sex. That's only a cut above Indiscriminate Screwing."

"Everytime I'm around her she wants it," I said. "She'll take her clothes off without any prodding."

"That's a pretty good sign she wants to screw. But it's still medicinal sex."

"Why?"

"How do you feel about her?" Spangler asked.

"Not good," I said. "I like her, but I wish I didn't know her."

"A sure sign of a medicinal screw," Spangler said.

"You opposed to medicinal sex?" I said.

"I'd like to be. It's like the first time I bought a whore. I thought it was a good deal at the time, and a bad deal afterwards. Sometimes you lead yourself around by your pecker. There's not much you can do about it, though. I think if you've got to go to medicinal sex, it means you're not moving around naturally enough. Like people who jog to keep their weight down. Nobody likes to take pills. But nobody likes to have a blue steel hard-on and no place to put it but your hand. There ought to be more women in the world."

"What about being faithful. To your wife?" I said.

"I don't know," Spangler replied. We made it to Woodbine before sunset.

# The Story of a Killing

We had gotten into White City early. After more than a week on the road we were on schedule, only a dozen steers had been lost, and we'd had no flat tires. The plan was holding together. We ate an early dinner at the White City Café: hamburger steaks, french fries, bread, salad, a cup of coffee and rice pudding—$1.85. The owner said she'd have to raise her price to two dollars after the first of the year. Jed and Opal joined Spangler and me in the Tavern, which was next door. There we met Edgar Flinch, who was a sheep rancher and offered to lend us his dog, Sally. Spangler didn't think she could help us much. Thank you, though. Edgar told us this story about the time he worked for Hardy (The Bear) North back before the war.

"As you know," he began, "the North place is outside of St. Peter. And in those days they had their own school there. North's was the biggest ranch in the country. He had gotten through the Depression because he refused to spend much on equipment. We did a lot of work with horses, right up to the war. He was a frugal man, and he didn't expand until those around him were going broke. He bought up their land cheap. I started work there in 1935. The dust was so thick when I got to St. Peter that we had our lights on and you couldn't see twenty yards ahead. That was in the afternoon.

The hired man before me had died. North had a son who was a little boy then. I watched him grow up. Such as he did.

"Well, those first years I worked for North we did all those things you don't get around to doing except when the weather's bad and you don't want to work anyway. We painted barns, we put up five wire fences, built corrals, dug wells and ponds, planted some of the government's trees, built drift fences and holding pens, put up a new shed. We even fixed up the house and the yard a bit. Of course, North had some cattle, and he was always building up his cow herd. But the grass was bad, and he couldn't put much out there. He didn't want to do the grass harm. He was out of wheat altogether. Said after what the wind did to his crop in 1932, he'd never plow the land again. He was getting ready for when the weather would change, and he was going to run his place full of cattle. It was twice the work of wheat farming. His son could help by then, he figured."

Spangler said he knew where that kind of figuring led. Opal frowned. Edgar went on.

"I think the boy got hurt when nobody was watching him. You know, maybe fell out of a tree or something. Only he never went very far. Some say he had a hard birth. Nowadays I guess they'd have him into the head doctor. I'd see him around the yard standing out in the middle of it, looking just past the fence somewhere. It didn't seem as if his eyes would see you. You'd wave, and it'd be just a moment later, and he'd wave back. He walked kind of goofy. His arms didn't swing right with his legs. I never said anything to North about it. The Bear, he never said anything about anything, except to tell me what to do at the start of each day.

"About 1940 North began taking Billy T. (the boy) along with him and me in the truck. I don't think the kid much wanted to go, but North would take him anyway. He wouldn't talk much to him. Only ask him once in a while how he felt. Or if he thought he could open a gate. Or would he like to go by the pond and see if there were ducks on it. The boy was about ten, you see. He'd shake his head to answer no, and it was like he couldn't stop it when he wanted to, so it'd wobble on. Once, he started giggling and drooling when we came up on a bull breeding a cow.

"After a while, most of the time North would take Billy T. along, he'd get me to do something else. After that year I don't expect I rode in the same truck with the boy six times.

"Times were coming along. Billy T. had better catch on or North would have to hire another man. If we hadn't spent the better part of five years puttering around that ranch, getting everything in perfect shape for the day things would either go right or they wouldn't, we'd have been in a mess about help before we were. I could handle the winter feeding pretty well. North and me could get the steers up to the main corrals for working, what with all those drift fences we had up. And the new fences all around didn't need much fixing. But when calving time came, we were running all the time and not keeping up. I said I wanted a bit more in the way of pay, if I was going to be working through the night most of the time. North said maybe Billy T. could give us a hand." Spangler poured another round of beers.

"There was a school just out of St. Peter then, and they had been sending Billy T. there since he was about seven. Every once in a while I'd notice the schoolteacher bring him home and she'd stay after supper for awhile. I thought the Norths were doing their part in giving her a decent meal every now and then.

"One day in the spring of about '41, a whole bunch of people showed up at the house. Right in the middle of the day. About four trucks plus the schoolteacher in her car, all coming up the lane. Billy T. was with the schoolteacher. I guess he was about twelve or thirteen then. They wanted to see North, they said, and I went down to the pens east of the barn and got him. He told me to take up where he left off fixing the hinge on the main gate. I could see they all went into the house. They were all the men who ranched around us. They stayed for about an hour, I guess.

"Billy T. must have been kicked out of school, because he was around the yard the rest of that spring, grinning at me everytime I'd come in sight.

"North hired another man. It was a nigger he got from Nicodemus, whose father was a dusty cowboy back with McCoy. Or so he said. That nigger knew a lot about cattle, I'll say that. It was all right with folks that we had a nigger out there. Unlike down at Hays, we didn't have no Negro problem. The nigger and I would ride together over the ranch on horses, and The Bear would take the truck, and every once in a while Billy T.

"Once I took the truck to town, and on the way back I saw Billy T. standing out in the road a mile west of the house. Just standing by the side of the road. I gave him a ride back to the house. He didn't say anything. Just looked at me kinda silly.

"There was a good deep pond north of the house that the government built and stocked with bass. I don't fish much, but that nigger did. He said it was pretty good. Other folks thought so too, and The Bear, he didn't mind people coming over and fishing. The ranchers' kids had been coming down there for some years now, and every once in a while the men themselves would stop by on a summer evening. I remember that summer started just as usual, with kids fishing down there most any time, but toward the end, say from about July on, you'd hardly see anybody down there. Except the nigger, of course. He'd go down there late when there wasn't enough light left to light a match by. That was all right with him, though. I got to know him pretty well." Edgar paused when he saw Jed get up to take a piss. Spangler and I followed Jed to the john. Spangler teased me about the rubber machines.

"We didn't pack any of those for you," he said. "But by the looks of a few nights ago, we should have." We pissed.

"Sounds like the North kid was as fucked up as my heifer," I said.

"Sounds that way," Spangler said. We went back to the table. Edgar started up again.

"One day Stevenson, the guy who lived to the east of us, drove over and wanted to talk with The Bear. I told him he was down south working over a windmill. Stevenson drove off in that direction.

"In September, I asked North if the nigger and I could shoot the doves that were coming through that year. He said that would be all right. The wife might cook them up for us if we wanted her to.

"The nigger and me shot a mess of doves the first day of September and gave some to North. He joined us the evening of the next day. As we walked back to the barn, North asked did I notice if Cooper's store had any single shots in. I thought they did. They usually kept a Winchester 37 on the shelf for the boys coming up.

"I guess North must have bought it sometime between then and the end of the month, because it was around the first of October that I saw him out with Billy T., down at the dump in the gully on the far east pasture. He was shooting tin cans and I guess teaching Billy T. how to use the new gun. I didn't see much of Billy T. after that. I hadn't seen much of him since about the middle of summer, come to think of it. They kept him up in the house. I didn't see how the boy was going to learn to handle a gun, as floppy as his arms were. But I didn't make that my business.

"I think the wife was upset about Billy T. learning to shoot, because when I got back to the main house she asked me if I had seen them, and I told her I had. That was about all she said, except thank you. She was polite to me, and the nigger, too. Though I never saw the inside of the house.

"Pheasants were thick that winter. We gave every third one we shot to North. He joined us a couple of times. The only kind of hunting he didn't want us to do was duck hunting off the pond. He wanted that pretty much to himself. That got under the nigger's skin. He used to drool about the thought of a duck roasting in the oven. I don't like ducks much, but they aren't as greasy as carp or possum. The nigger liked carp, possum, ducks. He'd even eat badger.

"One day North offered me and the nigger a couple of butter balls he had gotten. He said he shot a mallard, and the butter balls got up. Being stupid, they flew around once and came right back in. He shot them both with one shot. The nigger said he would be pleased to have those ducks. I knew the nigger and me would be eating different meals that night. A duck is one thing, but a butter ball ain't a duck. I think their stupid head turns their meat foul. Or something. And to top it, I knew that nigger would skin those ducks and fry them in possum fat.

"I guess it was in January. I know it was. Because hunting season was supposed to be over, but The Bear didn't pay that any attention because the big redlegged mallards were just coming down. Most every morning, we'd hear him shoot down on the pond. We'd wake up by it. He'd turn on the yard light when he left, and a little while later we'd hear some soft popping. If you're waking up anyway, you hear those little sounds.

"It was one morning in early January and redlegged mallards had been coming in a little. I heard the door slam again. I raised up in bed and looked out the window. In the yard light I saw The Bear with his Model 12 and Billy T. with his single barrel. I guessed The Bear thought maybe it was time to give him a real taste of hunting before the year was over. Billy held the gun too far back near the stock. The barrel would scrape on the ground. The Bear snapped at him about it.

"They went out the gate and I couldn't see them anymore. In a little while I heard the soft shots. I wondered if Billy got his gun off. The nigger woke up and said we had to tell North to get the vet out to look at one of the horses today. We dressed.

"When I went out to take a dump, I saw The Bear coming up the road carrying Billy T. over his left shoulder and holding him on with his left hand. In Bear's right hand he carried both guns. I guess Billy T. jumped up in front of Bear when the ducks flew. North never said how it happened. They buried Billy T. right there on the ranch in that little cemetery they shared with the Walters family. North said we didn't have to come to the service. We could take the day. Not many people went. Things were never the same between him and the wife, though. I can tell you that. I left to come out here when my dad died in 1951. The year of the flood. I think the nigger still works there."

Jed said he heard North died three years ago by his own hand. Spangler took a deep breath. Opal's eyes were glassy. It wasn't the kind of story they had wanted to hear. We never talked about it again.

# Spangler Talks about Jed as We Go from White City to Alta Vista

He's the only one that knows what we're doing," Spangler had said to me a couple of days into the drive, and again as we moved out this morning. "He took cattle from Salina west, and up into Nebraska and out to Colorado. He even took some to Montana. I remember him telling about a boil he got on his ass in Nebraska, and how he had to stand up in the stirrups for three days."

"You look like you know what you're doing," I said.

"I told you what I know and what I don't know. I remember drunken conversations even if you don't."

"About how you were close to mowing lawns instead of raising cattle? I remember," I said. "But what makes you think Jed is the only one who knows what we're doing? I'm getting the hang of what we're doing. You've taught me a lot of things."

"That's not the same," Spangler said. "Jed knows things about driving cattle we'll never use."

"So what?"

"I thought you were a teacher. That's a slim attitude for a teacher to have. You ever read an encyclopedia?"

"No."

"I have. *The Columbia Desk Encyclopedia.* Bought it for Harold, but he wouldn't read it. I read Bartlett's, too."

"What?" I said.

"I read *Bartlett's Book of Quotations.* I like quotations."

"I've never heard you quote anything."

"I don't. The ones I remember are about myself. I don't think it's a good idea to talk about yourself in a roundabout way like that." He paused. "I say them out loud when nobody's around."

"Tell me one."

"No." We rode on a little ways, keeping quiet.

"Did you buy *Bartlett's* for Harold?" I asked.

"Yes. He never read it."

"Why not?"

"I don't know," Spangler said. "He didn't read much of anything as far as I could tell. Not until he started reading about Zen and China. Opal said it was good that he was reading, no matter what. But I didn't say that. If you don't read anything, you're likely to be impressed by the first couple of things you bolt down."

"You read much?" I asked.

"Yes. But I don't want to talk about it."

"Why not?"

"Personal."

"I see." This time we rode nearly an hour in silence.

"What do you think of Harold?" Spangler said to me as we crossed an old high-walled wooden bridge.

"I don't know," I said.

"Would I say that, if you asked me what I thought of that ball-cutting bitch that keeps skirting around here in that sports car?"

"I guess not," I said. "I don't like Harold."

"Neither do I," said Spangler.

Spangler wheeled Canyon Snip off the left and cut behind the herd to bring up some stragglers. I stayed where I was, in the middle.

We had moved the truck forward after we crossed the I-135 and it led the way, flashers pulsating. It would come in and out of view as first it dipped into a draw, then rose out, and then we'd dip and rise. There is a lot of puttering to do when you drive cattle, and you can always find something to get done—which we needed to do in order to avoid a long, sloppy talk. Or you can let the puttering go and it will just about amount to the same thing. Spangler stayed on the left for quite a while, bringing the slow steers along. Jed was at the front, Duke in a slow walk. We ate lunch on horse back and kept up a long, slow pace. Around noon Spangler came back my way and talked about Jed again.

"Sometimes I think Jed knows more of what not to do. Like that damn horse of his. That horse hasn't wasted a step in twenty years. I rode him once last spring, and when we'd go through the draws where the volunteer wheat was greening up, Duke would tear off a mouthful on the run. I said to Jed, 'Goddamnit Jed, this horse shit machine you got eats on the run. I damn near pitched over his head and bought the ranch.' And Jed says: 'You should not ride my horse. You should ride your horse. I should ride my horse.' You know how he talks." I said I did.

Spangler continued: "Jed knows what you don't have to do to keep this herd going, and I don't. I push too hard and then I make more work for myself. I like work. I'm not old. But it's not being old that Jed has over us. The thing is, the old fart has driven cattle about as far as we've driven cars."

"Everything that's gone wrong hasn't been our fault," I said.

"Bullshit. Everything that goes wrong is our fault. My fault. I'd be a pig's ass if I'll let somebody else take credit for things that go wrong on my job."

"But Jed didn't keep those things from going wrong," I said.

"He's not in charge," Spangler said. "I didn't say he should be in charge because he knows more about what I'm doing than I do. I'm in charge. Besides, he keeps a lot of things from going wrong that I don't know about. That's what he's paid to do. I'd be a better man if I knew what trouble he was keeping me out of."

"What about me?" I said. Spangler grinned. Anytime I'd fish for a compliment, Spangler would run me down. I thought I might take that away from him by being direct.

"You're O.K. A little stupid around cattle. Weak in the arms. A bad drinker. Use too much medicinal sex. Can't handle a rope. Talk too much. A bad shot. And your ass never stays in the saddle."

"I see."

Late in the afternoon it was warm and sunny, and the herd was moving along well, so I took my heifer out of the pickup and let her walk the last hour before we camped.

# A Day's Rest Playing Kansas Thump-Thump

The day we took off, it rained. We had been lucky and unlucky. Some things, like the movie people and the motor home accident, made me think we were trapped with bad luck. But when it rained on the day Opal's plan called for a rest then I figured we were lucky. I was always encouraged when I thought bad luck and good luck balanced out in the end. But not Spangler.

"I'd rather the luck run all one way or all the other," he'd said about the matter once. "That way, you'd know where you are, and you can put up a fight or act cocky. None of this candy-assed things-even-out shit."

"Things do even out," I said.

"Maybe," he said. "But I don't have to like it. If you push things around a bit when the luck is running one way or the other, you look like you know what you're doing."

Anyway, it seemed to me lucky that it rained on our day off. We had stayed with some friends of the Tukles (Sally and George). The cattle were in a small pasture. We all turned in early—I slept in the truck. Jed, Opal, and Spangler stayed in the house. It was Jed who woke me the next morning.

"You are awake," he said, when he saw me stir after he had banged around in the back of the truck for a few minutes.

"Yes," I said. I sat up and looked over the side of the truck. It was a gray morning. About to rain.

"Don't you go to Junction City today?" I asked Jed as I yawned.

"No," he said, and went back of the horse trailer.

"Why not?" I asked. "I thought I saw on the plan you've got some relatives up there." He came back up to the truck.

"I do not have relatives in Junction City," he said. "My relatives in Junction City are dead."

"I see," I said. It started to rain. Not a drop here, a drop there, but a light spray that came with a little wind. "Does Opal know your relatives in Junction City are dead?" I asked, "or did they die since she made up the plan?"

"No."

Maybe Jed had decided I was his friend. At least he talked to me. I had the impression that an old friend of his might get some expanded answers. The best I'd get were one or two words and then a stare.

"What did you think of the dinner at Brookville?" I had said to him the day after that.

"Good."

"I thought you didn't drink," I said.

"Yes."

"Was it hard to keep the herd going without me?" I had said after I had rejoined them from Heather.

"No," Jed paused, "The woman in the car by the side of the road back two miles is not your wife." There wasn't a syllable that rose toward a question.

"Yes," I said. "No," I said. Jed stared.

It began to rain harder. Jed and I went inside, where everybody was up and getting breakfast.

"More than halfway there, pistol," Spangler said to me as I came into the kitchen. "How about a day in a bar? I've got some friends at the Army base and they know a bad bar in town."

"I'll go along," I said. "But I don't want to get drunk. I remember what it was like after Brookville."

"A limestone fencepost on your head and olives behind your eyes, and you've got a hangover," Spangler said. Opal pointed out that we'd all be better off if Spangler and I didn't go to the bars — and there was the matter of taking Jed to see his relatives.

"My relatives in Junction City are dead," Jed said.

"I see," said Opal. It looked like we were going to get to the bars on the wings of Jed's dead relatives.

It took a few phone calls, but in about an hour Spangler had made arrangements for us to meet his friends in the Twin Engine Tavern. Jed and Opal stayed in Alta Vista. Spangler and I got to the Tavern about noon.

"Good to see you," said Spangler to his friends, three rather dapper men in khaki pants and pressed shirts. He introduced me all around. There was a pitcher of tomato beer at the table and one of the men had a bottle of J.W. Dant on the floor underneath his seat. He said they'd laced the pitcher with the whiskey just before we got there.

"I want to drink to me," said Spangler as he poured himself a beer. "I'm about to kill a bear on this cattle deal." We all laughed and poured ourselves beers and drank them down.

I like taverns. I like sitting at big, round, wooden tables where maybe fifty men a day for a hundred years have sat. I never minded that in Kansas you couldn't get hard liquor over the bar — that all we had were beer taverns. I liked the brown bags of whiskey that we all kept in plain view under our chairs or between us on the booth benches. There was something rich in knowing the tavern owner well enough to get a pull from the house bottle now and then — it was like family in one way or another.

"Up Carrie Nation's ass," said Spangler as he poured a few more glugs of the J.W. Dant into the pitcher of beer. "Let's get it good and stiff for her sake."

I found myself missing the Palomino Bar and thinking that getting back home would be drinking Green Gables and red beer, and talking to Eddy while waiting for Ray Pratt to come. I could remember when we started the drive, I'd said to Spangler that when we got to Kansas City I'd show him my bar, Kelly's, on Westport Road. I'd thought then that to get to Kelly's would be to get home. Halfway down the road I didn't know.

I was thinking about all this when through the front door came Cue Ball and one of his sunglassed/moustached helpers. Before I thought about it, I said, "Spangler, there's Cue Ball." That was a mistake.

"Oh, him," said one of the men at our table. "He's with the movies. A friend of the General, who's a friend of Duke Wayne." Spangler stood up.

Cue Ball had walked along the bar, stopped for a moment to say something to the bartender, and then had gone on past us to a table near the back. Like a lot of men I know, just before Cue Ball sat down at the table, he looked the place over—just to see if there was anyone there he knew. He saw Spangler.

Cue Ball tried to be cool. The sunglassed/moustached man had sat down, and Cue Ball tapped him on the shoulder and tried to say something to him without being noticed. But it didn't work, and the sunglassed fellow stood up to hear what Cue Ball was saying. He saw Spangler, too.

The fight wasn't fair. It wasn't like the ones you see on T.V., where the whole bar jumps in, and guys who've had it in for the fellow drinking next to them take the chance of a general fight to beat the piss out of him. No. It wasn't like that. Only Spangler and Cue Ball. After Spangler had thrown the moustached fellow into a pin-ball machine and knocked him out.

Spangler walked across the bar, picking a path between the tables so he didn't disturb a soul. Cue Ball started to sit down, and then decided to keep standing. The other fellow sat down and Spangler came right up to him and pulled him out of his chair by his hair until he sprawled across the table. Then Spangler grabbed him by the belt and, still holding onto a fistful of hair, tossed him into the pin-ball machine. The tavern became silent with crash, and for a moment all you could hear was the sound of broken glass falling to the floor as the moustached man twitched. Then something broke in the machine, and all the steel balls fell out, one at a time. Whap. Whap. Whap. Whap. I don't know why, but I laughed. So did some other people. They laughed in a tentative way, but I laughed good and hard.

Cue Ball was looking at his friend sprawled out on his stomach on the pin-ball machine, his head rammed through the scoreboard, one leg off the side, the other off the end.

It seemed as if Spangler waited until I stopped laughing before he leaned over and said something to Cue Ball. Cue Ball shook his head no. The bartender had come around the bar. Spangler's friends got up from our table and walked over toward Spangler. Other people were standing up. There began general chatter, but nobody broke in. Spangler again leaned over and said something to Cue Ball and then pointed to the moustached man. Cue Ball nodded no. Spangler took him by the nose, pinching it between his index finger and his middle finger and led Cue Ball around the table into a clear space. Cue Ball tried to pull Spangler's hand down, but Spangler grabbed his ear and twisted it. When they got to a clear space, Spangler turned loose of Cue Ball and stood toe-to-toe with him, with his left hand behind his back. I laughed again. I knew what this was going to be. Kansas Thump-Thump. Cue Ball was in serious trouble. Some others figured it out and they began to laugh, too. Cue Ball looked around and started to turn away, but Spangler got him by the nose again and leaned into him to say something. Cue Ball put his left hand behind his back and looked up at Spangler. Cue Ball's belly was bigger and it pushed Spangler away a little, but Spangler was a foot taller—neither made any difference in Kansas Thump-Thump.

"You want to play Kansas Thump-Thump?" Spangler had said to me one day after work right in the beginning. I said sure. I had just gotten my horse, I had my own heifer, I was doing my job— why not play Kansas Thump-Thump.

"How do you play?" I said.

"We stand toe-to-toe and put our left hands behind our backs. You get the first swing. Hit me right in the chest as hard as you can. You win if you knock me off my feet. Unless we play Ellis County rules, and then you don't win until I bleed at the mouth."

I hit Spangler in his chest with my fist, bringing it forward like a boxer might. I hurt my hand. It sent a slight shudder through Spangler. He drew his right hand behind his head and brought it over the top and came down with a whomp on my chest, using the edge of his fist and his forearm. I toppled like a dead man.

"Let's not play Ellis County rules," I said from the ground. He grinned.

Not everybody in the bar knew about Kansas Thump-Thump. I had seen it played since my bout with Spangler, once in Hill City and twice in Hays. I wondered how Spangler would keep from killing Cue Ball on the first blow. I wondered why he hadn't kicked the yellow piss out of him right at the start. Those who knew about the game told others.

Cue Ball took the first shot. Spangler rocked a little. I think he was surprised that Cue Ball had any strength. Cue Ball's eyes got big when he saw how little damage he'd done. Spangler grabbed him by the nose when it looked like he might bolt. Then Spangler let go, and while Cue Ball was leaning slightly forward, Spangler brought his right arm around and caught Cue Ball at the top of the chest with a blow that drove him down more than backward. Cue Ball's knees buckled, and he clutched his throat. He was out. Spangler picked him up. He looked around until he saw me and jerked his head for me to come over. I made my way through the crowd.

"Work his arms for him," Spangler said in a even, almost soft voice.

"What?"

"Give me a good whap with one of his arms. I think he's a little unconscious." I took Cue Ball's right arm and, holding him up by the back of his shirt, used the arm to strike Spangler on the chest. The men around us laughed. Somebody passed Spangler a beer.

He tossed it in Cue Ball's face. I let him stand by himself. He wobbled a bit and then Spangler hit him again, this time lower on the chest, with a stroke that came by Spangler's ear as he cocked his head to the left side and brought his fist and forearm through low and even slightly on the rise just before it hit Cue Ball. The blow launched Cue Ball in a clumsy back dive. He lit on his head. I looked at him. He was bleeding from the mouth. It had only taken Spangler two blows to win by Ellis County rules.

Of course somebody had to call the cops. We could hear sirens in the distance. The men returned to their tables and some left. Spangler and I went out the back door. One of the men Spangler had met said he knew the bartender well, and he'd make sure he didn't talk. Spangler said to bill him for the pin-ball machine. I almost killed myself when I stepped on a steel ball on the way out. We had parked the truck a block away and we walked in a quick step through the rain to get there. The cops arrived as we drove away.

Opal said she was pleased we'd gotten back so early.

# The Tornado

## I

We were west of Eskridge. It was the afternoon of our twelfth day; the western sky was mounting thunderheads, white at the tops, black at the bottoms. We could see rain streaking down in patches. For a while, the sun would explode through, printing hot spots on the prairie we had already covered. Grave-diggers bolted down into Blackwolf and Brookville and Kipp and White City as the storm followed our trail. At sunset the light turned green against the clouds. It was still. We kept looking over our shoulders. Opal turned on the lights. Jed spotted a funnel dropping out of the clouds to the southwest.

It was high in the air and pulsed down, then up, then down. It seemed to float, as though in a news film, far away and not real. We kept on, circling back to the truck to get our slickers. The herd seemed dogged and resigned. I looked ahead. There was no place to hide, I thought. Then I thought: Is there a place to hide with two hundred and fifty steers and four horses, a truck, three men, Opal, a cat, and one bingy heifer? The funnel sucked itself back up into the clouds.

We could see the bottoms of the clouds bubble out and gather together in ripples. My impression was that the high, soft thunderheads had flattened. There was a ragged quality to the whole sky. Shreds of black clouds were breaking away from the thunderheads. The sun was setting, and selected bright beams would dart through.

"What do you think?" Spangler said to me, coming back to the rear of the herd.

"I think we got about an hour to go, and I hope the place in Eskridge has a basement."

Jed whistled and slapped his hat against his leg, then pointed the hat to the northwest, where a funnel had come out of the clouds about ten miles away and was surging toward the ground. It was growing thick toward the top like a weight lifter's thigh, but as it touched the ground, the bottom two-thirds was thin and lithe. We could not see the ground it touched.

"It's moving away from us," Spangler said. "We've got a problem if one comes out of the southwest like the first one."

"We tell the kids at school to move at right angles to them," I said.

"Section roads run north and south. Tornadoes run from southwest to northeast." Spangler diagrammed with his hands. "Our problem is going to be whether to go south against it or north in front of it, hoping it will cut behind us."

"Or stand still," I said. "Or cut this guy's fence and run the herd in and let them go until the morning. We can always pay the guy off. Have cattle got enough sense to get out of the way?"

"I don't think so. We better keep the whole shooting match together. Look at that son-of-a-bitch." The funnel was moving north of us now, its thick thigh moving the thin toe from behind it to the front, then back again—all in eerie slow motion, and silence and green light. Jed pointed to another one to our southwest. We felt a breeze cut across the road.

"Let's move up to the next section road and hold it there," Spangler shouted. Opal honked. I uncoiled the bull whip and began pressing the south side of the herd. Spangler pushed hard on the north, and Opal brought the truck up tight on their asses in the middle, the horn honking. The wind was picking up.

Jed had ridden up to the section road, about a hundred yards ahead and on top of a small hill. He was stretching the ropes across all three of the roads, the one ahead and the two at right angles. The idea was to bunch the herd there, in the intersection, and wait and see which way we should go. The problem was getting there. It wasn't raining, but the wind was kicking up the dust, and the steers sensed the danger and were turning in on themselves or looking with stricken panic through the fences into the open pastures. We kept the pressure on, not giving them time to make the move through the fence. But then they began to break forward on the run, and we could see the problem was going to be how to stop them. Jed was at the head of the road, past the intersection to the east. I was trying to get up through the ditch on the right to cover the road on that side. I could see Spangler on my left, cussing the steers and whipping them out of the way, as he plunged ahead trying to beat them to the top of the hill. Opal said later she eased off when they broke up that hill. From where she sat the dust exploded off the road, and all she could see was the three of us galloping after the herd.

I didn't get to the crossroad in time, but it wouldn't have made any difference. They ran right through those fake rope fences like they knew all the time they weren't real and had just played along with us. They ran past Spangler on the north, even though he beat them in their faces with the bull whip. They doubled back past Opal and went west. They ran past Jed to the east, as he beat his hat against his leg and drove his horse back and forth across the road as quickly as he could, trying to turn them. On my side they had all spilled through by the time I got there. In effect, I had driven them around the corner and down the road going south toward the black funnel we could now hear hissing about two miles away. Spangler called me back.

We were all in the intersection. The retarded heifer was thrashing with fright in the back of the truck, Rabies howling, Opal out of the cab and standing in the road looking with the rest of us at the funnel as it seemed stalled two pastures away. We could see our steers, their heads down, trotting in four directions away from us.

"Let's put these horses in the trailer. Right now," Spangler said. In a moment there were four of us in the truck. Opal was putting the things she had had on the seat beside her—her cigarettes, a comb, a map—on the dash. I sat on a lighter. Spangler was behind the wheel with Opal next to him. Jed was next to the window on the other side.

"We'll just sit here," Spangler said, "and see which way that nasty black bitch goes." It was coming right at us, but slowly. Churning toward us like a slow locomotive.

"We don't want to let that thing get too close," I said. "There's all kinds of pressure around those things."

"It's not like a bull, Spangler," Opal said. "Don't wait here until the last minute before you get our ass out of the way." Jed pushed down that broken window to get a better look.

"She is coming up the hill," he said evenly. "She is tossing wood in front of her."

"They're mercurial bitches," said Spangler. He put the truck in gear and eased through the intersection, east. "I don't want to get in front of her and have her chase us halfway across the country," he said.

"Step on it," I said, looking out the back window. We jumped ahead. Tree branches and sheet metal sailed onto the road in front of us.

"Spangler, you dumb son of a bitch!" yelled Opal, "you're going to get us all killed this time." She pushed her foot on top of his. The truck lurched forward, snapping our necks; then Spangler accelerated and elbowed Opal away. I looked out the back window.

"It's coming down the road!" I yelled. "On the right side—it's coming down the road!" Spangler looked in the mirror.

"Shiiiiiiit," he said. Jed opened his door and looked back.

"You turn right at the next road," Jed said.

"Yeah, yeah, but this fucking thing is hard to drive in the wind," Spangler said. He checked his four-wheel drive lever, out of nervousness—he had checked it several times before—and shifted into third gear. The horse trailer was whipping us.

"You turn at the road at the bottom of the hill," Jed said.

"I see it," Spangler said.

"Slow down, you son-of-a-bitch, or we'll never make the turn," Opal said.

"Keep going," I said, looking out the window.

"You swing the truck wide," said Jed.

"I'm not even there yet!" Spangler yelled. We could hardly hear him. He rolled down his window, and we could hear the hissing turning to a roar. I looked out the back window and could see wood and nameless junk tossed ahead by the upper part of the funnel. And clear as could be, I could see fenceposts and a water tank being sucked in at the base. Trees along a ridge were bending in toward the pasture. In the failing light that funnel was visible darkness. We made the turn, the trailer whipping behind us but staying upright. The funnel cut back of us. I looked in the bed for the heifer, but couldn't see her. Rabies' box was working loose. We drove a mile south and stopped and got out.

"Now we've got a fucking mess," Spangler said. "Cattle all over this country and it's dark." We stood there watching the funnel plow over a hill and then float in the air for a while, before blending in with the dark clouds in a dark sky.

The sun was down, and a string of trailing clouds was beginning to cover the horizon. It got dark quickly and then began to rain. In the quiet I could hear steers bawling in the distance. I walked back up the road to look for my heifer and found her where we made the corner, her tongue out, her head twisting in the dust. For some reason, when we didn't kill her that spring, we couldn't ever kill her. I dragged her back to the truck.

"Jed thinks we ought to round them up tonight. But I don't know," Spangler said. "We'll just have to comb the countryside all over again tomorrow."

"How far can they go during the night?" I asked.

"Five-ten miles, I guess." Opal was sitting in the truck; the three of us were sitting on the front bumper.

"Get that bottle out, Opal." She brought it to us. "You want a shot?" Spangler said to her before he drank. She did.

"Let's go into Eskridge and see Ted Wiggins and tell him what happened. Maybe we can call around to the farmers here and they can give us a hand in the morning."

That's what we did, but not until the four of us killed a fifth of Green Gables, sitting there in the dark and the occasional rain, not talking much, only to say that *there*, we could hear some over *there*, and that perhaps they'd bunch up once the night cleared. On the way into town the radio reported tornadoes west of Eskridge. There was an unconfirmed funnel on the ground. This was an alert; the radio beeped a while, then played a golden oldie, Pat Boone's "April Love."

After we checked into the motel, we went over to Ted Wiggins' house, and he called around for us and told the farmers in that area what the deal was. Some of them already knew; they had gone out to check on things after the twister went through and had seen bunches of steers in the road. One guy, just south of where we were drinking, had already rounded up about twenty of them as they wandered into his front yard. Things didn't look too bad as we got to bed that night. The next day we spent rounding up the herd. It took us all day, and we were short eleven by sundown.

# I Find Out Some Things about Myself

S ome days hardly anything would go wrong. The steers were getting trailbroke. They'd be a little hard to manage around cars, but they were even getting used to that. Our biggest problem seemed to be keeping ourselves going. We were getting beat. By the time we'd put up the steers, unsaddled the horses and put them up, checked out the feed situation, and eaten dinner, it would be nine or ten o'clock. Then nearly every place we'd stop, we'd have to have a drink with the local cattlemen. Or at least with the guy who was putting us up. Sometimes it'd be midnight before we got to sleep. Jed would usually get away before then.

We had problems with the heifer, too. Sometimes she couldn't make it until noon. She'd just stop. Right in the middle of the road. Kind of stretch out and try to hide her head between her front legs. I'd come up on her and I'd see one goofy eye staring at me. I'd have to hogtie her and drag her back to the bed of the truck, where she'd ride with Rabies.

Opal made Spangler clean the cat's box. Spangler didn't want to do it. He said the box was just punishment for the cat's biting him. He did it by hosing the whole thing out (with the cat inside). Some pretty nasty stuff came running out the air holes of that box.

Some days nothing would go right. We'd lose steers on every crossroad, and sometimes we couldn't get them back. We'd have to call somebody we knew, or the sheriff, and tell them if they found a steer, hang on to it. We'd be back. But for the most part, it got better the more we drove. Jed was getting worn out. You could tell by the way he didn't want to get in and out of the saddle. His legs were cramping on him. He never said anything, though.

We were getting some publicity. A local paper here and there would send somebody out in a station wagon to take some pictures. At Clinton there was this pleasant girl reporter from the *Kansas City Star*. It turned out we went to the University together. I knew which one she was, although I had never met her. It was kind of fun being news.

We were coming up from south of Lawrence to run parallel with Highway 10, but since the motor home accident Spangler would not drive on the highways when he could help it. We had left Clinton that morning and were trying for Eudora that night. It's silly, but I forgot that the University was over a couple of hills and ten pastures; I guess I knew it, of course, but I didn't think of it until I saw Harold pedaling up on a bike.

"Hi, there, hi," he waved an oversized engineer's cap at me.

"Hello, Harold," I said.

"Hi, Dad; hi, Jed; hi, Mom; hi, steers; hi, horses," he continued.

"We've got a short day; let's stop up here for a while and break for lunch," Spangler said. "There's some wide shoulders ahead. Eat lunch with us, Harold."

"Why not? I've come a long way, baby."

"Where did you get that bike?" Opal asked, once we had the steers up on the shoulder, and she was passing out sandwiches around the hood of the truck. Jed didn't like to be liked by Harold, so he ate up by the fence.

"Peugeot's just another name for freedom."

"Where did you get the money to buy the bike, Harold?" she asked firmly.

"Pushing grass," he said, giving her what he took to be the steady stare of honesty.

"Don't you have classes today?" Spangler said.

"It's Saturday," he said.

"Is it?"

"Yes. Have you lost all track of time? Night and day blending together? Have you become one with your herd?"

"Did you know we were down here?" It suddenly occurred to me to ask.

"I felt your vibrations deep in my castle: Ellsworth Hall, room 637."

"I called him yesterday," Opal said, talking to me but looking at Harold. "I thought he might give us a hand."

"That's all right, we've got plenty of help," Spangler said in a cheery way that reminded me of bright plastic. "Besides, Harold has his studies. It's all right."

"Rejection," Harold said and hung his head. It was quiet for a moment, until I took a loud bite of my apple. Harold peered at me through the hair in his face. I noticed a line of pimples cutting across both cheeks just where his hair did.

"Don't step on my lines," he hissed at me through the hair. I shrugged.

"Don't be nasty," Spangler said as he fixed himself another sandwich.

"How's Jed? Pure. Truth. Windweathered. Yang-full Jed."

"His legs cramp by the end of the day," Spangler said.

"Do you want to help?" Opal asked. "You can help Jed up in front."

"I don't believe in what you are doing," he said with his honest stare fixed at his mother. "I don't believe in killing these animals, and I don't believe in sick capitalistic motives."

Spangler went around to the back of the truck to check on the taillights, the tires, the trailer hitch, whatever needed checking on.

"What did you come for?" Opal said politely.

"I was going to try my new bike. It seemed like the thing to do. See the U.S.A. on your Peugeotlais." Jed had finished lunch and came back to the truck to get a drink of water.

"Jed full-life/life-full Jed," said Harold. Jed took off his hat and put it on again. He walked up the road to where he had tied up his horse and stood there, re-cinching the saddle.

"He's Claudius and I'm Hamlet, Mother," Harold said to Opal, pointing at me.

"What the hell does that mean?" she said.

"It means that Dad, super-Spangler, cowboy out of the past, is a ghost. Not the real thing." Opal began packing.

"We've got to get going. I wish you'd at least ride along for a while," she said. "Take some interest."

"You think my Ophelia's named Ralph, don't you?" he said to me, winking.

"Who cares?" I said.

"You do, Claudius."

"Get off my ass, you little shit," I said.

"My, my. Language makes the man," he said.

I could feel Jed looking at me from up the road and Spangler looking over the bed of the truck. Opal stood still.

"I'll wrap that fucking bike around your neck," I said.

"Give me a kiss first. Then we can go around once, with gusto." I jumped him and pushed him into the ditch. I picked him up and tossed him down again and picked him up again, this time by the shirt, with my left hand, and hit him in the face with my right, knocking him back into the ditch. I walked back up to the road and tossed his bike at him in the ditch. Nobody said anything.

"Let's go," I said, coming back to the truck. Opal was crying. Spangler was coming around the road side of the truck and taking long strides to get to his horse, tied on the other side of the road.

"I'm sorry," I said. Nobody said anything. I went up the road and picked up the signs and wound the rope around them and put them in the truck. On the way back I looked right at Harold, who was playing dead in the ditch with the bicycle on top of him. A mouse of a bruise was coming up on his left cheek. His shirt was ripped. Jed and Spangler were in the saddles. I got up and we started down the road. Nobody talked but in bits and pieces. It was like the first day out of White City. It didn't change everything between us, but it changed some things.

# II

That night I thought I better talk to Spangler about what had happened. I didn't know what I was going to say, and I don't know now. It turned out I didn't get a chance. Heather found me just after we got the cattle put up.

I had worked without pleasure that afternoon. I thought it would be good to be back in my part of Kansas. Maybe some of my friends would come down and see the drive. We thought the papers might be running a story on us here and there. A few sightseers gathered as we took the cattle across Highway 59, south of Lawrence, but that's about all. Nobody I knew. It didn't make any difference. All four of us had scattered to different parts of the herd. It turned out to be easy to be by yourself when you're driving two hundred and fifty cattle.

Beating up Harold was an ugly win, and I didn't like it. Right after it happened, I was confused about my feelings, but as the afternoon went on, I became less confused and more unhappy with myself. I didn't want my place with the Tukles set up because I had beat the shit out of their son. I thought I might be feeling sorry for myself. I should have seen it all through Spangler's eyes. But I couldn't do that then.

We brought the herd into the large field beside the Post Office. It was government land and so it was against the law to use it—unless you took Spangler's thinking on the matter, in which case all government land could be used by everybody. Opal had made a deal with somebody, and it worked out.

Spangler and Opal decided they were going into Lawrence that night. He told me to stay with the herd. The field was well fenced, but he wanted someone out there. Jed would be back with the truck. They'd get a ride out in the morning. I don't think they went in to see Harold. I think they just wanted to be by themselves. Jed and I might have been just like family, but that some-- times means it's important to get away from people like us. I think I'm right about that. I thought I might drive in and see them after dinner.

When Jed left to drive Opal and Spangler into town, I stayed around the herd for a while. I coaxed my heifer over to the fence and fed her some cattle cubes. She rested her chin on the bottom rail and ate from my hand. I thought she had gotten bigger since we started the drive, but she had grown in that way retarded kids do, a kind of fleshy, awkward growth. She made me sad. I had gotten used to taking care of her. She seemed to look for me to come by on Chief when she drifted out of the back end of the herd toward the end of a morning's drive. I thought she'd watch me over the edge of the pickup as I rode back up front.

"That heifer is getting along better than I thought she would," Opal said to me once as I came by the truck after loading Tic-Tac-Toe.

"I watch out for her," I said.

"I see you do," she said. "Don't get attached to a cripple, Leo. Nothing hurts more all the way along."

I thought about that as I fed my heifer the cattle cubes. I couldn't name the pleasure I got from taking care of her. I was glad to be alone so I could think of things like that. It was a way of not thinking about the day. After a while, I walked a couple of blocks into town and down the main street, looking for a place to eat. A block into town Heather drove up in the MG.

"Hi," she said brightly. The top was down, her arms were tan, and her face was sunny and warm. She was still a Renoir painting, still one of the best-looking women I'd seen. I realized that she had the ability to descend on me during my weak times—or if not that, make weak times for me. If I didn't know I was vulnerable,

I'd know if she showed up. The time I left her in Blackwolf was the only time I'd gotten away.

"I thought I'd never see you again," I said.

"After last time?"

"Yes." She turned off the engine. "Do you want to talk about it?"

"I don't think so," I said. "We've been going at this for more than a year now. Nothing is going to get any better."

"I know," she said. "That's what I want to tell you."

"Then there is nothing more to say," I said, and looked down the street.

"We could talk about it all. Remember a bit. It might be fun."

"One thing always led to another with you," I said. She smiled. "I have other things on my mind." She opened the car door on the passenger's side.

"Hop in," she said. "I won't hurt you. We can drive to Lawrence. See where we were good together. Visit some of our old bars."

I'm no good at winning and I'm worse at endings. I try to let things trail off, work themselves out, go their own way. I'm not like Spangler. I can't get the bull whip to pop like he does. "Snap it off," he once yelled at me when I was practicing and getting nothing but dull thuds. "Snap that son-of-a-bitch off clean."

"Leave me alone," I said to Heather and shut the door. "I don't want to see you." She looked at me and cried. She leaned her head on the steering wheel—her hair tumbled down through its spokes—and cried as she'd breathe in. I looked up and down the street. Then back at her. She was shaking, and it rocked the little car slightly. I walked away—into town, past stores, past a cafe, and to the end of the block. When I crossed to the next block I looked back. Heather had started the MG and was following me. I could see her eyes shining through the windshield. Her hair was blowing and she held the steering wheel with both hands. At the end of the block I went into a tavern and sat down. I ordered a red beer and the dinner special (meatloaf). I looked out the window and saw that Heather had parked in front of the tavern. She was staring straight ahead. I went outside.

"Go away," I said. She didn't look at me. I went back into the tavern and drank my beer and ate dinner. I bought a sixpack and walked outside into the street. It was about seven or eight by then. The shadows that were long when I had gone into the tavern had stretched into evening. Heather was still there, now more poised, her back straight—but still looking straight ahead. I started to walk.

I walked north across the railroad tracks and toward the river. She started the MG and followed me, keeping back about fifty yards. I thought if I walked south to the herd, she'd follow me there too, and stay the night and make a scene. I didn't want go through it all in front of the Tukles. Not after what they had gone through with Harold still so fresh with us all. For my own sake, too.

In less than a mile I came to the river. The moon was up, and I walked down a dirt road that I knew would take me along the bank. The road ran from Eudora to De Soto, and I knew about it because I used to take my old Studebaker out on it and park with girls. Heather was still behind me. I was getting tired of walking. Two weeks on horseback had spoiled me.

The moon had gotten high enough to be reflected in the river. There was the steady hum of river noises—frogs in the reeds, a locust clinging to a cottonwood, night birds. Behind me, the steady noise of the MG was out of place. I saw a skiff tied to an old duck blind on a point of land. I walked off the road and down to the river and along the river to the point. Heather stopped the car on the edge of the road and turned off the engine. She could see me from there, but because the moonlight on the water was not reaching as far as the road, I could not see her—only a lighter place against a string of dark trees that lined the road behind her.

There were no oars in the skiff. I looked in the duck blind and found a canoe paddle, old and warped. There was also an anchor. When I came out of the blind and got into the boat, Heather honked the horn. When I paddled into the river, she flashed the lights. The Kansas River is calm and easy through here. It is broad and sandy and shallow. You can find eddies along the side where you won't move much at all. If you toss an anchor out, you can stay there for days. I rowed across to the other side and found a still place and tossed out the anchor. She must have heard the splash. She said something, but I could not understand her. I felt the bottom of the skiff and it was dry, so I stretched out in the bottom and hung my hands over the side and propped my feet up at the end and looked at the sky. I could never tell the constellations, I realized, and so I had no stories to go with late summer stars. But they seemed to me to be helpful in their silence. I knew if I thought about them long enough, I would scare myself with the notion of death. I closed my eyes and listened to the river at night. I must have fallen asleep. I didn't hear the car start or Heather leave. I slept and woke in short stretches, but I didn't go ashore until the morning light let me see Heather was not there.

It took me an hour to walk back to where the herd was pastured. By the time I got there, they had left. They had tied Chief to a fencepost, and he whinnied when he saw me, and tugged at his rope. He was saddled and ready to go. It took me another hour to catch up with them, but then I didn't run all the way. For some reason, we had all decided not to ask anybody any questions about what had happened the day before. I worked right in. It took the day to get things even again.

# We Tangle with the Law

**T**he drive from Eudora to where Highways 10 and 7 meet was uneventful, except that at lunch Spangler noticed the cat was getting mucus in his eyes.

"Is that the first sign of rabies?" he asked as we rode. "How do my eyes look?"

"Maybe it's just a cold."

We stayed on the dirt roads a mile south of Highway 10—our usual strategy. We were getting more onlookers now. They were about as thick as when we first left Hays, only now they came in station wagons and four-door Fords and Chevys with drooling children leaning out the back windows. Small boys with silver six-shooters would leap from behind fenceposts and do us in with twenty or thirty methodical shots. Fathers loomed nearby, snapping pictures. Nobody had a bottle to pass around, and we didn't stop and talk to any of them. It was as if we were in a movie and we had to act out our parts, and that meant ignoring the fans along the side.

It was a short drive. We got to the intersection about four in the afternoon. Ahead you could see that the sky had a gritty look about it no matter how clear of clouds it was. I knew that's what the city sky always looked like on clear days, like a window cleaned with a dirty rag. I had lived with such a sky for most of my life, but since I had been away, I couldn't readjust to it. That night we shared a pasture with a growing mobile home business. They fenced off about twenty acres back of the scattered truck campers and horse trailers (the homes were strung out along the highway where passing motorists could get a look at them). Spangler's brother had arranged the deal with the manager and owner, a Mr. Hopewell.

"This horse trailer isn't as good as the last one we bought from you," Opal said by way of greeting, when meeting Hopewell. "It doesn't track well, the bearings weren't packed, and the latches are plastic."

"Nylon," Hopewell said politely, but with some confidence. "Nylon, ma'am."

"They don't work," Opal said and lit up a cigarette.

Hopewell was pleasant enough. He thought that having us camp there might bring in some business. He had put out signs: RESTING PLACE OF THE TUKLE CATTLE DRIVE/STOP IN AND SEE A MOBILE HOME.

That night Opal drove into Bonner Springs and bought some food, and we cooked dinner in the Tukles' trailer. After that, Spangler broke out the Coors and the Green Gables and poured half-and-half drinks into the plastic tumblers we found in the cupboards. Jed said no. But Opal nursed one drink through till I left, and Spangler drank three. I put away two and it only made me a little tight.

We spent about two hours after dinner sitting there in the narrow naugahyde-and-foam-rubber-and-plastic (and nylon) trailer. It seemed to me to be the oddest place we stayed. Only the smell of our feet as we took our boots off to relax seemed to let me know we were the same four who had spent nearly two weeks behind a herd of steers. But even that odor was gone when Opal found an exhaust fan, which seemed to suck the trailer clean in a moment.

We talked. Spangler wanted to know how Jed felt. Jed had fallen asleep. Opal suggested that they better call Harold when they get to Kansas City. It was her way of trying to get that issue back on the table—or at least talk about what happened and get Spangler to unload his mind. He only said, "Don't spill your guts, Opal," and glared at her when she told me that Harold had not always been a disappointment to Spangler. But we smoothed over the matter, and by the time we were relaxed enough to go to sleep, we had talked about parts of the trip—the parts that amused us now that they were back down the road: The way the tornado seemed to chase us around, how Spangler bluffed out Officer Stiltson, the look of terror on the fat boy's face in Brookville when Spangler grabbed him, how Jed wouldn't stay in the Garden of Eden, and the gentle good will right at the beginning, when all those ranchers came out to see us work during the first days and gave us a pull from their bottles. I remember that coyote going up that hill and looking back at us, as if somewhere in his racial memory he'd seen us before. But he couldn't have.

Nobody talked of the incident at the lake. Or the story we heard at White City. Or Cue Ball. Even then, our stories about what we had done began to grow away from fact, but we never corrected each other. Jed slept the entire time. I woke him to take him to our trailer.

That night I couldn't get used to the whine of cars and trucks on the highway outside my window. I hadn't thought about it before, but what's not there in the west is that permanent drone of machinery that you get in the cities—the muzak of the industrial world. I didn't sleep well. Jed got me up by hitting me across my chest with his hat. Breakfast was ready at Spangler's trailer. Jed had eaten. Get up.

**II**

"Not too far today," said Spangler over his cup of coffee. I think we should make it to the Hall of Fame."

"You've been thinking that for two hundred miles now," Opal said. "Did you ever call them?"

"No."

"You said you would."

"Well, I didn't," he said. "We better load that heifer of yours in the horse trailer for the next two days," he said to me by way of trying to change the subject.

"O.K."

"Why didn't you call?" persisted Opal. "That wouldn't have been too much trouble."

"How's the cat this morning?" Spangler asked me.

"He's got a nasty whine," I said. "And I think I still see mucus around the eyes. It's not easy to get a look at him through those holes. The smell's so bad you don't exactly want to get right down and stare."

"How many days?" Spangler said.

"If he's alive when we reach the stockyards, you're in good shape."

"You're not going to be in good shape if we don't have a place to put these cattle tonight," Opal said.

"Opal, my sweet, leave it to me. Leave it to Spangler, sweet bitch." Her eyes dilated. "There is no way that we can't put these cattle up at the National Headquarters for the Agricultural Hall of Fame. Right there in Bonner Springs. They'll be glad to have us. We'll be an attraction. Leave it to me."

"Leave it to you!" she said to Spangler. "The things I've left to you over the years. How about the wedding rings? And getting the paint for the house? And picking your mother up at the bus station that time in Kansas City?"

"Back off, bitch. I told you for twenty years I was sorry about the rings. And you know I never heard you say anything about picking up Mother. Now what's this shit about paint for the house?"

"You were supposed to get the paint for the inside of the house, and you didn't and I had to wait all day with nothing to do. Finally, I got Ted to bring it out."

"When did all this happen?"

"The second year we were there."

"You mean the farmhouse?"

"Yes." She lit up a Salem.

"You mean in 1948?"

"Yes."

"Don't you think you've been keeping that one back a little?"

"I don't bitch about everything that goes wrong."

"Shiiiiiiit."

I left to go find Jed. We didn't have far to go, but it was all on the highway and it would be a problem. We'd better get ready. Besides, it looked like Spangler and Opal were heading for a good one, and I didn't want to be around holding it down to a smoldering fire. In the hundred and twenty or so days I had been working for them, I had learned it was best to let them explode into hot flames. I found Jed tying all his short ropes and long ropes and pieces of cloth to his saddle.

"Morning," I said. He beat his hat against his leg. "Cops going to help us today? Going across the bridge?"

"Yes."

"Did you talk to them yesterday?"

"No."

"How are you feeling?"

"Good." He spat.

"Two more days," I said, and began to get my gear together.

"Are you going back to Hays?" Jed asked. I had ceased to be surprised that Jed would talk to me. But I was a little surprised that he'd ask me a question.

"Guess so." I hadn't thought about it. Or rather I hadn't thought about not going back. Maybe I had. "Spangler wants me to go to Montana with him to buy a new herd. That might be fun. Then, too, I've got a job teaching when I get back." It would have been too obvious that I was just making conversation if I had asked Jed about his plans. Of course he was going back. He had no other place to go. That was one way to look at it.

"Maybe I better get Spangler and Opal out of the trailer. I think they're having a fight."

"Yes."

I told Spangler that we were ready and that we better get going. Those cops weren't going to wait all day at the bridge. He agreed. He was glad to get out of there. I think Opal had him confessing to his sins of the early fifties. Whatever they were.

"How about the cops?" I asked. "What's the deal on the cops?"

"That's Opal's deal. She's the one that talked to them. I guess they're going to meet us at the bridge and stop traffic and let us go over. She worked the whole thing out. I don't think we're supposed to be there any special time. I don't figure they can miss us."

Jed had opened the gate. "Just leave it open after we get out, Jed," Spangler said.

We rode to the back of the herd and eased them out of the pasture, but held them in the wide ditch on the right of the road. Opal was behind us, the truck flashers going. Spangler and I rode on the left side, Spangler near the front, and used the fence to flank them on the right. Jed rode behind. They came out easily. I thought they looked pretty good. Their weight was down, but they were moving together and quickly. Today would be a short drive, and we would have enough time left at the end of the day to drive the route to Kansas City and talk to the stockyard boys.

It was eight miles to the bridge over the Kansas River and into Bonner Springs. We covered it before noon. On the way we saw some cops come by us and slow down and talk into their radio mikes. Overhead a news helicopter circled. When we came over the last hill just before the bridge, Opal drove ahead in the truck. I hoped we wouldn't have to stop and have a conference. It would be tough getting them going again. I could see Opal talking with a circle of Highway Patrolmen. Along the right side of the road there was a long line of blue cop cars. They'd have to move those, I thought.

"I hope all this official help does this right," Spangler yelled back to me.

"I don't think we ought to stop. Do you?"

"I guess not. These steers have been pretty good to put up with some of the shit we've stacked on them. I don't know how they are going to take this bridge. I don't think they're going to take it, if we give them time to look at it long."

Opal was getting the cops to move the cars out of our way. Two of them went across the bridge. Two others pulled onto the bridge and started their roof flashers going. Two more swung around in the road and circled in behind us, way back.

I think she's got those sons-of-bitches working," Spangler yelled. "She'll chew their asses if they don't get it right."

"She didn't spend it all on you this morning?" I said. Spangler grinned.

"No. I don't think so," he said.

We were coming to the bridge. There were cop cars on the left, two behind us; the truck was blocking off the right where the fence was falling away from the bridge. Ahead were two other cop cars, their lights blinking, the driver checking us in his mirror, the partner leaning back out his window. The helicopter returned. Opal waved at it. The river looked bigger than I remembered it. The bridge looked more temporary, more a man-made thing than it does from a car, where it seems as natural as the car itself. From horseback, behind a herd of steers, the whole thing looked oddly like a toy, and shaky, like something too big for itself. It made strange noises when we took the herd onto it. The cop cars in front started up. Opal pulled in behind us and in front of the trailing cops. We filled up the bridge from side to side.

The cattle on the edges were spooked. They'd trot along the edge, and then look out over the river and then bust back into the middle of the herd and never come to the edge again, if they could help it. Nobody wanted the rail. We could hear our hoofs on the bridge and it seemed to echo even though the bridge was open. Chief was edging sideways on me; Spangler's horse was giving him fits. The helicopter was hanging back and holding off high. Just as we got to the middle of the bridge and things settled down a little and we could see the other end, the helicopter dropped down level with us, off to one side and out in front. That did it.

Our horses turned. Mine went up on his hindlegs and spun around. He had taken a lot of new things these last two weeks, but a ten-ton horsefly waiting out there was too much. He started running back off the bridge. I was loose in the saddle, and all I'd learned about riding during those months deserted me, and I grabbed the saddle horn with my left hand just before my horse came to an abrupt stop. A cop car had turned on a siren. I vaulted over frontwards. My arm didn't hold the weight and it broke. Clean off.

All the childhood fears I had accumulated about breaking a bone, something I'd never done, vanished. I was going to be all right. I said to myself as I got up, my wrist limp as I held my arm with the other hand. Chief bolted past the cop car and off the bridge, tossing his head wildly, his reins down on his neck, the ropes and stirrups flapping absurdly.

Most of the herd had turned back. Spangler was nowhere in sight. Jed was coming along the rail, trying to turn them with his hat. Further back, Opal turned the truck sideways on the bridge, but half the herd had gotten by her. The other half now broke forward across the bridge as the helicopter put on a surge of power and rose out of the air beside us. Opal jumped out of the truck with the Model-12 shotgun in her left hand. She took one shot at the copter as it crossed high over the bridge, pumped once, and took another shot as the copter turned east toward Kansas City. She pumped for a third shot when one of the cops grabbed her in a bearhug from behind. She back-kicked him in the shin. I looked down the bridge and saw Spangler coming at full speed. Two other cops were pinning Opal to the truck. The one with the split shin had the Model 12 in one hand and was pulling up his trouser leg with the other. The copter was a dot in the sky. I looked down the bridge. Someone standing by a silver Audi had my horse. I walked to the truck.

"She took a couple of shots at that helicopter," the cop with his pant leg around his knee said to Spangler.

"Did you get the son-of-a-bitch?" Spangler said to her. Opal was loose now and standing against the truck.

"Too far away." Spangler looked at the gun the cop was holding.

"Should have used the rifle. That might have dumped the pig-fucker in the river," he said. "What's the matter with you?" He looked at me.

"I lost my horse."

"Shiiiiiiit."

"Somebody's got him," a cop said, pointing down the bridge.

"You can't shoot at helicopters, mister," the cop said.

"You sure the fuck can't bring them down with a shotgun," Spangler said. "I wouldn't worry about it. What's the matter with you?" He looked at me again.

"I broke my arm."

"Shiiiiiiit."

"We can take him up to the hospital in one of the cars," a cop said.

"No you don't," Spangler said. "Tie that fucking arm up against your chest," he said to me. "We've got to get these cattle over this bridge while we still got some to get over."

"The lady is going to have to come with us," the cop holding his leg said.

"What the hell for?" Spangler yelled. "Taking a wild shot at some fairy in a helicopter? Did you see what that shit-for-brains did? I've got cattle all over this bridge. I've got a man with a busted arm. Are they going to show all this (his arm swept both ways on the bridge) on the evening news? Hell no. Can I sue them for weight loss, personal injury, defamation of character, embarrassment of my professional life? And you want to take my truck driver to jail?"

"I thought she was your wife," said the cop.

"She is, she is. But she's driving this truck across the bridge. Right now."

"O.K. But when we get to the other side, she comes with me."

"Shiiiiiiit."

Another cop brought me my horse. Opal tied my arm against my chest. Spangler told her to get the truck going and rode back to join Jed, who, with the help of curious spectators who had gotten out of their cars along the backup, was driving the steers back toward the bridge.

I asked a cop to help me into the saddle, and then I rode across the bridge to see what the deal was with the steers that had gone that way. They had been blocked from going off the bridge and were now ambling back up toward me. I let them come, thinking they might attract the rest of the herd from the other end.

I could see Spangler and Jed and half an army of kids and men and women edging the steers toward the bridge. I could see the steers tossing their heads back and turning the whole front part of their bodies. I couldn't see their eyes rolling, or the drool in long slimy lines coming out the sides of their months, but I'm sure it was there. When they decided to come onto the bridge, they charged. I was in trouble for the second time in half an hour.

The cattle down at my end looked up and saw the others coming. Mine turned and ran. I tried to beat them, but I only drove them faster. I looked ahead and saw that the barricade at the end of the bridge wasn't much: cop cars shoring up the sides and some saw-horses in the middle with folks standing behind them, taking pictures of me and two hundred and fifty steers about to run them over. Photographic dedication turned to panic.

"Pull those cars over." I began yelling. But everybody was running, even the cops. A guy in a truck drove it up to the barricade, but it didn't do much good.

I couldn't turn the herd. I had galloped through most of them that had been in front of me, but I wasn't good enough to turn them. The rest of the steers had caught up with us, and I led them all right through the barricades, my horse cutting to the left of the truck at the last second when the lead steers took out the saw-horses.

All up and down the road people were screaming and running for their cars. Doors were slamming, windows were rolled up. Cars began to honk in hopes of keeping the steers away. One woman turned her windshield wipers on.

The herd spilled off the bridge and out into the town. I finally got Chief stopped and turned back to see Spangler and Opal and Jed coming slowly over the bridge. Behind them were cop cars, their red lights pulsing. It looked like a Western Day parade.

We had a short conference at the busted barricade: I should go to the hospital and have my arm set. Opal said she wanted to go to the courthouse and clear up this matter about the helicopter. Jed and Spangler would check with the Hall of Fame and see if they could get some help rounding up the steers. After we loaded our horses, the cops led us our separate ways. Steers in bunches were everywhere.

### III

They had to put me out to set the arm. I didn't wake up until after dark. Nobody was there. I found a button pinned to the sheet and pushed it. A nurse came.

'You're awake," she said.

'What time is it?"

"Nine. How do you feel?"

"O.K. How about helping me get out of here?"

"Not until morning."

"Does that mean a little after midnight?" I asked.

"After the doctor makes his rounds in the morning."

"Those doctors don't get around until the middle of the day. I've got to be at work by sunup."

She left. I couldn't stay awake and fell back to sleep. I woke in the middle of the night with the throbbing in my arm. It would be that way for days, but I got used to not thinking about it. I pushed the button again. A flashlight came into the dark room.

"Yes?"

"How about a couple of aspirin?" I said.

"Are you allergic to them?" the voice behind the flashlight asked.

"No. But I take them to get a buzz on." The flashlight left. I was going to ring again, but another flashlight came in. Bigger.

"What's the problem here?" she said.

"I want a couple of aspirin."

"What for?"

"I broke my arm." I held it up so she could see. "It hurts."

"Aspirin is not on your chart. We can give you something to make you sleep."

"Forget it."

She turned out the light. I didn't sleep the rest of the night. About five I got up and took a shower and dressed. I was waiting on the edge of the bed when, an hour later, Spangler came in.

"How you doing?" He turned on the light.

"It hurts." I held my arm up.

"Did you take some aspirin for it?" he said.

"I guess not," I said. "Did you get the herd rounded up?"

"Yes. Yesterday. Took hours. Opal's in jail. I'm out on bail. We had a fight with the Hall of Famers. You know that five acres of original prairie they got? It seems the board read our letter and said that if my steers shit all over the original prairie, then it wouldn't be original anymore. 'Now if you'd been a buffalo herd, Mr. Tukle, we could accommodate you.' That's what some shithead told me. One thing led to another. You know how it goes. I hit him with a bronzed statue of a turkey. Aggravated assault. Five hundred dollars bail."

"Where is the herd?" I asked.

"We fenced in a cloverleaf. Right where we turn east. Worked out well. Lots of grass. They never settled down, though. One housewife lost her station wagon through the fence, she got to looking so hard."

"What's Opal in jail for?"

"Seven charges. I think the one that did her in was the Obscene Gesture one. She did that in front of the judge. I think we can get her out this morning. What about you?"

"I'm supposed to wait here until the doctor comes."

"Can't do that. We got to get going."

"How did you get in here?"

"Walked. Front door."

"Let's walk out," I said. We did.

The girl at the front desk asked if she could help us and I said no, that we wanted to see a friend with a broken arm, but that he wasn't awake yet. She suggested we come back during normal visiting hours. Ten to noon. Two to four. Seven to nine. We said we'd do that.

"It's raining," I said.

"Yeah. One of those hurricanes broke up over Texas, and this is what we got left. I guess we better go by the jail. Jed's there too."

"Jed?"

"He's just sleeping there. Five dollars and meal. I slept in the truck. Down in the cloverleaf."

It was nine o'clock before we got going. The judge dropped all charges. He said he had seen the evening news and appreciated what happened. There were unusual circumstances, he concluded. And since there had been no property damage (Opal had missed), he'd drop the matter. She ought to watch her temper, though.

The judge had a message that they wanted me back at the hospital, if I was there in the courtroom. I told him I wasn't.

# "I Have a Feeling We're Not in Kansas Anymore"

**D**o you know what that is?" Opal said to me just before she stepped out of the courthouse into the rain.

"It looks like rain."

"Wrong. That's zero to five percent chance of rain."

"It looks like it's going to be zero to five all day," I said. "It looks like one of those three-day drizzles."

"The judge took away my shotgun shells," she said. Then: "It's supposed to clear up."

"We can get some more," Spangler said.

"I don't think so. You got to sign for them now, and he put me on a list that goes to gun stores so they won't sell them to me. If that copter comes back, I'll use the rifle on him."

When we got to the herd, there were Highway Patrolmen everywhere. They even had a mobile office set up. Opal said they wanted to have a meeting with us before we got going that day, so we'd all know how we were going to work the last stretch. A man who looked absurdly like Rod Steiger did the talking.

"My name is Becker, Lieutenant Becker," he said.

"Do you raise chickens?" Spangler asked.

"No," said Becker, puzzled.

"Go ahead. Just wondered."

"This is Officer Crocker, Officer Waters, Officer Beam, Officer Tills, Officer Stiltson."

"I have a brother who works out of Russell," said Stiltson.

"We've met," said Spangler. "He's known for the fine work he does out there. He helped us get started." Spangler shook Stiltson's hand more firmly than he had shaken the others'. Stiltson beamed.

Becker said: "Now, as we told your wife last month, this cowboy-cattle drive of yours puts us in a difficult situation. We'd rather you just load these cattle up here." Spangler frowned. "But I don't guess you plan to," Becker said. "Got to take them all the way. Right? Just like the old days."

"What kind of bugs you got in your ass?" said Spangler.

"Mainly you. And the morning paper," said Becker. "That's why we can't let you sink or swim out there. Or the headline to-morrow would be POLICE DEPARTMENT TURNS BACK ON RANCHER / CATTLE SCATTER THRU CITY."

"It's good of you to help us," I said. Becker glared.

"Here's how it's going to work," Becker said to Spangler. "We'll patrol Highway 32 along the river edge. Put a string of cars along the shoulder. You keep well down below the roads, next to the rail-road tracks. We figure there's fifty yards of grass between the tracks and the road on the river side. You take the herd along that strip. About ten miles up the road the strip narrows down, but you'll have to make do."

"Until a train comes along and makes a fucking circus of the herd," said Spangler.

"No trains," said Stiltson. "We've got cooperation there. You've got until five this afternoon to get your cattle off the right of way."

"Do we follow the tracks all the way in?" asked Spangler.

"No," said Opal.

"Naw," said Becker. "You follow them for about fifteen miles. Then we take you off the right of way and under the turnpike and right down the middle of 32, through City Park, through

Clifton Park, across Eighteenth Street, and onto Central Avenue."
I nodded.

"What are you nodding about?" Becker said.

"I figured that's the way we'd go. I used to live around here."

"Then why the hell didn't you tell these friends of yours what a mess this is going to be?"

"Because I knew you could handle the job, Lieutenant Becker." He tried to stare me down. He succeeded. He continued.

"Once we cut away from the river and get past the turnpike, we're going to form a moving box around the herd. We're going to clear off Central—the merchants aren't all too happy about this—and we're going to put cars behind you and cars in front and motorcycles all down the sides. And we're going to move right along. Right snappy. This ain't going to be no parade."

"It sounds like we're getting rushed through town," Spangler said. "I hoped we might take it easy so Opal could do some shopping." Becker didn't even bother to glare.

"After we get on Central Avenue, might as well get off your horses and climb in one of our cars for all the cattle driving you're going to be doing. It's all going to be for show," Becker said. "We'll have those cattle boxed in all the way across the Central Street Bridge. We might let you drive them the last ten yards into the pens to see if you still remember how."

"My taxes at work," said Spangler.

"There's a donation involved—now, didn't your wife let you know about that?" said Becker.

"You want a steer? Leo, cut the officer out a steer."

"We'd rather have money. Not for us. We got a softball team. Make it a hundred to the softball team. We need new bats."

"Shiiiiiit." Opal told Spangler to give Becker that other movie hundred-dollar bill.

"Another thing," said Becker. "The guns."

"What about them?" said Spangler.

"We want them. Just like on television, Tukle. Check your guns at the edge of town. You want to play cowboy—that's fine with us.

But we know how the act goes. So Officer Stiltson will keep the guns till you leave town. Got it?"

"We can always throw horse turds at the helicopters," I said, trying to put an ironic glaze on the proceedings. It didn't work. Spangler was getting claustrophobic. He was tapping his foot and scratching his sides.

"I don't like you," Spangler said to Becker.

"That's too bad," Becker said.

"No. That's about right. You ought to be disliked by everybody in the world about the same way I dislike you."

"How's that?"

"About the same way I don't like bird shit on my windshield." Spangler led us out.

## II

We didn't have far to go, but we were getting a late start. It was nine before we were on the road. Stiltson took the rifle and the shotgun. He didn't know about the pistol. We were in our slickers; the sky was gray and shot through and through with water. It seemed not so much to be raining, as water suspended in the gray air around us. It was cold. My ass wouldn't settle in the saddle right; the leather was stiff and tight. My arm hurt and I felt awkward and out of rhythm with what I wanted to do.

On the right as we left Bonner Springs we could see the bridge, a ridiculous white slab over the gray river. Blue Highway Patrolmen were everywhere we went. Cars moved around us with the caution of the curious. I had the feeling we were trapped in a slow-motion rerun of a slightly out-of-focus home movie. I could see us through the lens of a Kodak movie camera pointed at us from a passing Cadillac from Maryland. We were bent over our saddle horns; the heads of the steers were low. We were not looking beyond the brims of our hats; our horses' necks were loose and low, the bridles were slack. Opal was peering blank-eyed through the streaked windshield of the truck. Nobody waved, and there wasn't much you could see in the background, because it was raining and it was dark.

The cops helped. They stayed clear of us and cut people off before they could get onto the roads that crossed from the main highway across the right of way to the tracks and the river. We all agreed there was nothing left to do but get where we were going. The last day was going to be a job.

Way over above the river I could see a helicopter. So could Opal; I saw her reach across the seat into the glove box for the pistol. I pointed the copter out to Spangler, who shrugged.

"Opal's got the pistol," I said, "and I think she'll take a shot if he comes over."

"I believe you're right," Spangler said. "I hope she gets him this time." But the copter hovered way out there, then turned away from us and went back toward the city.

Every once in a while we'd see jets, big Boeings, come up the river and then climb into the ceiling. The railroad track that had followed the river had doubled and then doubled again. There were switch engines working flat cars. I could hear the clang of couplings and the surge of engines beginning their pull.

To the north was the Interstate, and slowly it converged on us. At first the noise was a distant hiss, but by noon I could hear the whine of individual trucks. It was as if we were going down a funnel. The river and the railroad tracks angling in on one side and the Interstate on the other. And in the gray, wet air an occasional plane climbing out of the city. A sign told us we were on the Kaw Valley Scenic Highway.

The first thing we saw of the city as we came in was the Channel 5 TV tower—or at least the red light on it, blinking like a tired eye up near the bottom of the sky. Within the hour we could see the gray slabs of buildings across the river; we could see cars crossing and crisscrossing roads and underpasses and bridges and sliding in and out of the rain and the mist. Several roads began to parallel us. On one there was a funeral procession.

"We're lost," Spangler said as he rode back from the truck, waving a limp map. "Those goddamn cops got us off on this road and then jumped us for that fucking funeral. Now I don't know where I am."

We stopped. The edge of the road above us was no longer lined with cop cars. Ahead, the right of way turned into a thin path along a bluff, the railroad track falling below. Another jet climbed into the haze, but this time it didn't disappear. We hadn't noticed, but the sky had begun to clear, leaving only the naturally dirty air of the city and the slight grayness that rainy days sometimes leave behind for a while, like the echo-pain of a mean headache that has gone. Jed had ridden up to the front of the herd. Opal was in the truck on the highway. I rode up to her to see what was going on.

"Where do we go?" I asked.

"Wait there," she said. "Becker said wait where we are until they get the funeral out of the way." I rode back down and told Spangler, who was sitting on his horse in the middle of his herd reading the map, for all the world like a lost tourist with a station wagon-load of screaming kids.

"Keep them here," I said. "Becker told Opal to keep them here."

"Sure. Two hundred and fifty steers are just going to stand still between the Interstate and the train tracks and an ILS approach over their heads." He pulled a bottle from under his slicker. "Want a drink?" I did.

The Green Gables bubbled in the green bottle. The sun broke out behind our backs. It must have been about two in the afternoon. We had been lucky in a way. The rain had kept the cattle quiet. Now if we could get all the help the cops had promised us, we could make it through the city in the sunshine. The girls from the pool might recognize me after all.

"Here's Becker," I said as I spotted him up on the ridge, looking down at us. Stiltson was with him. Becker had on aviator glasses. They were waving us forward. We cut to the back of the herd, shouted at Jed up front, and began to ease them forward, around a slight bend. Just before the right of way became very narrow there was a cut in the bluff, and we drove the herd up the hill through the cut and onto the highway. For the first time since we had left Bonner Springs, the three of us could see what the world up on the highway was like. In front of us there was a double line of cop cars, making a narrow lane about fifty feet wide. At the far end there were three city tow trucks with big wooden rear bumpers made of two-by-sixes that extended two feet out on each side so that nothing could get through them. On one bumper somebody had put the sticker: I'D RATHER BE SAILING. The whole thing looked like a moving corral.

We brought the herd up and into the lane. Opal brought the truck in behind us. I could hear the spare horse thumping around in the trailer as Opal let the clutch out and lurched slightly. Behind Opal the cop cars closed in, and in between them motorcycles. Becker was right, I felt I wasn't needed. Jed looked around at me and shrugged his shoulders and came to the back of the herd. Becker turned on his blinker light as a signal to the wreckers and the cars on the sides to get going. We were off.

This moving car-truck-motorcycle box took us down Highway 32, which cut under the Kansas Turnpike. I looked back at the Kaw River we had been following all morning, and I could see that the sun was doing its best to turn off the gray, musty air that had accumulated in the long, low valley. It had its work cut out. The further the sun moved toward the west, I thought, the brighter it must get. But my view was abruptly cut off by the underpass bridge and the trucks that rumbled over it, taking one thing and another into the city, including cattle going to the stockyards.

We bent up through City Park, where I used to go with girls after I had been drinking. I had still lived at home but was too old and suave to use the car. There were no roads cutting into the highway here, and I thought that was good until I realized that now it didn't make any difference. The herd had nowhere to go except forward. There were people in the park, and they waved at us and we waved back. They seemed friendly, and it looked as if they were there just to see us go by—they had brought lawn chairs and blankets and cameras. I looked at them and waved. Jed kept beside me and held his eyes on the herd. Spangler was back by the truck talking with Opal. We got through the park and went a few blocks, where there were houses lining the street and people on porches and stoop steps. Soon we cut back into another park, Clinton Park. It was on our left, and there were people all along the edge and up the small hills that lead back into the woods. There were men selling balloons to the children, and there were young couples leaning against trees drinking beer. While we were going along this stretch, the cops began to make some moves.

More motorcycles were coming from behind, and the cars along the edges were dropping back. They wouldn't be able to fit cars on both sides of us and get the herd down Central when it turned into a city street—which would happen just as we left Clinton Park. For a moment we felt needed again. Some steers got up on the sidewalk when a couple of motorcycles didn't get in place in time. Jed worked them back, beating his hat against his leg as he urged Duke up on the sidewalk and then back down again.

"Wooo-eee, cowboy!" yelled one young man standing there with a beer in his hand. "Go get 'em. Wooo-eee!" His wife came up to quiet him. Motorcycles closed the gap and Jed came back to ride with me. Spangler moved up to the front of the herd.

We came out of the park and into the city, here a city of small shops with modest old office buildings rising only a half-dozen stories into the bright sunshine. Ahead there were banners strung across the street: WELCOME TUKLE HERD. SHOOT ANOTHER COPTER. DRIVE 'EM. GO, GO, GO. Along the side there were kids on bikes who'd ride ahead and then come zooming back down, scattering the people who were standing on the sidewalk. A woman about Opal's age (but bigger) held up a sign that read: HAMBURGER'S HALF FAT. A man I took to be her husband held one that read: WHOSE GOING TO CLEAN THIS UP? But most of the signs welcomed us, praised us, urged us on: STICK IT TO 'EM, TUKLE. THE GOVERNMENT. NEED A HAND? EAT MEAT. I don't know if Spangler or Opal saw it, but I did, and I never said anything about it, but about three blocks into the city I noticed a sign hung from the roof of a two-story sewing machine company building: THE ROOKIE'S PLASTIC, MRS. ROBINSON. I wondered if Harold was in the crowd, but I didn't see him. It didn't matter. We were heroes.

We didn't know it, sleeping out with the herd and not reading papers and getting to bed before we'd watch television, but the whole city had been hearing about us coming across the state. And the night before, when they'd seen the film of the drive and heard about Opal taking a shot at the helicopter, they had decided we deserved a welcome. We were what they had always threatened to be in the grumble-gripe-talk of coffee breaks and back-of-the-store gossip sessions. They were glad to see us. We were a parade. Spangler led the way down Central Avenue, keeping Canyon Snip's head high by pulling back the reins. He looked over his shoulder and waved for us to come forward, up through the herd, but we stayed back. He pointed at Opal and waved his arm for her to come forward.

"He wants Opal up in front," I said to Jed. "I'll drive the truck."

"No," Jed said, and got off his horse right here. He waited for the truck to pull even with him. It stopped. He talked to Opal a moment. She shook her head no. Becker honked. Jed opened the door. She paused and got out. Jed gave her the reins to Duke, and she swung into the saddle. Jed climbed into the truck and began to drive. Opal joined Spangler at the front.

The afternoon sun was still high enough in the sky to clear the low city buildings. We had gone about ten blocks; we had about fifteen to go. We crossed the Eighteenth Street Throughway, which had been blocked off by barricades. Up and down the side streets I could see kids scrambling to get a better view, first coming up close and then backing away. Smart ones climbed the rusty fire escapes that scaled the sides of buildings. The crowds were getting thicker. Police lined the route. Behind us I could see people filling in the street where the herd had passed. A small boy stood looking at a steamy trail of horse turds. He kicked one with his tennis shoe. It didn't roll like a rock or clang like a tin can, so he squashed it flat in a one-jump, one-foot stomp and ran after his friends who had gotten ahead. In a vacant lot a high school band played the Marlboro theme. The cornets were screeching like fingernails on a blackboard.

All this time the herd trotted on. Every time they'd look one way or another, there'd be a line of motorcycles, or the tow trucks, or Becker and his men in a row of patrol cars behind us, their flashers flashing. The herd was being pushed hard. They had been in a trot for nearly five miles now, and their heads were beginning to hang. And then they'd snap them up again and look around in a wild way to see if there was any place to stop, any place to go to get out of the way of the wave of people and cars that rose behind them. Saliva strung out of their mouths in thin, long lines. Occasionally one would stumble, and I'd cut over to it and block off the rest of the herd and let the fallen steer get back up. The ones on the edge of the herd had that wild look in their eyes that they got when they were on the bridge. Not much farther, I thought.

Ahead, Opal and Spangler were leading the herd, and Spangler was waving now and then to the crowd. When the procession came to a stop for a moment (I didn't know why), he reached under his slicker and brought out the Green Gables. The crowd cheered as he tipped it up. Opal turned it down. He rode over to one side and passed the bottle into the crowd and rode back into the herd. Opal had lit a cigarette.

We started up again. The herd milled and would not drive. Becker honked. Jed slapped the side of the truck with his hat. Spangler and Opal rode on for a moment, and then Spangler looked around and saw the herd stalled. He came back, uncoiling his bull whip from the saddle ties. I started to do the same, but my broken arm wouldn't take the reins. Before, only the pain had bothered me—now the fact that it was broken was getting in my way.

We eased back of the herd. Becker pressed in too close and Spangler told him to hold his horses. He snapped the whip over the heads of the herd. The crowd cheered as the cattle began moving forward again, slowly.

"We better cut the pace," I said to Spangler.

"Slow it down," Spangler yelled to Becker and snapped the bull whip over the hood of his police car. Becker took off his aviator glasses and threw them down on the seat and leaned out the window to give us one of his glares. He yelled something, but we couldn't hear him. We rode up on either side of Jed, bringing the cattle that had gotten behind him to the front.

"How's it going?" Spangler yelled at Jed.

"We are going too fast," Jed said.

"Slow the truck down," Spangler said. "That way Becker will have to run you over if he wants to hurry us." Opal had stayed up front, smoking. Spangler waved her forward. He stayed back, snaking the bull whip out over the herd, not snapping it, but rather sailing it out there like fly-fishing line. Back at the ranch I'd seen him pop sunflowers off their stalks as we'd ride through a field. He'd uncoil the whip and snap it out over the heads of tall sunflowers and pulverize a big one ten feet away, its yellow and black flower becoming confetti in the western afternoon. He'd grin and pop another one, the sound like a rifle shot. The tip of the whip breaks the sound barrier, he once told me. That's the noise. But here on Central Avenue the whip eased out over the cattle like a sluggish black snake in the afternoon sun. It was just the right touch. They moved forward as a herd.

We didn't have far to go. Five, six blocks. This was my end of town. There was the Dew Drop Inn. The Five O'Clock Shadow with its blue Hamms sign in the dirty window. I wondered if Normal Jones, who runs the place, was there. He left the bar for nothing. Once, there was a fire next door and all the fire trucks were right there in front of his window, and still he didn't leave from behind the bar. His patrons copied him in this. I didn't see him on the sidewalk.

It's funny and sad. How you can live somewhere else and get to not liking where you've come from. I remember thinking that when I first noticed the change in the color of sky back there at the mobile home junction. I thought then that I was glad I had found a place for myself where there wasn't a city to mess things up. Where there wasn't a traffic jam three times a day. Where there weren't winos drinking melted-down deodorant sticks. Cops two to a block and black-and-whites as thick as bind-weed. I thought it was good not to miss any of that. Nor the bridge table suburbs where my parents lived, barbecues flaring up like camp-fires in the summer evenings. But there was something about being right back in the middle of the city that made me wonder. This was home. Of a kind. I wished I could stop the drive for a moment and take Opal and Jed and Spangler and show them around. They should meet Normal Jones. And Tim "Crackers" Bracken, who once played a pin-ball machine for thirty-one hours straight. He didn't win many games. He just got into the rhythm of it and couldn't quit.

There were people to meet here. The men put salt in their beer and complained about the government. Spangler would get on. I'd show them around tomorrow. I was getting it in my head I was glad to be back. I wondered if I'd look as stupid in my cowboy hat and boots to these men as I had to Spangler when he picked me up that day over a year ago. Kangaroo shoes.

I could see the Central Street Bridge. As a kid I had tried to shoot pigeons with a slingshot off that bridge. And LeRoy Parker and Wanda Flowers had once dropped a stolen rubber machine off the bridge onto the tracks below. It broke open and they were caught picking up the rubbers and the quarters. Wanda had been in charge of the quarters.

There was a new sign since I had been here last, one that told us to stay in the left lane if we wanted to go over the Lewis and Clark Viaduct. We didn't. The cops had the bridge well blocked in. Some of the motorcycles zoomed on ahead at the last minute in order to be in place on the other side. Others trailed behind— there was no need of them on the bridge. The herd balked, but only slightly. The bridge rose gently up in front of them, and in their mind's eye it must not have looked so much like a bridge as like a hill of some kind. It was not long and flat and open like the one the day before. They went on it with a clatter. The moment they did, pigeons from beneath the bridge flapped into the air, the flock coming out both sides and swinging wide over the tracks below before coming back to take a look. They had grown used to the sound of cars going over and that would not send them up, but this constant clatter was a new noise and they wanted to see what made it. They came back, then banked away, first one flock, then the other.

We were up high on the bridge. I could see the stockyards ahead and to the right. Further up in the city I could see the statue of the golden steer that rose on a pillar a couple hundred feet above the Cattlemen's Association Building. The sun shot off its flanks.

There was nothing but railed-in road all the rest of the way. A hundred yards more on the Central Street Bridge. Fifty yards on the flat, and then up and over James Street on that short bridge they built the year I went away to the University. The herd was beginning to trot now. When we topped the James Street Bridge, I looked back and I could see the parade strung out behind us. The high school band was leading the way. There were cars and people on bicycles, but most were walking. The pigeons had banked away again.

Just off the James Street Bridge there was a large sign with an arrow at the bottom of it: THE GOLDEN OX RESTAURANT. The arrow pointed right. Beyond that sign was a smaller sign put up by the city which said: STOCKYARDS RIGHT LANE. Opal led the herd down the James Street Bridge, and with the motorcycles and barriers closing in on the left, she turned us hard to the right and down the wide brick road that ran parallel to the stockyards on the right side and the meatpacking plants on the left. A block down we could see there were pens open and saw-horse barriers forming a funnel. We picked up the gait even more. Spangler popped the whip. The spare horse whinnied at the noise. Jed lurched the truck into second gear. Opal was being passed on both sides by drooling steers on the trot. I dropped back to drive a straggler. He slipped on the bricks, but then regained his feet and caught the others just as they were entering the funnel. Opal wheeled out of the herd, and the three of us pressed our horses close to the back edge of the cattle. Spangler popped the whip hard, and in a rush the last part of the herd surged up the funnel and into the pen.

The stockyard cowboys slammed the gates shut.

# Television

What was the most difficult part of the trip?" a sandy-haired T.V. interviewer asked Spangler.

"Night before last," Spangler said. "We had steers to hell and gone in Bonner Springs." The newsman winced. A woman behind the camera held up a blackboard sign on which she had hastily written "LIVE."

"What's that mean?" Spangler asked, pointing to the sign.

"Are you glad to be in the city?" the interviewer pressed on.

"I will be after I sell these steers. We'll have a shitpot full of money then." The woman with the sign was shaking it at Spangler.

"Live," he said. "Am I supposed to say live or live? What does she want?" The woman reddened and dropped the sign in exasperation.

"They don't want you to swear," I said to Spangler. We were just off camera. The man had told us he'd have us join Spangler after a few questions. Opal was smoking a cigarette and Jed was standing with his hat in his hands.

"Don't you want me to swear?" Spangler asked the interviewer.

"It upsets some of our viewers," said the man.

"I see," Spangler said. "Maybe you better ask someone else the questions," he said, and walked over to where the woman was standing and picked up her sign and handed it back to her. The camera swung to us. The interviewer back-stepped our way.

"Your name?" he asked me.

"Leo Murdock."

"And what did you do to yourself?" He pointed at my arm.

"I broke my arm."

"How?"

"I fell off my horse."

"How did that happen?"

"It's a long story."

"Oh. Well, what's your name?"

"Jed."

"Jed what?" There was no answer. "Well, uh, Mr. Jed, what did you do?"

"What?"

"What did you do on this drive?"

"I rode my horse." Jed dropped his hat. Opal picked it up for him. Spangler had gone over by the truck and was digging under the seat for another bottle of Green Gables.

"I'm Opal Tukle," Opal said rather smartly, even before she was asked. She smiled and brushed her hair back with her cigarette hand.

"Is it true you shot a helicopter?" the man asked.

"I guess it is. Didn't hit it, though. Spangler said I should have used the rifle." Spangler was coming back from the truck with the Green Gables.

"You want a snort?" he asked the man as he came back on camera.

"No thank you." Quite a crowd had gathered around us, and when we each took a snort (even Jed), Spangler passed the bottle around. It came back our way once, but then we never saw it again.

"You finished talking to us?" Spangler said, after he had taken his gulp from the bottle.

"This is *Eyes and Ears News. Action Camera Spotlight.* With the Tukle herd here in the stockyards. Max Marx reporting. Back to you, Ed." He turned to Spangler and said, "Now I am, Mr. Tukle."

"O.K. Hope we didn't get you in trouble." The woman who had held the sign chuckled in a condescending way. I thought that was too bad, because she was good looking and I was thinking about trying to meet her. But just the way she laughed, I knew she thought we were all hicks. I wondered if I would have thought that in her place.

After the interview, lots of people came up and talked to us. There were kids who wanted Spangler's autograph. Some women gathered around Opal and talked to her for a while. There were even a few people my own age (guys with bellbottom pants and dry-look hair styles—girls with white jeans and solid-colored blouses) who talked to me. Mostly they wanted to know how hard it was. How many steers died (five), how many we lost (about twenty), and how old Jed was. Jed had gone back to the truck for a nap. After about twenty minutes of milling with the crowd, we were told by one of the officials at the stockyards to come with him. We woke up Jed, and the four of us followed the man through the maze of gates and lanes until we came to a rundown one-story frame building pretty much in the middle of the stockyards.

"We killed a bear, pistol," Spangler said to me as we went inside. "And here is where we collect the hide."

# The Grade of Meat

They're not CHOICE of any kind, Mr. Tukle," said a tiny man with a crew cut and a cigar, who sat behind a card table of a desk in a box of an office. "You see, we had the computers over at the packing houses check this out. And every day you drive them, well, that cuts them back, now doesn't it? I mean, they lose a little weight. Now hold on. Yes, yes. You're going to say they get it back a little at night. They do. That's the problem. See, our computers tell us that's what causes gristle. See, when the steer loses weight and then puts it back on again, there is a line of gristle. Now, the packing house boys, well, they're mighty proud of what you did. I mean, you brought the romance back into the cattle business. But they figure the meat you got there is mostly gristly. Fifteen lines of it, at least. See what I mean? But you'll have no problem selling them as CUTTERS. Lots of dog-food buyers here."

There were five of us in the office. The tiny man was the only one sitting down. He was looking up at us in a steady stare. I thought he was sure he wouldn't get hurt because he was so small, and after all his office was humble, his desk flimsy. Besides, it was all out of his hands. Jed spat on the floor near the door. The tiny man peered over and looked at it, then at Jed.

"What's the price of CHOICE cattle?" said Spangler.

"You haven't got CHOICE cattle, Mr. Tukle."

"Let's start off finding out the price of what I haven't got."

"Fifty dollars a hundred. That was closing today. It's after time."

"What's GOOD going for?" Spangler asked.

"Now maybe you got that. See." Jed spat again. "About thirty dollars a hundred. See. There's the difference. I mean, you made a lot of news. But that's not money. I mean, it's out of my hands. We had the computer check it out. That's what the big boys in the packing house tell us, and we've got to deal with them after you leave. See?"

I could tell by the way Spangler looked out the window that he had stopped listening to the tiny man. I looked out the window, too. It was greasy. Outside I could see that it was getting into the late afternoon. Long shadows of gates and chutes stretched across the open pens right next to us. We could not see our herd from where we were.

"You'll have no problem selling the herd, Mr. Tukle. Tomorrow. But we'll have to have storage fees. It's after closing." I quit looking out the window. The tiny man's cigar had gone out. Spangler was silent.

"What's the problem?" I asked. Spangler turned and glared at me.

"Makes no difference to you that your heifer winds up as dog meat?" he asked.

"I hadn't thought about it," I confessed. I hadn't thought about killing her at all, I realized.

"It's a matter of money, boy," the tiny man said in a fatherly way. "Mr. Tukle here thought he had CHOICE steers. That's one thing. See."

"That ain't it either, ass-hole," said Spangler. The man relit his cigar, using a butane lighter that he had been fiddling with for some time, but which I just noticed when it shot into flame.

"What is it, Mr. Tukle?" said the tiny man.

"I don't think we want the herd to be dog food," said Opal from where she stood.

"That's stupid, ma'am," said the tiny man, and spit out a flake of cigar. Spangler took one long step that put him in front of the card table. The man looked at him for a moment and drew in on his cigar. It hadn't lit. Spangler picked up the card table, turned it over, and rammed it down over the man's head and shoulders. There was a pop of fabric and a puff of dust. It rested flush with the arms of the chair; the canvas had split like old paper. The four legs of the table wobbled around the tiny man's head. The cigar rolled on the floor up to Jed. He stomped it. Spangler stalked out. Opal and Jed followed, Opal talking. I tripped on something as I was trying my best to stalk out with speed and power.

"That man's made a mistake," said the tiny man. "That's a mistake. See. He's made a mistake. He doesn't know who I am." I saw Spangler cross in front of the window. I had tripped around the office so long I needed an exit line.

"You look pretty dumb," I said. Harold could have come up with a literary allusion. I wasn't equal to the task. I left.

Spangler was taking long strides through the boarded alleys of the stockyards. Opal was running to keep up, but Jed had fallen behind.

"What's he going to do now?" I asked Jed when I caught up with him.

"I do not know."

When Jed and I got to Spangler, he was standing by the truck. Opal was talking to him. He was staring out over his cattle. It seemed to me he was trying not to hear her.

"You either sell the herd, Spangler, or we ship them back to Hays," she was saying.

"That's not a choice," he said softly.

"Get in the truck, Spangler," she said. "Let's go and have a drink and talk it over."

"No."

"Yes." She sounded more firm than I had ever heard her. Jed got in the truck on the other side. We all waited.

"O.K.," Spangler said. Opal got in first. I got in on Jed's side. Spangler slid behind the wheel and slammed the door.

I had never seen him so grim. His fingers were digging into his palms around the steering wheel. I looked out in the herd and saw my heifer mingle and disappear among the tired, dirty steers. Suddenly, Spangler got out and went back of the truck. He smashed Rabies' box with his fist, and picked the cat up by the scruff of the neck. He gave it a hard jerk. Rabies' eyes bulged and his mouth opened in a silent howl. Spangler stalked to the gate and threw the cat into the cattle.

The cat crouched for a moment before he ran off. Spangler went up to the pen and leaned over the fence and looked at his herd. The three of us sat in the truck. It was getting dark.

He came back to the truck and stared at us through the windshield. He twisted the outside mirror in his hands—back and forth—until it broke off and then broke, mirror glass tinkling on the bricks. Jed grunted. Spangler kicked the truck. He got in. We swung around in the wide street and went down the road that ran perpendicular to the cattle pen where the herd was. At the first intersection Spangler swung the truck back around and took dead aim on the cattle pen. We must have been going fifty by the time we broke the gate down. Opal was screaming. We killed a few steers outright, but most of them bolted to the back of the pen. In an instant Spangler reached over and got the pistol out of the glove compartment and jumped from the truck, shooting the pistol in the air. The steers knocked him down as they rushed through the broken gate. Jed tried to get out his side, but he couldn't. Opal was crying. I got out and tried to find Spangler. I heard a shot from the milling cattle just behind the truck. They bolted against the ones who hadn't gotten out yet. In a moment all but the dead ones and my heifer were clear of the pen. Spangler was on his back on the brick and mud and cow shit floor of the cattle pen. He rolled over on one side and shot my heifer through the neck. She toppled over and twitched.

When I came near, he pointed the gun at me. I backed away. He got to his feet. People from around the cattle pens were running at us. Spangler fired a round into the air and then threw the pistol at the truck. He collapsed.

# The Last Night

It is later that night. Much later. Near midnight. I am in Kelly's Westport Inn, drinking Jameson's and Guinness out of a beer glass. Opal has been in three times since ten. Looking for Spangler. Jed, she tells me, won't check into the Muehlebach. He is asleep in the truck. She is worried about him because he is breathing funny. She can't describe it any other way. The police are looking for Spangler. I have been here since nine. Stationed. Waiting for Spangler.

The herd had bolted down the streets with the shots from Spangler's pistol. The stockyard cowboys tried to bring them back by using trucks and cars. They only split the herd even more, so that in about fifteen minutes the steers were poking around the short streets just east of the stockyards. We could hear sirens coming at us from all parts of the city. Jed and I had unloaded our horses, resaddled, and mounted up. Opal had rolled Spangler over and he came to. He got up and walked over to the corner of the pen and propped himself up like a boxer on the ropes in a ring, leaning back against the corner and stretching his arms out along the sides. He yelled at Opal to leave him alone. When we got back about an hour later, he was gone and Opal didn't know where he was. He had taken out his horse shortly after we'd left, and ridden off into the city. It was absolutely dark when we got back.

Jed and I had no luck trying to bring the steers back. We'd find them in bunches of five and ten, and without any more than that they wouldn't herd up. Even when we'd get some to drive, the stockyard cowboys or the cops would come roaring up behind us and then the steers would spook. The city people weren't much help, either. Always yelling "Giddy-up, little dogie" and waving their arms. I saw steers everywhere. Standing alone in doorways. Knocking down *Kansas City Star* newsstands. Trotting single file down Santa Fe Street. Twenty of them tying up the entry ramp onto the Lewis and Clark Viaduct. A trio of them placidly eating grass in Observation Park. A large steer dead on the side of Twelfth Avenue, two Negro boys poking it with sticks.

I was tired. My horse was tired. Jed's legs were cramping up. (I could tell by the way he'd shake them out of the stirrups and stretch them out, trying to get them untied.) I tried to bring some steers back, but I thought there wasn't any point to it. I knew that's what we were supposed to do. We had brought the herd back together many times before. But this time it was like it couldn't be done, and not because we couldn't do it. It was as if it wasn't meant to be done. Those steers trotting in bunches through the city didn't seem like the Tukle herd anymore. We had delivered the Tukle herd a few hours ago. It's hard to say. Only it seemed just as natural for them to be browsing around the city as it had been for them to be scattered around the ranch. When we got back, Spangler still wasn't there.

The truck was ringed with cop cars. There were maybe twenty steers in the pen. They had drifted back on their own. Opal was talking to a circle of men. A tall policeman in a Smokey-the-Bear forest hat came up to me while I was still on my horse. He wanted to know if Spangler had been with me. I saw the tiny man sitting in his car. A dark Mark IV. His cigar glowed. No, I hadn't seen Spangler. We loaded the horses. Jed went and sat in the truck. I didn't want to talk to anybody, so I joined him. My arm hurt and I was hungry as hell.

I have eaten. I brought in a pair of double cheeseburgers from across the street. Kelly usually doesn't let you eat in the bar, but in my case he made an exception. I have taken off my boots, and I am sitting at the big round wooden table near the phone booth. Opal has said she would call to find out about Spangler. Or to tell me about him. But instead she has been in three times. She won't sit down for a beer. The police are going to hold her if Spangler can't be found by midnight. She tells me the cops are picking up the cattle in paddy wagons.

The herd scattered way across the railroad tracks and into the main part of Kansas City, Missouri. The radio is giving half-hour reports. There is a number you can call if you find a steer. The police are looking for a tall man on a white horse. I am remembering that on St. Patrick's Day you can get free green beer in Kelly's, and that they always have to close the place by noon, it's so full. Cops help Kelly keep people out. I get there first thing in the morning and stay all day. I am thinking this when Spangler walks in.

"It costs just as fucking much to park a horse as a Lincoln," he says. "What are you drinking?"

"Boilermakers, Guinness and Jameson's."

"You can get pretty drunk drinking those things," he says. He takes a drink of mine.

"They're going to put Opal in jail," I say.

"That's what I hear," he says, looking for the bartender. "The cops are paying five dollars a steer reward. Find a thousand-pound steer and you get five bucks. Does that tell you something about the price of meat?"

"Somebody's going to turn you in," I say.

"I don't think so. No reward. Besides, I'm a hero. The guy who charged me two-fifty to tie Canyon Snip to a chain-link fence told me I was a hero. He said he didn't believe in heroes, though." I get Kelly over and order two more boilermakers.

"Is this the fellow?" says Kelly. I say it is. "There's going to be a cop around here before long."

"I know," says Spangler. "I thought I'd have a few belts in me before I go downtown and talk to some candy-assed judge. I don't know why I haven't been caught. I'm not exactly hiding."

"Where'd you go?" I ask. Kelly stays to listen.

"I just rode around and looked at the herd. I saw you and Jed a couple of times. Didn't look like you were getting much done. You haven't learned not to push the steers around. Still stay too close on their butts. Can't pop a whip. Ass never has quit bouncing." He tries a grin.

"I do all right," I say.

"Maybe you do," he says. He looks into his boilermaker, dark brown and foaming at the top. He drinks it off in one long pull. Not a gulp. He gets a breath or two around the edges of his mouth, but he never puts the glass down until it is empty.

"Good," he says. "Don't believe I've had one quite like that. Tastes like a proof of God." He turns to Kelly. "Can you mix me a batch in a bottle to go?" Kelly hedges.

"Do it for him, will you, Kelly?" I ask. Kelly agrees. It is mixed in a McCormick's whiskey bottle. Spangler smells it. Then takes a pull.

"I better save it for the road," he says and caps the bottle. Kelly stands around. Spangler stares across the table, but he is not looking at me.

"It was spooky out there in the city," he says. "Just poking around in the streets, looking at my cattle. Watching you guys work a couple of blocks away." He pauses. "I'd see a bunch of steers down a street and I'd ride down to get a close look at them. I'd hold off of them aways so they wouldn't spook. I wanted to look at them. Canyon Snip couldn't figure it. He wanted to drive them, or cut one out. I just wanted to see if they were really my steers. They had my brand on them. Every bunch I'd see would have my big star brand. I don't know who else has cattle pastured in Kansas City. Some of them would try to follow me as I'd ride away." He pauses. "We did it and we didn't," he says to me. Then: "Sorry about your heifer." He takes a deep breath and puffs it out the corners of his mouth. I can't talk. We sit.

In comes Opal. "Spangler Star Tukle—get your ass out of this bar and get in jail. I'll be damned if I'm going to spend my time in Kansas City behind bars because you lost your mind and ran our cattle all over the city. It's a mess out there." She points out the door. Through the front window we can see two steers crossing Westport Road. Opal is pissed.

"We're going home," Spangler says.

"We're going to jail first," Opal says. "Either you're going to jail, or I'm going to jail—and I'm here to tell you that it's not me."

"After jail we're going home," Spangler says.

"Not before we sell the cattle," Opal says.

"No."

"Yes."

She pauses.

"I'm running an auction," Opal says. She smiles. "Tomorrow. Every B-B-Q owner in Johnson County thinks Spangler is a big hero. All those years of him bitching about Kansas City dentists, and he turns out to be their man. I've got a place for the auction. The cops are bringing in the cattle. With all the publicity we're getting, I'll have it packed. I'm selling them one steer at a time."

"I'll buy one," says Kelly. Spangler looks at him. Opal lights a cigarette. "Why not," says Kelly. "I've got a freezer. Besides, I can have some of it stretched to jerky. Every drinker in here would buy beef jerky off that herd."

"See, Spangler?" says Opal. "That's the kind of thinking I'm working on. Every golf hat dentist in Kansas City will want to turn a steak on his B-B-Q off that herd. Even if it is full of gristle."

"They'll say that gives it character," I say.

"The fucking deal smells," says Spangler. "You're making a circus out of my deal, Opal."

"I'm making some money of it," she says. "We both got our jobs and yours is to get in jail. Nobody's asking you to this auction. What you don't know won't hurt you. I've heard that often enough." She takes a deep drag and blows the smoke out across the table. Spangler glares. She says: "It's my turn, Spangler. I get to stick it to them. Those are my cattle, too." She gets up and leaves, the cigarette smoking in her right hand. At the door she tells Spangler to get his ass in jail.

Spangler looks at me. He twists off the top of the McCormick bottle and takes a pull. "She's a mercurial woman," he says. "But she's a piss cutter."

In a moment he will leave without saying anything more. He will go across the bar with the McCormick's bottle of boilermakers in his hand and out the door and across the street. He will ride Canyon Snip down Westport Road until he gets to Main Street. People all along the way will wave at him in glee. Cops on Main Street will pick him up and lead him downtown to meet the judge. Crowds follow. To start with, the charge will be multiple counts of disturbing the peace. He is guilty with pleasure.

# Where I Am Now

I look out my window and across the dirt street here in Gorham and see my red jeep parked down from Betty's Tavern. Spangler is not there yet. Jed has died. It is spring and blizzards lurk in the Dakotas. Spangler and Opal have moved from the big house in Hays to the ranch house where Jed had lived. I am teaching school and working for Spangler. Things are as they were, save for Jed. Nothing is the same.

Later that night in the bar, Kelly says I have a phone call. It is Heather. She wants to know if I am all right. I know she wants to ask about seeing me again, but I won't let her. I say I'm going back west. We hang up.

Spangler spent a night in jail. For rudeness and arrogance, if for nothing else, said the judge. Spangler was pleased. The next afternoon we drink in Kelly's again. Jed joins us and has an apple with his beer. He cuts the apple in slices and pulls the flesh off the skin with his teeth, leaving a small pile of apple skins in front of him. Opal comes in after the auction and buys a round of tomato beers for the bar.

We have some fines here and there — there was some property to repair. But it was nothing. Lawyers squabble for a few months about one thing and another, but it comes to a stall. We are clear.

There have been giant thunderstorms in recent days. Gravediggers bolt down over Natoma and Hill City. The price of cattle is low and Spangler will keep this year's herd through next winter. We know we can't do it again. His truck pulls in at Betty's. There is nothing more to write.

THE END

# Some Notes on the Writing of *The Last Cattle Drive;* Or, My Life as Fiction

## The Route of *The Last Cattle Drive*

One autumn day in the early 1980s I took my pickup truck along the route of *The Last Cattle Drive.* I wanted to see what mistakes I had made in the details I had used in the novel. And what fiction I had mapped for the drive to follow. Was the schoolyard in Paradise, Kansas, the way I recorded it? More or less. Was there a boardinghouse down the road should the characters want a place to stay that first night? No. Was it possible to have a motor home run into the herd near Lake Wilson? Yes. Was it probable there were pheasants near Blackwolf?

"We don't get many pheasant hunters around here," said a rancher I met at a coffee shop in Wilson. "Better shooting north and west. Try Hays."

Later that day I drove into Brookville and, like the characters in the novel, had a chicken dinner at the celebrated Brookville Hotel—

albeit without Opal, Jed, and Spangler. Or Sissy. Just as I was paying my bill someone from the restaurant asked me to sign the guest book located on a stand by the door. I did so, writing in the names of those who had been on the cattle drive. I wonder if anyone has ever noticed that in that act fiction has been converted to fact. It is something I do every day. My life is fiction. That's a fact.

## THE MOVIE AT THE END OF THE WORLD: TAKE ONE

All through the 1980s and even into the '90s, whenever I've give a reading (usually not from *The Last Cattle Drive* but from my novellas or short stories) there would be questions from the audience about the movie of *The Last Cattle Drive*. When was it going to be made? Was it true that Jack Nicholson was going to star? Or was it George C. Scott? Who would play Opal? Faye Dunaway? Meryl Streep? Who would play me (I was less the model for Leo than readers seemed to suppose, but privately I was hoping for Richard Dreyfuss).

Most authors don't mind being asked questions about writing or literature, but most of us wince when the literary success of our work is measured by nonliterary commercial success. And movies made from books are the most obvious indicators of such success. Also, some of the best movies are made from some of the worst books. That said, I of course knew that a movie staring Jack Nicholson was being planned and in fact had almost gotten made (see my essay in this book "The Last Cattle Drive Stampede"). When that project failed, there were other attempts to make the movie, most notably with Sean Connery as Spangler. But the Connery movie was to be retitled and moved from Kansas to Montana. That prompted the following editorial published by the *Wichita Eagle Beacon* on March 10th, 1990.

### BOO! Outrageous That The Last Cattle Drive Will Be Re-titled and Filmed in Montana

What could be worse than 20th Century Fox's plan to change the name of the movie version of *The Last*

*Cattle Drive*, Robert Day's classic Kansas novel, to "Road Show"? Fox's plan to shoot the movie in Montana instead of Kansas this summer, that's what.

This makes about as much sense as calling the movie version of *Lonesome Dove,* Larry McMurtry's classic novel of the Plains, "Two Guys Who Want to Move to Montana" and filming it in New Jersey.

After all, Mr. Day's novel, published in 1977, is the tale of a crusty Western Kansas rancher who, appalled at modernity, decides to drive his cattle to the Kansas City stockyards instead of shipping them there by rail. The tale is told from the perspective of a young city slicker from Kansas City, who gets an education in what Kansas is really all about.

None of this matters, apparently. According to the Kansas Film Commission, actor Sean Connery is slated to star in the movie, and the producers want "mountain looks to go with Connery," whatever that means.

Well, excuuuse us for not having any mountains. And excuse us, too, if we boycott the movie once it's released. Why shouldn't we? It won't have anything to do with Kansas.

As it turned out, the Sean Connery version of *The Last Cattle Drive* was not made in either Kansas or Montana. However, in the meantime there had been a lawsuit over the Nicholson/Hutton version of the movie that precipitated the bankruptcy of MGM. More on that in The Movie at the End of the World: Take Two. And on *City Slickers* in The Movie at the of World: Take Three.

## ANTHONY BURGESS AND MY CHANCELLORSHIP OF THE UNIVERSITY OF KANSAS

I met the writer Anthony Burgess in the early 1970s when I was a guest speaker at the University of Richmond. There was a lunch for Katherine Anne Porter (who had given me helpful advice about my writing when I was a student), the poet Richard Wilbur (who remains a friend after all these years), the great literary critic I. A. Richards, myself and Anthony Burgess—newly famous for *Clockwork Orange*. I remember Burgess was smoking the cigars I later gave to the cattle buyer in the Kansas City stockyards at the end of *The Last Cattle Drive*.

Burgess and I liked each other immediately because (as Montaigne says about friendship) of who he was, and who I was. One result of our kinship was his vivid and lovely praise of my novel ("written in remarkably fine North American English") that has appeared in the many editions of the book, both in America and England.

Over the years, Burgess and I stayed in touch, and when he came to the University of Kansas to give a reading and meet with students and faculty he asked his hosts if arrangements might be made for me to join him. As it happened, I was then living in Western Kansas and so, along with my friend Ward Sullivan—who is rightly thought to be the model for Spangler in the novel—we drove the ranch pickup to Lawrence one afternoon after we had moved cattle that morning. The roundup had taken longer than we thought, so when we finally arrived at the Chancellor's House on Lilac Lane in the heart of the University's campus we probably still smelled of work. For sure we were not essence of lilacs blooming in the dooryard as we barged into the house. For sure we needed a drink. More than one. But there was no strong drink to be had.

We sat down with Burgess and a variety of professors and deans, all of us assembled on couches and comfortable Morris-like chairs. Someone offered us iced tea or hot coffee. Or water. I remember Burgess looking grim. Still we were pleased to see one another again, and we traded stories back and forth about our trips, what writers' paths we had crossed, and what books we were reading. Maybe there would be wine at dinner. Or at least tomato beer. That, too, was not to be the case.

In those days the fine biologist Del Shankel was the acting chancellor of the University of Kansas and there was a search being conducted to find a new Chancellor. That was the topic of discussion at dinner. What kind of chancellor would best suit the university. A scholar? A business man or woman? A leader from the world of politics? The deadline for applications and nominations was that very day. In a moment of levity, I nominated Anthony Burgess.

"I'll accept," said Burgess, "if I can get a drink."

"I second Mr. Burgess' nomination," said Ward, "but I need a drink as well."

"I don't think we have much by way of liquor in the place," said Del, who, after all, was just more or less house-sitting until the new chancellor was chosen. And besides, the university was no doubt officially dry at the time.

"We've got a bottle of Green Gables in the truck," said Ward. This was true. Before *The Last Cattle Drive* was published, Ward and I drank Jack Daniels Black, but because the characters drank Green Gables, we switched brands. Burgess, with his prodigious memory (he could recite most of *Ulysses*), knew right away the whiskey came from the novel. Ward went to the truck and brought back a full quart of Green Gables.

"Since we are drinking the fiction of whiskey from Bob's fact of a book," Burgess said as we started in on the bottle, "I withdraw my name to be chancellor of the University of Kansas and nominate Robert Day." Ward seconded the nomination. Now the professors and deans looked grim.

"You'll need to put that in writing before midnight," said Del. He seemed amused. "Do you want a piece of paper?"

"I'll use this paper napkin," said Burgess. We had put the Green Gables on an official University of Kansas paper napkin and some of the whiskey had run down the bottle so that the university's red and blue Jayhawk had become besotted.

"Curious creature," said Burgess looking at the Jayhawk. "One of your prairie birds, I expect. Are they good to eat?"

"They're imaginary," I said.

"More's the merrier!" said Burgess while writing my nomination on the napkin as if it were spoken, cartoon-like, by the Jayhawk. "I hereby nominate Robert Day to be Chancellor of the University of Kansas," he pronounced with a flourish, and handed the napkin to Del Shankel.

I was not invited for an interview.

## THE WRITING OF *THE LAST CATTLE DRIVE*

I wrote most of *The Last Cattle Drive* the summer of 1975 in a small farmhouse on the Smoky Hill River south of Gorham, Kansas. I did the first draft on a Hermes 10 typewriter I still have but now only use for letters and postcards. I revised the manuscript the following spring in Chestertown, Maryland. I reworked it again after it had been bought by G. P. Putnam in New York. Some of the rewriting I did on the typescript in my own hand which often I could not read. My guess is that over a third of the novel was not in its present form when I finished the initial draft. Writers are first of all (and finally as well) rewriters.

I remember that summer on the Smoky Hill was hot with the heat being broken now and then by violent storms ("thunderheads that climbed past twenty thousand feet"). I was at the time reading the novels and literary essays of Vladimir Nabokov and it is his remark that "weather is the first refuge of a sentimental writer" to which I allude at the opening of my chapter "Weather." I was also reading Andy Adams' *Log of a Cowboy* (which I did not understand was a novel until his cattle drive reached a nonexistent bog in Western Kansas) and *Huckleberry Finn*. Astute readers will spot fragments of sentences ("There is nothing more to write . . .") lifted from Mark Twain. And other elements as well.

Every morning after my writing I would drive the dirt roads of Western Kansas to take notes on the physiognomy of the land: limestone fence posts, creaking windmills, cottonwoods more in bunches than in groves. Doves in pairs on power lines. Grain trains. Stock racks in the beds of pickups, sometimes with a few head of low dollar steers heading to market; sometimes with a horse saddled and standing catty corner.

I had lived in the area in the late sixties when I was a teacher at Fort Hays State College and was more or less run out of both town and gown because of my antiwar activity as well as the production of my play *No Negro Problem in Hays*. (Among those attending the three packed performances of the play were KBI agents wearing ponchos, skimpy-brim hats and wing-tip shoes. I suppose they thought the ponchos were a good disguise).

While teaching and causing trouble, I worked for Ward Sullivan, and in so doing came to learn about cattle and ranching. But writing a novel about it made me focus on the precise nature of Western Kansas life. It wasn't the research that Tom Wolfe advocates for writers of fiction, but more noting the details of the daily life I had lived and that I now needed to make my story vivid. I am of the school of E. M. Forster who, when asked if he had researched *Passage to India,* said: "That wouldn't be fair, now would it?" Still, you don't want to have bogs in arid Western Kansas if you can help it, and you don't—as Eudora Welty once admitted to me she had done—make moons rise in the west.

Over the years I've gotten letters (and now e-mails) from readers of the novel telling me their favorite part and in turn asking for mine. Some readers like the moment at the start of the drive when Leo gets drunk and half falls off his horse. Others like the helicopter scene toward the end. Still others like the toast Spangler gives: "Friendships wane and friendships grow." For me, two moments stand out. One is when the tall man outside Lucas stops the herd and after some argument tells Spangler to kiss his ass, and Spangler says: "I don't stand in lines." The other is when Spangler sees the movie company filming the Western Kansas countryside and says: "I hope they leave the place the way they found it. . . . Nothing's the same after you take a picture of it." Here, he spoke for me.

In fact (as well as fiction), it was the movie *Paper Moon* they were making in and around Hays and Gorham when I was writing

*The Last Cattle Drive*. Unlike the characters in the novel, I never saw any of the film crew. However, I once heard a public service announcement on the radio asking listeners to keep on the lookout for a poodle named Minnie that had been lost by one of the movie people. Ward named all such tiny, decorative dogs "bobcat-bait." As Minnie probably was.

## THE MOVIE AT THE END OF THE WORLD: TAKE TWO

One day I got in the mail a book titled *Fade Out* that was an account by Peter Bart of how MGM went bankrupt. A friend of mine had sent it with a note that I should read the chapter titled "Euphoria." I do judge books by their covers. And their blurbs. I have never read a book that was called "gripping." Nor one not written (nor read) by its author, usually some "celebrity." When I looked at *Fade Out* I could see no reason why I should spend even a tiny fraction of my life reading a story of how a movie company went broke. But I did. At least I read the chapter "Euphoria" as my friend had suggested.

According to Peter Bart, I am the principal reason MGM went belly up. The story is Hollywood's version of my fifteen minutes of fame. Apparently MGM needed a blockbuster movie to save it from financial collapse, and the movie of *The Last Cattle Drive* (re-titled *Road Show*) was galloping to the rescue. Marty Ritt (*The Molly Maguires, The Front, Norma Rae*) was going to direct. Jack Nicholson and Timothy Hutton were the co-stars. Everything was "bankable": the director, the stars, the story. Even Kansas was bankable. At least Topeka, Kansas where—I am told—the city passed a special law saying that yes, MGM could drive a herd of cattle through downtown. The movie was a "GO" project if there ever was one.

Then Marty Ritt quit and Richard Brooks (*In Cold Blood*) took over. Brooks quickly said the script was sick unto death of mad cow disease and the whole premise of the novel was nuts and stupid, and that was my fault. All of which led him to have a heart attack high enough on the Richter scale of heart attacks for MGM to cancel the picture (two days before it was to begin shooting) and collect the insurance. But not so fast, said Timothy Hutton, who smelled a fake heart attack. He sued. The rest of the story is *Bleak House* peopled by swarms of sun-tanned California lawyers. Finally, MGM has to pay. And goes belly up. The End. Of my fifteen minutes of fame included.

## WOMEN AND PROFANITY

I am told the book has a "tude" about women. At a reading I gave in Berkeley, California, a woman in the audience asked me how she could "cleave the attitudes of the characters from those of the author." I was more than a little worried about that word "cleave"; it's what you do to the testicles of a bull calf to make a steer. Also, she wanted to know, was it necessary to have so much profanity? And finally, she asserted, you cannot hum the theme of the movie *Giant*, nor say the word "shit" in seven syllables.

She was right about her final two complaints (it was the theme of *High Noon* I had in mind, but somehow got as wrong as west-rising moons and bogs in Western Kansas). And as to "shit," the best I can do is get five syllables out of it. I am told, however, there are seven-syllable shit swearers out there. They must have the lungs of Mario Lanza.

About the other complaints, it seems reasonable to point out that it was a woman, Opal, who organized the drive, and who solved the problem of what to do with the cattle once they had been scattered—by men—across Kansas City. In the meantime, the men in question (as Kansas's Carry Nation could have predicted) retire to Kelly's Tavern to piss and moan about the world. And drink the night away.

I should also note that it is Spangler who observes to Leo that he won't fully appreciate women until he notices their faces instead of gawking at their breasts. I created Spangler as well as Leo. These points made, there is some truth in the observation that the book portrays the world of Western Kansas as a man's world. Just as there is some truth that Western Kansas and working cattle is a man's world. Wives are called "The Wife." Not "my wife Opal," nor simply "Opal." I have heard conversations among ranchers where I could not tell if the pronoun used referred to the man's horse, his pickup, or The Wife:

"How's yours this morning?"

"A little cranky, but after awhile, just fine. Yours?"

"The same."

Why should I cleave such scenes from their source? The first duty of a writer is not to lie about experience.

As to the profanity in *The Last Cattle Drive*: I like the story about the Western Kansas girl who went to Hollywood and became a starlet. One day she got out of a limousine and put her stylish high-heeled foot in a fresh pile of dog. "Oh, shit," she said, "I stepped in do-do."

## A Sequel to *The Last Cattle Drive*; or, What Have You Written Since?

I once wrote a long story using the characters of *The Last Cattle Drive* to see if they could live beyond the end of their book. They cannot. I placed them in Topeka, Kansas, at a luncheon in their honor. They were served beef hearts. And tomato beer. Fancy women fussed about. There were speeches by political leaders who gave them "official recognition" (the first sign of "fatal misunderstanding," according to the American writer James Agee). But there was no action in the story. Ergo, no reaction. The story was as dead as a suburban dinner party where there is nothing to drink and you don't talk politics or religion.

Beyond that one failed story, I've not tried to write—or even much imagine—what a sequel might be. It can't be another drive because that would not only defeat the title of the book, and also what Leo writes two sentences before he rips off Mark Twain: "We know we can't do it again." Besides, I've had other stories to write, to wit.

For a number of years I worked for the *Washington Post Sunday Magazine* as what the editor called "a chronic contributor." I also wrote for *Smithsonian* and *Forbes,* and even the old bland *Modern Maturity.* These days I contribute essays to The Prairie Writers Group. In the meantime, I have been writing stories and novellas, some of them collected in a book titled *Speaking French in Kansas.* It is the novella (or what Katherine Anne Porter called The Long Story) that I like best. It is also the form that publishers, and thus probably the American public, like least. Who am I to tell that to my muse?

## The Dedication of the First Edition

"Virginia" was (and is) Virginia Wilds, my wife at the time I wrote the book. I have heard her say that living with me then was like living with a bear. Presumably not one in hibernation. "Edgar Wolfe" and "Edward Ruhe" were my professors; Edgar Wolfe taught me the value of precision in prose, Edward Ruhe showed me the breadth and depth of the literary life. Ward and Treva Sullivan are the models for Spangler and Opal; however, Ward once observed it might just as well be the other way around. His life was fiction, too. Opal was always pretty sure she could tell fact from fancy.

By the power invested in me to write "North American English" I now add to the original dedications Fred Whitehead, Perry Schwartz, and especially Kathryn Jankus Day (a.k.a. The Wife). How lovely to be able to do this.

## The Movie at the End of the World:
## Take Three: *City Slickers* and Art Buchwald

The reason these sections are titled The Movie at the End of World is because my agent once noted that so much money had been spent to not make the movie of *The Last Cattle Drive* that it would be the "end of the world" before it was finally made. It is also a title I've borrowed from the writer Tom McGrath. These are Hi-Signs from the Deities of Daily Living and Previous Literature, as we shall see in the following section.

One assignment I had for the *Washington Post Magazine* was to write a piece on how much the movie *City Slickers* was indebted to *The Last Cattle Drive*. I am not an investigative reporter. The stories I wrote for the *Post Magazine* were mainly literary nonfiction, often about Kansas, but also about France, where I live part-time. In the case of *The Last Cattle Drive* and *City Slickers*, I was curious to know only what had been taken from my novel and used in the film. And I would learn this, not by traveling to Hollywood and doing interviews, but by watching the movie. Which I did.

I was struck, perhaps more than most people might be, at how *City Slickers* used aspects of my story: The modern-day cattle drive. The experienced rancher matched with a rookie hand. The calf that needs care. There were many dissimilarities as well. About this time I got a call from the same lawyers in California who had represented Timothy Hutton in his successful lawsuit with MGM. They wanted to know if I had seen *City Slickers* and did I want to bring legal action against the producers. To answer that question, and to add a back story to my piece for the *Post Magazine*, I flew to Martha's Vineyard to interview Art Buchwald, who was then suing Paramount Pictures concerning *Coming to America*. The conversation over hamburgers in Art's kitchen was long, funny, and finally precise. He had detailed the misery and money he had spent pursuing his own lawsuit.

"Do you think I should sue over *The Last Cattle Drive*?" I finally asked.

"It depends upon whether you want to be a writer for the next five years or a litigant," Art said. "Which is it?"

It turned out I wanted to be a writer.

## The Story of *The Last Cattle Drive*

Two questions I have been repeatedly asked about *The Last Cattle Drive* are: Is it true? Or if not, where did I get the story?

By "true" I think people mean: Did the drive really take place? Put another way, is the book nonfiction? Or thinly disguised nonfiction, as if the annals of Kansas in the mid-seventies will show that a cattle drive went from somewhere north of Hays, Kansas into the Kansas City stockyard? The highways along which *The Last Cattle Drive* traveled, and the towns through which it went, are "real," therefore the drive itself was "real." All the author (one Robert Day, a.k.a. Leo Murdock) did was keep a journal, change a few names, and get it published as a novel. You might even be able to find evidence for this "reality" by checking the guest book of the Brookville Hotel restaurant. If the characters are listed there, that is prima facie evidence that the drive "existed." In fact, the drive was "real." I know because (to steal a line from the writer Truman Nelson) I made it up. But from where? From my life. Which is fiction.

The story of *The Last Cattle Drive* came from, as most of my stories do, a holy trinity of literary deities. The Deity of Previous Literature. The Deity of Daily Living. The Deity of Invention. These gods are not jealous gods to a writer—at least not to this writer. There are some stories I write that ask little of Daily Living. There are some that are deeply indebted to Previous Literature. But no story I have written—and certainly not *The Last Cattle Drive*—is bereft of any one of these deities. It is the way art is made: one part life, one part art, one part the energy of the artist—all mixed in some potent proportions as The Muse (the Mother of all Deities) dictates. It is T. S. Eliot's formula of "Tradition and the Individual Talent," with Invention as a catalyst.

A word about Invention. First, it is to be contrasted with Inspiration, which is a false deity. Those of us who write as a calling cannot trust our work to flourish though spasms of inspiration. Ask a Kansas rancher if he needs to be inspired to feed his cattle, check his fences, or break ice on the stock tanks after a hard freeze, and you'll get some inspired gruff profanity. If you write a thousand words a day, you don't wait to see a white dove at sunrise to wire your fingers to your brain. My motto is: type, type-a-writer.

Then what is Invention? It is the leaps of imagination brought about by your own writing (or painting, or composing). In literature we see that Henry Fielding jumped into his invention of Parson

Adams as he was riding in the otherwise dull carriage of Joseph Andrews not talking about politics or religion. Picasso attached bicycle handle bars to a bicycle seat and it became a bull's head. True, Picasso didn't get very far into his work when Invention made him leap, but that sometimes happens.

In *The Last Cattle Drive*, there are many moments of Invention: The baseball gear that Leo wears. The pheasants near Blackwolf (a mistaken invention as it turned out). Sissy. And there are moments when the Deity of Invention holds hands with Previous Literature: The scene where Leo is in the trailer toward the end of the drive and remembers (for the reader, of course) all that has happened before. That technique of knitting the book together I stole from Heinrich Boll's *The Clown*. Just as I stole the "This Book is for Jed" preface of *The Last Cattle Drive* (where the entire novel is coded, and which turns the book into a "document"—the ultimate nonfiction "reality") from Nabokov's *Lolita*.

In the end I am amused (and mused) to think that a Western American cowboy novel has stuffed into it not only my red jeep (from my callow youth), but hunks and chunks of German literature, American Mississippi River literature, and a previous cattle drive story all dancing *ensemble* with a Russian author's nymphet in her "circular skirt and scanties." I wonder what Spangler would have thought had he met her. Or Leo, for that matter. My, my.

"I SHALL TRY TO TELL THE TRUTH, BUT THE RESULT WILL BE FICTION."—KATHERINE ANNE PORTER
There is nothing more to write.

Robert Day
Bly, Kansas
Winter, 2005–2006

# The Last Cattle Drive
# Stampede

I forget how I first heard that my novel *The Last Cattle Drive* (an account of a modern-day cattle drive from Western Kansas to Kansas City complete with accounts of famous Kansas-Thump contests) was being considered as a film project, but I remember hearing that Xerox copies of the typescript were being sent to the West Coast by plane. Not airmail. And not Federal Express because this was in the late '70s and before all that. My impression was that some Great Film Company had booked a seat for a stack of typescripts on the evening flight from New York to L.A. First class, no doubt. There was, I heard, to be an auction. Unless someone—A Great Movie Someone I was led to believe (and at one time I even knew his name)—unless A Great Movie Someone decided instead to go to the South of France to play boules. Weeks went by and nothing happened. All was quiet on the rumor front. My book went through the normal publication processes. Apparently boules was being played in the South of France. Or maybe there had been an auction and nobody wanted to buy my particular kind of bull. I was told the novel would now go around the lot. In any case, not to worry. My book had rooting interest.

In retrospect I recognize a basic absurdity that should have foretold for me the future: it never once occurred to me that The Great Movie People were in fact reading my novel—in Xeroxed first-class typescript or in its final published form. What I thought was that the Great Movie Someone needed a stack of pages to wave at a Great Movie Someone Else and talk a lot in movie mumble about taking meetings on this coast or that coast baby until finally A Not So Great Movie Someone got a Monarch Notes report from someone who had in fact read the book (that someone is so far down at the end of the reel that he doesn't even get an adjective—and besides he is probably a she). In the end lots of typescript waving goes on until say, George C. Scott says yes. Or no. He said no. But not before he said maybe. But that comes later.

I must admit two things: one, this was in the days shortly after *Annie Hall* came out and so my picture of the movie business is shot through Woody Allen's camera, and two, there are a few good guys in all this: my agent, for one. He told me in the beginning many are called and none are chosen and Hollywood is all madness. Go back to your typewriter, he would say. Of course. Easily done when your novel is being considered for a movie. Right. My agent lives in New York; he's not sure Los Angeles exists but if it does he doesn't approve.

"I just had a talk with the movie people," I said to him one day.
"Yes," he said.
"They didn't seem to know how matters stood. I got angry," I said.
"Yes," he said.
"I might have been rude," I said. "In how I talked to them."
"They wouldn't know," he said. "They have no culture and no conversation."

The other good guy is a good lady: an independent producer who did in fact read the book, bought it for her Great Film Company, and as far as I know to this day thinks the novel would make a fine movie. Along the way she had a heart attack and 10 to the power 20 anxiety attacks. Her story is no doubt more maddening than mine. But first in print as we say in the writing business.

Sometime after *The Last Cattle Drive* was published and long after the Great Movie Someone had come back from his boules I was standing in a friend's car repair garage when his phone rang. It was for me. The switchboard operator at Washington College in Maryland where I teach had tracked me down to say that Hollywood was on another line and did I want to speak to them. She hoped I did because by now they had invested a few dollars on the wait. Put them on, I said. Hollywood calling, I told my friend who was rebuilding a splendid old Morgan.

A woman agent I didn't know wanted me to hear the news hot: *The Last Round Up* had been sold. For X dollars with various options. It was a great day. She had been told it was a great book. It would make a fine movie. It had rooting interest. On behalf of her agency (who was aligned with my agent) she wanted to thank me. I was impressed. Even if she'd gotten the title wrong. I'd never earned X dollars before and although I understood that only a tiny millimeter of the X's leg was to come my way at the beginning, still I thought that when the whole X gets in my pocket I'll be a rich man. And that, I knew, was only the beginning. Your mind does funny things at a moment like this. I'd always wanted an airplane. I saw myself at the controls of a Lear Jet going toward Cannes.

A day later the woman agent called back to say that she had boosted the price to a slightly bigger X. It was a great day. The more X's loaded on the film the better. Still, all these X's, much like the verbs in a German sentence, came at the end. A few days later the lady producer called to say she had been the one who had bought the book and how pleased she was at having done so. It had been sent to her by an urban cowboy from Texas who thought it wonderful in spite of its slanderous attitude towards Texans. She'd let me know when there was more news. A few days later my agent called to tell me that all the film people who had been calling me during the previous week were for once in their lives correct about something: the book had been optioned. Not sold, he pointed out. Optioned. They are renting it with an option to buy. It might take years for them to make up their minds, and just because they got something right the first time around don't count on the second time around. Go back to your typewriter, he advised, and forget about it. Right. Just forget that your book is going to be made into a movie and that one day you'll be sitting in the theater watching Robert Mitchum, Cloris Leachman, Jimmy Stewart, and Timothy Hutton (my ideal cast in those days) parading across the screen on your words. That vision and the vision of all those X's just dropped out of my mind. Right.

Months went by. I called the Great Film Company. It was a good thing, too. George C. Scott was 90-percent a sure thing to play the lead. With him in the picture all else would fall in place. It would be the Patton of Westerns. Richard Nixon would watch it. If I had not called I might have begun a slow drift toward my typewriter. Four days later came the only letter over a period of five years that I was to get from Hollywood. George C. Scott had advised The Great Film Company he was not going to do the picture. It was a matter of creative control—whatever that was. Out the window went my idea of Scott doing a parody of the scene toward the end of Patton where he gives an interview on a horse. Or having him say as he drives the steers through the streets of Kansas City: "I love it, God help me, I love it." George, how could you? Poor Richard Nixon. If he finds out he'll have a seventh crisis.

Several more months go by. I get a message to call a number in New York. I am to ask for a Mr. Skins. It is about the movie.

"Al's," says a voice. There is music in the background and loud talk.

"Mr. Skins, please," I say.

"You want Skins," the man says.

"I'm returning his call," I say.

"He's in the head," I can hear someone in the room say. I take it I have reached a pay phone. The man who has answered has apparently let the phone drop to the end of its cord. It swings back and forth and I hear its thud when it hits a wall.

"Hello, Skins here," says a man who turns out not to be Mr. Skins but just Skins.

"Robert Day returning your call," I say.

"Yes," he says. "Glad you called. I've got a partner and we've got a little showcase picture business whereby we use a dynamite story like your *Last Round Up* book and plop one of our actors down in the middle and take it the film festival route. Cannes. Venice. South Florida."

"It's called *The Last Cattle Drive*," I say.

"Fine. Good. B plus title. We might have to nix that. Westerns aren't hot right now. But what do you say you come up to New York and we treat you to a little meal and talk the matter over."

"I have an agent," I say. "You should call him."

"I can't do agents," says Skins. "I think it's best we work this ourselves. Agents get in the way. We can spring for your train ticket here. You in Kansas, right."

"Maryland," I say.

"Really. Drive up then. We'll pay gas, tolls, the works."

"Can't do it," I say. I was about to tell him the book had already been bought, but there was some commotion in the bar and he said he had to go. He'd call back. It will take a while but he will.

Many more months go by. By now the rent on the book is up and The Great Film Company either has to pay X or let it go. Or, as it turns out by the contract, they can rent it again for another year while they get their act together. They do the latter. About the same time I get another phone call—this time from the lady producer. Good news. They've hired a screenplay writer. I didn't know they wanted a screenplay writer. I thought they were looking for cattle and actors. If they wanted a screenplay writer why didn't they call me? I could have done that. But they are happy. They have Robert Getchell. *Bound for Glory. Alice Doesn't Live Here Anymore.* He grew up in Missouri. Missouri, I say. My book is about Kansas. Not to worry he knows about Kansas. We are lucky to get him. He cost us a pound of flesh and two pounds of X's. But the more X's we load on the picture the more likely it is to get made. John Travolta is interested. I am amused. I call my agent.

"Who is John Travolta?" he says. You have to know my agent. He likes books above all. It would ruin his day to know about John Travolta. Never mind, I say. Go back to your typewriter he says.

Six months later I get a call. They have a script. They are pleased with it. I will be pleased with it. It even has some of my own words therein. I will recognize my story. Paul Newman is interested. Burt Reynolds is interested. They've changed the name of the project. *Last Cattle Drive* sounds too much like a Western. It's called *Road Show*. They'll send me a script.

True, the script does have some of my words and true as well I recognize the story. Some of the characters, however, are a bit more difficult to find: my 40-year-old Cloris Leachman is now a 25-year-old Jessica Lange and my old cowboy's prostrate cancer becomes the nameless dread (Jimmy Stewart groans and bends over out of the frame now and then, but nobody says anything). But the thing that really irks me is that my great game of Kansas Thump-Thump (you have to read the book to understand the rules) is changed to Missouri Mule. Who ever heard of Missouri Mule? Everybody knows about Kansas Thump-Thump. Six more months go by. I get a call.

John Travolta is no longer interested but we didn't want him anyway. He's going to do another western: something about a city cowboy. Paul Newman thinks the project will be too easy. Cher is a picture away from a major role and she's ready to take Cloris Leachman's part if Faye Dunaway doesn't want it. Sally Field has turned down the female lead but accepted the male lead. The picture is on the board to be made in Kansas in September or Texas in November depending on how things break. It's a GO project for The Great Film Company. About this time *Heaven's Gate* opens in New York. The silence for the next year is going to be astounding. No Western will be made anywhere, no matter what month, no matter how things break, no matter how GREAT the film company or how GO the project.

"They want to renew the option," says my agent late that summer.

"What about my X's," I say.

"It's bad for writers to think about X's," says my agent.

"Are they going to make the picture this fall," I say.

"Nobody's going to make a Western ever again," says my agent.

"*Heaven's Gate?*" I say.

"It used up all the Western's money until the turn of the century," says my agent.

"Why do they want to extend the option," I say.

"Madness," he says.

The picture was not made in Kansas that fall. Or in Texas. *Heaven's Gate* was a Black Hole for X's, down which my movie fell and out of which came no sound from anyone in Hollywood. One winter night Skins calls back.

"We're still interested," he says.

"Talk to my agent," I say.

"We still don't talk to agents," he says.

"A Great Film Company has bought the picture," I say. "They're making the movie."

"We could do a showcase half hour with Teddy Grumpelt. You heard of Teddy Grumpelt?"

"No," I say. There is some noise in the bar and shouting. I think Skins wants more change for the phone. On credit, no doubt. Then I hear the click of coins.

"You come to New York," he says. "We'll spring for a dinner at Chez Poulet. You heard of Chez Poulet?"

"No," I say.

"It's a steak place," he says. "Got good Kansas City steak. That's what a good Kansas boy needs. Kansas beef. Don't take your book to Hollywood, kid. They'll break your heart." In the background there is more noise. I suppose his credit runs out. The phone lines turn to a buzz.

Many more months go by. Another option is renewed. Then the option is picked up. By now 18 percent inflation and four years have raised hell with my X. One whole leg is missing. But not to worry: the big basket of X's is to be gathered when the picture is made. Paperback editions in seven languages. T-shirts and cowboy dolls. My Lear Jet takes off in many directions.

The Great Film Company fires the lady producer. She leaves with the picture as part of her golden parachute. She starts all over, this time on her own. She calls to tell me that Marty Ritt is interested in directing the movie. That is good news. If Ritt takes the project it will get made. There is no mention of actors which, I am beginning to think, is the real good news.

In the meantime, not only have I been getting calls from a bar in New York, but I've been getting them from Ireland as well. The connections are never good and the brogue is thick so I'm not entirely sure what gets said, but the gist of it is that the caller, an Irish producer, knows an English director who in turn knows some French actors who once played boules with a Great American Movie Person in the south of France and between games they discussed the possibility of making a modern Western in northern Italy. I can't puzzle out if the cowboys will be bossing my herd in Italian, French or the Queen's English, but somehow I get the impression they are going to make their movie version of my book no matter what Hollywood does. This I know is wrong, a violation of international rights that will keep plagues of California movie lawyers busy for generations. I know as well I should tell my Hollywood producer, my agent, maybe even Rona Barrett. I say nothing. Your mind does funny things at moments like these: I see myself smiling as my cattle drive roars through the Chianti wine district toward Siena. Prego, prego, says a tall Italian cowboy.

It is about this time Jack Nicholson enters the picture. He and Marty Ritt have lunch in the Russian Tea Room and a deal is cut. A Very Great Film Company will bank it. Timothy Hutton is on board. They are looking to rope in a rising star of a woman. Cher's name comes up again. *Variety* says she's taken the part. *Variety* says she's not taken the part. The picture is set for Kansas in May. I get lots of calls. One day driving along in a friend's restored Morgan I hear on the local radio news more than you'd ever want to know about the making of my picture. A week later in an airplane the hostess hands me a copy of *USA Today* where I find the movie is a front page story: Nicholson and Hutton are in Kansas. There is a map of the state in case the rest of the nation doesn't know where it is. Nicholson buys sweatshirts at the University of Kansas bookstore and flirts with the cashier. Hutton takes pictures of the prairie so he can have them blown up and hung on the walls of his Malibu beach house. He wants to get the feel of Kansas, he says. The Very Great Film Company gets Topeka to pass a law allowing cattle to be driven through its streets. The Very Great Film Company buys a herd. It is a GO project. My basket of X's is getting full.

"Any difference between steers and cattle," says a man's voice at the other end. "This is pre-production calling."

"Yes," I say. "The words are different, that should tell you something."

"We bought cattle and someone says your book says steers. Have we got trouble?"

"Do the cattle you bought have large bags hanging between their legs?"

"I don't know," he says. "I'm in California."

"Call your man in Kansas and ask about the bags. No bags, no trouble. Unless you got sold 250 bulls, which I doubt."

"You are our man in Kansas," he says."

"I'm in Maryland," I say.

"What a mess," he says.

Months go by. More newspaper and television stories. The movie gets put back until late summer. They want the feel of heat in the footage. Marty Ritt quits. Health reasons. Who can blame him. He probably had a clause that said any place but Kansas in late summer. Not to worry. Nicholson is driving the picture. It is going to go. The Very Great Film Company office in New York calls to thank me for writing such a filmable book. It has rooting interest. Some day he hopes to read it.

In mid-summer they hire another director. I forget his name. Nobody important. He looks over the script and says it's sick. Then he gets sick. Or so *Variety* says. He says he's not sick. The script is sick. But no matter, the cattle are ready to go, the streets of Topeka have been cleared. Movie production is to begin on Monday, August 25th.

It is Sunday, August 24th. The phone rings. It is difficult for me to write this. Hello, I say. It is a pal in Kansas.

"They are selling the cattle."

"What cattle?" I say.

"The picture's cattle."

"Why?" I say. Boy am I dumb.

"The radio says it's because they're not going to make the movie after all."

Your mind does funny things at moments like this. There are no words in my head. I see, however, an Italian cowboy riding up to a New York café—Chez Poulet. He throws a boule through the window. Great Movie People dressed as steers rush out into the street. Crowds of bystanders root them on. My agent is there, trying to pull me out of the way. To no avail. I rope a steer as a souvenir of what might have been. When caught it is lighter than air and floats upward taking me with it.

"What movie," I say.

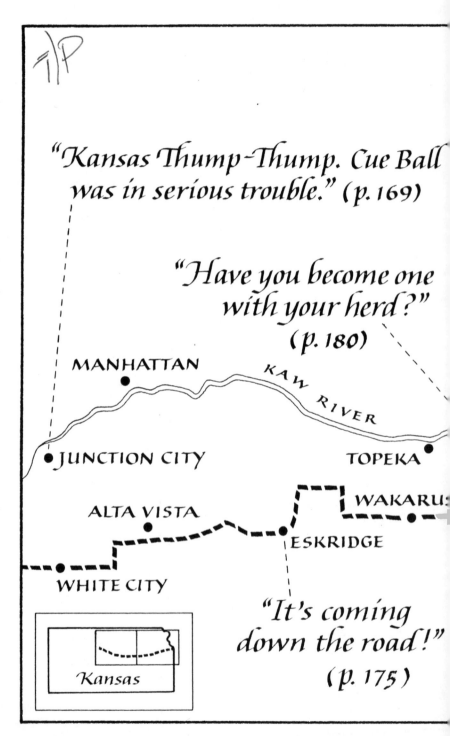

"*Kansas Thump-Thump. Cue Ball was in serious trouble.*" (p. 169)

"*Have you become one with your herd?*" (p. 180)

MANHATTAN

KAW RIVER

JUNCTION CITY

TOPEKA

WAKARU:

ALTA VISTA

ESKRIDGE

WHITE CITY

Kansas

"*It's coming down the road!*" (p. 175)

*continued from front*

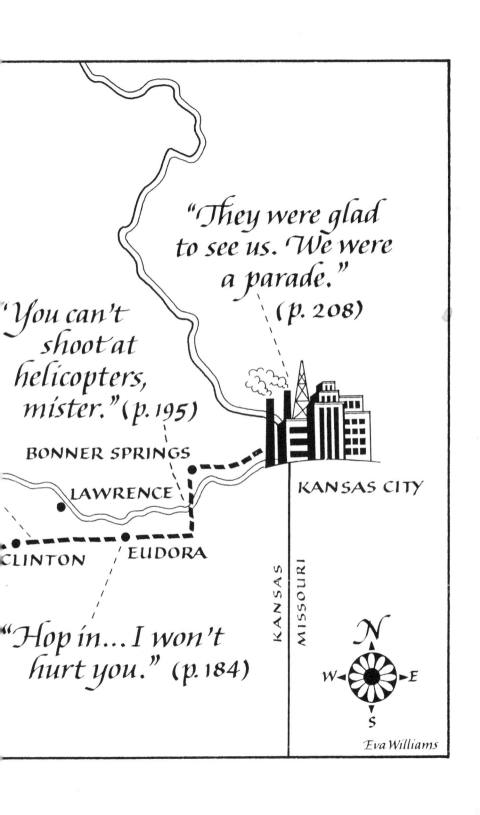

"They were glad to see us. We were a parade." (p. 208)

"You can't shoot at helicopters, mister." (p. 195)

BONNER SPRINGS

LAWRENCE

CLINTON    EUDORA

"Hop in... I won't hurt you." (p. 184)

KANSAS CITY

KANSAS    MISSOURI

N
W    E
S

Eva Williams